CAST OF CHARACTERS

Helene Hardaway has been married to Merrick for nearly fifty years. Will her daughters put aside their differences long enough to celebrate the golden anniversary?

Merrick Hardaway loves his wife more today than he did when he first married her. He knows how she misses their children, and he'll do anything to make her happy.

Megan Hardaway is the oldest of the Hardaway sisters. Her marriage to Noah Carson fell apart after her son was kidnapped twelve years ago. Now a teenager has come to Hurricane Beach looking for his parents—Megan and Noah.

Noah Carson hasn't been back to Hurricane Beach in years. But if this is really his son, wild horses couldn't keep Noah away.

Derek Carson is sixteen years old. He's had no contact with his family since he was four. Can he convince them he is who he says he is?

Amy Hardaway is the middle daughter. She's still playing the role of peacemaker—trying to get her family reunited.

Jon Costas had married one Hardaway girl when they'd both been too young to know better. Then he'd fallen for his ex-sister-in-law, Amy.

Lisa Hardaway is the baby of the family, the one who's always been protected. She's still learning to share her painful secret with her family.

Matt Connell never knew the consequences of his teenage love affair with Lisa. But now he wants to make amends.

Dear Reader,

As some of you may already know, "Marisa Carroll" is the pen name shared by both of us. For almost fifteen years we have been writing partners as well as sisters and best friends. That means we've shared the joys and sorrows of a joint career, as well as the joys and sorrows of growing up in a large, close-knit family. We have two other sisters—and two brothers—and are happy to count them as friends, not just siblings.

Perhaps writing about that special sister bond is what has made this trilogy such an enjoyable project for us. We've come to love Amy and Lisa and Megan almost as much as our own sisters. We hope you have come to love them, too, and we hope you enjoy Megan's story.

Sincerely,

Carol Wagner and Marian Scharf.

Books by Marisa Carroll

HARLEQUIN SUPERROMANCE
598—WEDDING INVITATION
635—MARRY ME TONIGHT
655—PEACEKEEPER
718—THE MAN WHO SAVED CHRISTMAS

HOMETOWN REUNION
UNEXPECTED SON
MISSION: CHILDREN

Don't miss any of our special offers. Write to us at the following address for information on our newest releases.

Harlequin Reader Service
U.S.: 3010 Walden Ave., P.O. Box 1325, Buffalo, NY 14269
Canadian: P.O. Box 609, Fort Erie, Ont. L2A 5X3

Marisa Carroll

Megan

Harlequin Books

TORONTO • NEW YORK • LONDON
AMSTERDAM • PARIS • SYDNEY • HAMBURG
STOCKHOLM • ATHENS • TOKYO • MILAN
MADRID • WARSAW • BUDAPEST • AUCKLAND

ISBN 0-373-70742-8

MEGAN

DEDICATION

For our sisters,
Joann Selhorst and Lynette Badenhop.

May we spend all our summers at the lake
and may we never have to go shopping for
bathing suits together.

PROLOGUE

HE STOOD on the wide deck overlooking the Gulf of Mexico, squinting against the fierce August sunlight. The afternoon was hot and bright, and the beach was an endless stretch of sugar-fine white sand. He remembered playing there, building sand castles with his grandmother, taking piggyback rides on his grandfather's shoulders.

Didn't he?

"I remember," he whispered fiercely. *"I do."*

But he didn't remember enough. Only bits and pieces of a dozen years ago when he'd been a little kid of three or four. He didn't remember his aunt Amy. Or the one they called Lisa, whose picture was on the piano in the formal, richly decorated living room of Sea Haven, his grandparents' home. They were watching him now, Helene and Merrick Hardaway, from the windows of the big white house that loomed behind him. He could feel their eyes on him—curious, wary, wondering if they could believe he was who he said he was. Right now he figured they were getting ready to call his mother. Tell her he'd shown up on the doorstep. Come back from the dead.

He couldn't even remember what his mother looked like. Only the faint echoes of her voice, soft and loving, and her arms around him, warm and strong, protecting him from monsters under his bed. Make-believe monsters, not the real two-legged one who had ruled his life for the last twelve years. And his father? Just hazy recollections of a photograph of a man in a blue uniform on the table beside his mother's bed that he used to blow a kiss to at bedtime every night.

Megan and Noah Carson.

All the rest of his memories had been beaten out of him years ago. Even his name. He was Erik now. He was afraid to answer to anything else. But deep inside, in his heart, he'd never forgotten who he was. Never. He was Derek Noah Carson. And once, long ago, he'd lived here at Sea Haven, Hurricane Beach, Florida.

CHAPTER ONE

HER SON WAS BACK. Megan sank to her knees and wrapped her arms around herself, trying to hold in the shock, trying to quell the excitement, the joy she could feel beginning to surge. She had dared to hope so many times since Derek had been abducted twelve years ago. And each time her hopes had been shattered.

She closed her eyes for a moment. *Derek was alive.* Her mind echoed the words again and again as she stared blankly down at the carpet, barely noticing it was beginning to show some wear. It had been here for almost seven years, as long as she had owned the small condo on a quiet side street in the Omaha suburb of Papillion, Nebraska.

"My baby." Her words were barely audible. "My baby is alive?" She waited for the tears but they didn't come. She'd cried too many tears. She had none left to shed.

"Megan? Are you all right? Megan, answer me, please."

Her mother's voice sounded faint and faraway. Megan blinked, not realizing for a moment that she had dropped the receiver. She picked it up with shaking hands. "I'm here, Mom." She was surprised to find her voice wasn't shaking as badly as her hands. "I'm okay. I...it's hard—"

"I know. He...he just showed up on the doorstep. It...it was such a shock," Helene murmured.

"How?" Short questions. She could manage those while she fought to get her heart rate back to normal, her breathing under control.

"He hasn't told us much yet, Megan. He's exhausted and half-starved. He's come all the way from Michigan. Way up north in Michigan. He hitchhiked most of the way, I think. He doesn't seem to want to talk about it. Your father said not to pressure him, not right away. He...he said he remembered our address. He said he remembered learning—" Helene's voice broke and Megan sucked in her breath and held it to stifle a wail of denial as familiar nightmare memories stirred to life.

"That's what we were doing." Her mother was whispering now, too, as though she couldn't trust her voice any longer. "You remember, don't you? Just before we went shopping that awful day. He was drawing pictures in the sand with a stick. He was only four. But so quick and so smart. I...I was teaching him our address. So that if he ever got lost—"

My name is Derek Noah Carson. I live at Sea Haven, Gulfview Road, Hurricane Beach, Florida.

Megan would go to her grave still hearing that little-boy voice. She had relived every moment of those last few days she'd spent with Derek again and again. Noah had been away on one of his navy SEAL deployments. Megan and Derek had come for a visit to Hurricane Beach. She'd learned not even to ask where Noah was going. He couldn't tell her. She hated what he did for a living, but she had loved him, and had wanted to look nice for him when he came home.

So she and Helene had gone shopping for a dress, taking Derek with them to the mall in Tallahassee. The little boy was cranky and hungry.

"Go see Grandma," she'd said. Her mother was only an aisle over, only a few feet away. Who would ever have thought they would lose him forever when they were both in plain sight of each other? The pain and guilt, old and familiar, stabbed at her again. She *should* have been more careful.

She'd turned her back on him for a moment, a blink of the eye and he was gone. He wasn't with Helene. He wasn't in the toy department, or at the pretzel stand, or watching the other children ride the mechanical toys near the fountain. He had simply disappeared. Until today.

"Derek." She didn't even realize she'd spoken his name aloud until her mother answered her.

"He doesn't want to be called Derek. He says we should call him Erik now. He...he won't say why." Helene began to cry softly.

He had a different name. This boy, this stranger on her parents' doorstep didn't even go by the name she'd given him. How did that feel? Did it hurt? No reaction penetrated her numbness.

Derek. She'd named him after a character in a soap opera. She couldn't even remember which one. A bad boy, dangerous and charismatic, just the type to appeal to a too-serious and studious high-school senior who longed for love and romance.

At nineteen she'd met Noah Carson, just as charismatic and even more dangerous than her TV heart-throb. She'd fallen head over heels in love with the young navy commando and never thought of the De-rek character again. Until her son was born and Noah—whose name had been given to him by a caseworker in a Methodist orphanage—didn't want his son named after him.

"Mom, please don't cry," Megan whispered. She could get through this. But only if her mother wouldn't cry. "It's just a name. It's a small price to pay to have him back with us."

"I'm okay." Helene sniffed and cleared her throat. "It's just such a shock. And Megan. He…I think he looks like Noah."

Noah. Oh, God, she was going to have to get in touch with Noah.

"Do…do you want me to call Noah and tell him?" her mother asked, reading her mind.

Megan's eyes lifted to the legal-size envelope sit-ting on the end table beside the telephone base. Di-vorce papers. Although she'd been legally separated from Noah Carson for nearly a decade, they'd never been divorced. Now, after all these years Noah wanted to take the final step. She hadn't even told her parents yet. She didn't know why. It was to be expected one of them would want to be free sooner or later. Perhaps he'd found someone to love? If he had, she was glad for him, but still it was unsettling that he was the one who wanted to sever the last tie between them.

"No," Megan spoke into the receiver. "I'll tell him."

"When can you come home?"

"I'll call the airline right away. I'll be home as soon as I can get there."

"Your father will drive into Tallahassee and pick you up at the airport."

"No. I don't know if I can even get a flight out anymore tonight. I'll rent a car and drive down from Tallahassee."

"We...we thought it would be best to wait to tell you until you got home from work. Now I wish we'd called earlier. Right away. But it was so—"

"It's okay." Megan was glad she hadn't had to deal with this in her office. She didn't want any of the one hundred and fifty residents and staff of Graceway Retirement Center to see their director of nursing a shivering, shaking, emotional wreck.

"Would you like to speak with him now?"

"No, not yet." Megan's answer was almost an involuntary reaction. "I need some time, Mom. And I'd rather see him when I first talk to him."

"I'll leave the door unlocked," Helene promised. "Your room is ready and waiting."

The sunny blue and yellow room that had been hers all through high school. Megan closed her eyes and pictured its serenity. The windows faced inland, away from the gulf, looking out over the acres and acres of pine and live oak that had been in her mother's family for generations.

"Fly safely," Helene was saying. "Be here soon."

"It's a miracle, Megan," her mother said fiercely. "A miracle. After all these years."

"I know, Mom."

She broke the connection and sank onto the couch.

She, too, had given up hope years before, but now she felt it stirring, and she pushed it back into the darkness with a ruthlessness born of too many disappointments. She wasn't ready to believe, she dared not believe. Not yet.

"COMMANDER, there's a call for you."

Lieutenant Commander Noah Carson, United States Navy, turned away for a moment from the Hell Week endurance exercise taking place against the backdrop of a spectacular Pacific sunset on the beach below the berm where he was standing. He eyed the young sailor waiting respectfully at his side.

"A phone call?"

"Yes, sir, Commander. You can take it in the support vehicle." The support vehicle was a naval ambulance on standby in case any of the SEAL students—now forty-eight hours into Hell Week, the most physically demanding and intensive week of training in the United States military—needed aid.

"I'm busy, sailor," Noah barked, his eyes returning to the line of shivering, yelling students walking, arms linked, into the water. Automatically he checked his watch. Hypothermia was always a danger in water-torture exercises, or evolutions, as they were known in Navy Special Warfare circles. And it *was* torture standing in chest-deep, sixty-degree surf. He knew that from experience.

Over the years SEAL instructors—the acronym stood for Sea, Air, Land—had calculated to the split second the amount of time a human being could stay in the cold Pacific waters off Coronado Beach, California, without endangering life. Noah knew that his

instructors, wearing blue and gold T-shirts embla-
zoned with the trident seal of the Navy Special Warfare teams, would keep the sailors standing in the
crashing waves exactly that long, not one second
more, nor one second less.

"Commander."

"I told you I'm busy, sailor. Unless the call's from
Captain Mannley himself, I don't want to be bothered with it." Harrison Mannley was Noah's boss,
the officer in charge of SEAL training, and he
was not happy with the dropout rate in this particular BUDS—Basic Underwater Demolition/SEAL—
class. When the old man wasn't happy, Noah wasn't
happy. It was his job to figure out what it was about
this class that made it different from the rest. So far
he hadn't come up with any answers as to why these
particular young men were less motivated, or less
physically prepared than the ones before them. All
he knew was that the failure rate in this class was
twenty percent higher than the norm. And that wasn't
good.

"The call's not from Captain Mannley, sir." The
sailor cleared his throat. "The call's from a woman,
sir."

Noah swung his whole body around this time. "A
woman?"

The sailor gulped. "Yes, sir. A woman. She…she
says she's your wife, sir."

"My wife?"

Megan. A quick fragmentary vision of laughing,
gray-green eyes and silky, ash-blond hair flashed
through his thoughts. He pushed the tantalizing, for-
bidden image away with an almost-physical act of

will. Was she calling him about the divorce papers? It didn't seem likely. Surely she would handle the final dissolution of their marriage through her lawyer. "Are you sure she said she was my wife?"

"Yes, sir."

"Then I think I'd better take the call."

Noah walked around to the front of the ambulance and put the receiver of the cellular phone to his ear. "Carson here."

A portion of his attention—the portion that was all navy—continued to focus on the young sailors in the water. One of them broke ranks and began to struggle back to shore despite the pleading of his classmates and the bellowed insults of the instructors. But the youngster had reached his limits, both mentally and physically. He stood shivering and shaking in the fading light, refusing to reenter the water. Finally the instructor signaled for a medic.

"Damn." Another one. Mannley was going to have his hide.

"Noah?"

He hadn't realized he'd spoken out loud until he heard Megan's voice. "I'm here."

"Noah? It's hard to hear you. We must have a bad connection."

"It's the middle of Hell Week, Megan. I'm out on the beach."

"Oh. Of course. I'm…I'm sorry to interrupt you."

"Megan, what's wrong?" The medic was approaching the shivering dropout. Noah eyed the line of trainees standing fast against the surf. A second student broke free of his comrades, and then a third.

Damn, Noah thought. *This class is losing sailors faster than we can count.*

"Noah, did you hear me?"

He turned his back on the ocean and the men in it. "I hear you, Megan," he said. It had been eight years since they'd spoken last, but it might as well have been eight minutes. Her voice, low and smooth as honey, still affected him like a shot of adrenaline injected straight into his heart. "I thought you'd want to handle the divorce through your lawyer."

"Lawyer? Noah, it's not the divorce I'm calling about." There was a short silence on her end of the line, as though she was steeling herself to speak. "It's Derek."

"Derek." He felt his stomach knot. A steel band tightened around his chest. Had their child's body been found after all these years? "What about...our son?"

"He's alive, Noah." Her voice broke. He heard her draw in a long ragged breath. "He showed up at Sea Haven this afternoon. My mother called about an hour ago. I...I've been trying to track you down."

"Are you sure, Megan? Are you sure it's Derek?" He couldn't take it in. He didn't know what to say, how to react.

"I don't know. Mother thinks it's really him. But Noah, how can we be sure? I...we lost our little boy. Now he's almost a grown man. A stranger. How can we ever be sure?"

"When does your flight leave?" He didn't have to ask if she was going to Hurricane Beach. There was no question of that.

"I can't get out of Omaha tonight. I've booked a seat on the first flight out in the morning."

"I'll be there as soon as I can get leave."

"Noah, I don't—"

He heard the reluctance in her voice and overrode it. "He's my son, too, Megan."

The tears were gone. Her voice was flat and hard, but she couldn't quite hide another shaky indrawn breath. "I'm aware of that, Noah. I'll tell Mom and Dad to be expecting you."

She broke the connection. Noah was left standing with the cellular phone still against his ear. As he lowered his arm and handed the phone back to the obviously curious, but silent sailor, he was amazed to find his hand was steady.

Inside he was shaking like a leaf.

"GOOD NIGHT, Erik. I hope you sleep well."

"Thank you, ma'am." He pulled the sheet up to his chest. He didn't have anything to sleep in but a T-shirt and his shorts. He didn't think Helene Hardaway was used to having people in her guest room who didn't even own pajamas.

She was staring at him again with those sad blue eyes as though trying to see something—someone— in him. He tried not to stare back. His grandmother. He didn't remember much about her, only her hair, not quite as white as it was now, and the words she'd taught him, the words he hadn't dared say aloud for all these years, but kept alive in his heart, his talisman against the darkness.

My name is Derek Noah Carson. I live at Sea Haven, Gulfview Road, Hurricane Beach, Florida.

"You sleep as late as you want," his grandmother was saying. "Your grandfather and I are usually up by seven. But you come down to breakfast whenever you're ready."

"Thanks. I don't usually sleep in very often, either."

His grandfather, tall and stern-faced, came up behind her and peered over her shoulder. "Good night, son."

"Good night, sir." He didn't know if the Hardaways believed he was who he said he was. After all, he didn't even answer to the name they knew him by. Byron Fielder had seen to that.

"Is there anything else you need?" his grandfather said.

"No sir. Thank you."

His grandmother was watching her husband from the corner of her eye. Erik had noticed that they didn't touch, or even talk to each other very much. For some reason, that made him sad. He didn't know why it should. Fielder and his moth—Fielder and his wife—*never* touched each other. Fielder hadn't even cried when Diana died.

"Good night," Helene said again. "Sleep tight. Don't—" She stopped talking, looking hopeful, obviously waiting for him to say something.

Don't let the bed bugs bite. Diana Fielder, the woman who'd raised him, the woman he'd always called Mother, but couldn't anymore, used to say that sometimes. Had his grandmother said it, too, when he was little?

"You always used to finish that little rhyme," Helene explained, lifting her shoulders in a shrug. "You know. It goes. Good night. Sleep tight. Don't let the bed bugs bite.''

He shook his head. "I'm sorry. I don't remember.''

"That's okay.'' Her smile was sad, like her eyes. "It was a long time ago. We'll leave you now. It's getting late.'' Her husband stepped aside and let her precede him out of the room. He flipped out the light and closed the door without another word.

"I blew it,'' Erik whispered into the darkness. "I blew it.'' Why couldn't he have just said the words to the stupid poem even if he couldn't remember his grandmother ever saying good-night to him with it?

He lay in the wide bed and stared at the ceiling. He couldn't sleep. The bed was too soft, the room too large and unfamiliar. Everything was unfamiliar. He thought he would remember more. But he didn't. Sea Haven was a big white house with green shutters. But it was not the magical palace he'd conjured from his fragments of memory. The focal point of the half-remembered world of sighing waves, soft, white sand and endless sunshine. How many times had he closed his eyes and gone there to escape the bewildering violence and grinding poverty of his life? Erik sat up and punched the too-soft pillow with his fist. He was safe now. Fifteen hundred miles away from the man who had snatched him that day, moving so quickly and holding him so tightly that Erik hadn't even been able to cry out.

With any luck, Byron Fielder would have forgotten where Erik came from. His kidnapper—he'd never, ever, thought of the man as his father, never!—had always been a little crazy, a lot scary.

He'd bullied and threatened Erik so that the boy had never dared to tell anyone who he really was. Since Diana died just before Easter, Fielder had been worse—angry and more violent than ever. The woman who'd raised him, who'd done her best to protect him from her husband's abuse, was gone. Erik used to dream of somehow getting enough money scraped together for both of them to get away.

But three years earlier, when the idea had really begun to take shape in his mind, Diana had developed heart trouble and their hand-to-mouth existence and lack of medical care had hastened her death. He couldn't abandon her. So he'd bided his time and hoarded what little money he had until the only person he cared about was beyond hurting. Then, as soon as the opportunity presented itself, he stole Fielder's rattletrap old car, and headed south for Hurricane Beach.

They'd moved around so much when he was little that there was a good chance Fielder had forgotten where he'd found Erik. With any luck, his tormentor would never find him.

He closed his eyes, tried to sleep.

He was safe now.

He was home.

CHAPTER TWO

"HE'S WAITING FOR YOU." Helene was sitting on the edge of the double bed, which was covered with a yellow and blue starburst quilt, in Megan's old room. The coverlet—already much-washed and somewhat frayed around the binding—had caught Megan's eye at a craft fair when she was a teenager. She'd bought it with the money from her first summer job.

She looked around, avoiding her mother's eyes, searching almost desperately for some small task. There was nothing left to do. The one good dress she'd brought with her was hanging in the closet. Her shorts and sleeveless tops were in the second drawer of the tall mahogany bureau, her underwear and nightgown in the top. Her toilet articles were neatly arranged in the mirrored cabinet above the double sink in the adjoining bathroom. She'd combed her hair and touched up her makeup.

"It's time, Megan," Helene prompted softly. "It's time to see your son."

"I know."

But she wasn't ready. She didn't know if she'd ever be ready. Helene was watching her closely. Megan forced herself to smile. She knew her mother was anxious, but there was little Megan could do to allay those anxieties. She was scared. What if she didn't recognize the boy? Or what if she did recognize her son, and then went to pieces, unable to hold back the emotions she'd kept bottled up inside her for so many years? She shook her head. She would never let that happen. She would be strong, because she had to be. "I'm ready. Let's go down."

Helene slipped her arm through Megan's as they descended the wide stairway to the lower floor. "He's out on the beach," she explained, not for the first time although Megan didn't tell her so. "He's been out there most of the afternoon. Your sister brought him a pair of jogging shorts and a couple of T-shirts from one of the shops near hers. What few things he has are entirely unsuitable for August in Florida."

"Does he need more clothes, Mom?" Megan asked. She was paying scant attention to what her mother was saying. Her heart was beating so hard and so fast she could barely hear Helene's words over the rush of blood pounding in her ears.

"He needs everything. It will be something you can do together. Shop—" Helene bit off her next words with a stricken little sound. "I'm sorry. I—"

"Don't, Mom. Don't start remembering. For both our sakes."

Helene nodded. "I'm not going to look backward anymore," she said. "Only forward." Her mother's words held meaning on several levels. They could just as easily apply to Helene's own unhappy situation with Megan's father.

Megan had only arrived in Hurricane Beach half an hour ago. Her plane had been held up by bad weather in Saint Louis, and the drive from Tallahassee had been slowed by vacation traffic and road construction. She'd had no time to talk to Helene about anything but the impending meeting with Derek. Still, the strained atmosphere of Sea Haven had been evident. Her parents' house was no longer the happy home of her childhood memories. It was suddenly too big, and too imposing without the warming echoes of her father's booming voice and her mother's laughter. Both Helene and Merrick now spoke only in cool, level tones and only when necessary. Obviously their marital difficulties, which seemed to have started a few months ago, had escalated.

"I'd hoped you two could talk over lunch," Helene went on, her fingers tightening on Megan's arm. "It might have been easier that way. With your father to fill in the gaps. You were so late I was afraid that Noah would be here before you. Of course, he's flying into Pensacola and that's a longer drive..." She must have realized she was rambling and stopped talking. Megan squeezed her hand to show she understood.

Merrick was waiting for them at the bottom of the stairs. "He's back from his walk," he said without preamble as they approached.

"I wish he had asked one of us to go with him," Helene fretted. "He's not familiar with the area. Or with the tide or the currents running along the shore. Did you remember to warn him to stay away from the old pier? That relic is a death trap. We should have had it torn down years ago."

"He's back safe and sound." Merrick's tone was soothing, but the furrows between his eyebrows had deepened farther. In the past he would have reached out and patted Helene on the shoulder or taken her hand. Today he did nothing, just stood awkwardly a few feet away, offering only the comfort of his words.

They'd reached the French doors leading out onto the second-story deck. Megan stopped short. Beyond the glass, the restless blue-green waters of the gulf stretched to the horizon. She had always loved the ocean. Until Derek had been taken from her. And then she had begun to fear it. She had terrifying visions of walking on the beach and finding the murdered body of her child washed ashore by the waves.

She took an instinctive step backward. Helene's hand tightened on her arm. "Go on," she urged. "Go to him."

Anxiety and elation warred within her. "Come with me."

Helene shook her head. "No, dear," she said, smiling gently. "You two should be alone this first time. Go."

A male figure wearing a white T-shirt and navy blue running shorts stood at the water's edge. Megan didn't move. "What does he look like, Mom?" she asked, her voice barely above a whisper.

Helene reached for the curved brass handle of the French doors. "See for yourself."

It was one of the hardest things she had ever done, walking from the dim, cool living room into the blinding bright Florida sunshine. The heat and humidity hit her with the power of a steam train, taking her breath away. She pulled her sunglasses out of her skirt pocket and put them on. They cut the glare. And more important, they provided a shield to help hide her emotions.

The sound of the ocean concealed her approach. Megan stopped a few feet behind the still figure of the young man who claimed he was her son. She swallowed hard, shoving her hands into the pockets of her cotton skirt to hide their shaking. Somehow she had imagined he would be facing her when she first saw him up close. Instead, she was presented with a broad back and narrow waist and hips.

He was hunkered down now, his weight resting on the balls of his feet as he studied something in the sand. He picked it up. Megan caught a glimpse of a sand dollar in his hand. Derek had always been fascinated by shells of every kind, but especially by the small sea urchins that so resembled a piece of pirate gold. A sob worked its way into her throat, cutting off her breath. She willed it away.

"Derek?" No response. She wondered for a moment if she had only imagined she'd spoken his name out loud. "Derek," she said again, louder this time so that it would carry over the sound of the waves and the cries of the gulls overhead.

He stiffened, dropped the sand dollar as though he'd been caught with something he shouldn't have. He looked at her over his shoulder. He wasn't wearing sunglasses as she was, and his eyes were narrowed against the glare of the afternoon sun. She couldn't see their color. He rose slowly, unfolding until he stood several inches above her five and a half feet. He moved with unstudied rawboned grace, all arms and legs and wrists and hands. His hair was long and shaggy, dark brown, without a hint of the auburn highlights Helene insisted were there.

Megan's feet were rooted to the sand. She couldn't speak. Couldn't move to embrace him. Now that the day she'd waited so long for was finally here, she didn't know what to do, what to say next. She was staring. He seemed to grow uncomfortable under the scrutiny and took a half step backward. A wave, bolder than the rest, washed over the heels of his scuffed running shoes, drawing her attention to his legs, lightly furred with dark hair.

A man's legs.

Her little boy's legs had been pink and chubby and smooth as satin.

How could she ever know for certain if this almost-man was her lost baby? How could she ever believe without reservation?

That way lay madness. Megan pushed aside her doubts and made herself smile. "Hello, Derek," she said, her throat tight and aching with tears long suppressed.

"Don't call me that," he blurted out. "My name is Erik."

"I'm...I'm sorry."

His hands curled into fists at his sides, just as her own had done. "I...I didn't mean to scare you," he apologized, his voice cracking on the last word. "I...I'm just not used to that name anymore."

"I...yes, of course," Megan said, feeling her nails bite into the flesh of her palms. "My mother told me that. I'm sorry, too. I'll try to get used to calling you...Erik. It's...it's not so different a name, after all."

He dropped his eyes to the sand for a moment, then looked back at her face. His eyes were gray, so dark a gray they were almost black. Her son's eyes had been gray, but the soft gray of a rainy sky, not the color of dark storm clouds. "Thanks," he said. "I appreciate that. What should I call you?"

"I'm Megan," she said, aware her voice barely carried over the ocean sounds. "I'm your mother."

"I guessed that," he replied, still watching her.

Guessed. The word stung. He didn't remember her, it was obvious from his expression. "You don't have to call me Mom." She hadn't realized how much it would hurt to say that, but it did. She plowed on, ignoring the new ache in her heart. "You can call me Megan if you like." She held out her hands. "Welcome home, Erik."

He didn't move for an endless few seconds and then he stepped into her arms. His body was tense and tightly coiled. She reached up and touched her lips to his cheek. He put his hands awkwardly around her waist and let her hold him for a brief moment. Sensing that he was holding himself rigidly in check—on the verge of bolting—she let him go. He stepped away.

"Let's go sit under the deck," Megan suggested, her voice rough with the tears she refused to let him see. "It's cooler there. There's always a breeze. You can tell me how you found us."

She hadn't allowed herself to dream of this meeting for many years. She had no expectations, she told herself. She was not disappointed in his reticence. But, *Oh, God,* she had thought *she* would know that he was hers the moment she touched him. Yet touching him had changed nothing. He was still as much a stranger to her as she was to him.

Erik walked beside her in silence. She motioned him to one of the chairs grouped in the sand under the high deck floor, but he didn't sit down. There was a breeze just as she had predicted and behind them the concrete wall of the garage provided the privacy she sought. Megan had felt her parents' eyes on them as they walked from the beach to the house, knew they were anxiously watching this first meeting from behind the hurricane-shuttered windows. And Erik obviously sensed it, too. She had seen him flick a surreptitious half glance at the second-floor windows as they walked.

"Is this okay?" she asked. "Would you like me to get you something to drink? Iced tea? A soft drink."

He shook his head. "No, ma'am. I'm fine."

"Do you think you could call me Megan?"

"Okay...Megan."

"D—Erik," she corrected herself. "Have you been Erik—ever since we lost you."

"Yes."

"Erik who?"

"Just Erik."

He set his lips in a tight line. *Dear God*, the same way Noah used to do when she quizzed him too stridently about his SEAL deployments. She tried a different tack. "Where have you been all these years?"

"A lot of places," he said.

"Who...who took you?"

"A man."

"Who, Erik?"

"I don't want to talk about it," he said. His jaw clenched. He refused to meet her eye.

"All right," Megan replied calmly, as another sharp, stinging pain circled her heart. He didn't want her to know who had taken him. He was trying to protect the monster who had stolen him away from her. "We won't talk about it until you want to." She held out her hand. "Please. Sit down. Don't go."

"Okay." He did as she asked, but he perched on the very edge of the cushion.

"Did…did the people you were with treat you well?" She thought for a moment he would refuse to answer that question, too.

"They were okay," he said. He watched her warily.

"Did you go to school?"

"My m— I learned at home," he said.

"In Michigan?"

"Yeah."

"I've never been there."

"It's a big state," he said as if to forestall any more questions about the location of his kidnapper's home. "Would you take off your sunglasses?" he asked suddenly.

Megan lifted shaking fingers to her face. "I'd forgotten I was still wearing them."

She took off her sunglasses, folded them carefully in her lap and then slowly lifted her face to his.

He was studying her very closely.

"Does this help?" she whispered. "Do you remember me?"

"Your hair. I remember it was light-colored like

that, like moonlight." He colored slightly, then frowned. "But short and curly, I think."

She nodded. "It used to be."

"Your eyes are kind of green. "I thought—I thought they might be gray like mine."

"They look gray sometimes," Megan admitted. "Depending on what color I wear. Yours are nearly the same color as your father's."

"I don't remember what he looked like."

"What do you remember, Erik?" She wondered how long it would be before she could say that name without hesitation.

"The sea and the sand. White like snow. And the sun shining on it, bright and hot. This house." He lifted his shoulders. "I mean that it was big and white and when I ran through the rooms looking for you or my grandmother there were echoes."

Megan nodded. "Go on."

"And the address. I always used to repeat it at night, after I went to bed."

"And it brought you back to us." She couldn't stop the tears that rolled down her cheeks. "No one will ever take you away from us again, Erik. I promise. If you just tell me who they are. Where they've been keeping you—"

He shot out of the chair. "No! I don't want to talk about it. I don't know if I even want to stay here. This isn't where you live, is it? Grandma said you live in Nebraska."

"I do." As far away form the sea as she could get.

"And my father. She said my father's in California."

"He is. But he's on his way to join us. He should arrive soon."

"I thought—I thought we'd be going to one of those places."

"I...we will. I've taken a leave of absence from my job for a couple of weeks. I'm a nurse. An administrator at a senior citizens complex. Did your grandmother tell you that?" He nodded. "I thought we could stay here, get to know each other a little better—"

He sat down again, his hands balled into fists on his thighs. "Yeah. Sure. That's fine. I'd like that."

Megan nodded. The glare of the sun off sand and water, the heat and humidity, the strain of holding her emotions in check were giving her a terrible headache. Erik looked pretty strung-out himself.

"Are you and my father divorced?" he asked suddenly.

"No. We're not divorced. We're separated."

"Did you break up because of me? Because I got kidnapped."

"No," Megan assured him, although her words were only partially true. "We did grow apart after we lost you. But it was mostly because your father was away so much. Did your grandmother tell you he's a SEAL?"

"A SEAL?"

"Yes. Special warfare. A commando."

"I know what you're talking about. I've read about them." He was frowning again, harder than ever.

"He's a lieutenant commander now," Megan explained. "He doesn't go on missions anymore. At least I don't think he does. I...I haven't seen him in a long time.''

"Did you look for me?" His voice was gruff, but he couldn't quite hide the tiny catch in his words.

"Oh, God, yes, Erik. We looked everywhere. For years. We passed out flyers. Your grandfather hired private detectives. We had your picture added to the files for Missing and Exploited Children.''

"What's that?" he asked suspiciously.

"It's a network of people who help parents search for kidnapped or abducted children.''

"You mean I was one of those milk-carton kids?"

Megan smiled. "Yes. Twice. Once when you were six and again when you were twelve. They computer-enhanced your photograph, hoping someone might recognize you as an older child.''

"Did the picture look like me?" he asked.

Megan cocked her head, studying the square chin, wide-set eyes, the too-large nose he had yet to grow into. There was a faint fuzz of a mustache on his upper lip. This young man, *her baby,* was old enough to shave. So much time had been lost, so many years stolen away from them.

"Yes," she said. "I think it did. I'll show it to you someday if you like.''

"Yeah, okay.''

"Erik, do you remember anything about what happened that day at the mall?"

"No. I don't remember.''

"Why won't you tell me about the people who took you? They should be punished.''

"I don't want that.''

"Erik, don't protect them. They stole you from

me." Megan knew she was skating very close to the edge but she couldn't stop herself.

"Why didn't you watch me better?" he retorted.

"I...I only let you out of my sight for a moment. Only a moment." Megan clamped her teeth on her lower lip to keep from lashing out in her own pain.

His eyes narrowed. He shrugged. "Yeah. It probably was only a minute. But it seemed like forever when I couldn't find you. All I remember is someone picked me up and held me so tight I couldn't even say a word. Then he started walking really fast." He ran his hands through his shaggy hair. "Walking and running and driving for a long, long time in a car. I still dream about it sometimes."

"Oh, Erik. I'm so sor—"

"I'm going to my room," he said abruptly. Then, perhaps realizing how harshly he'd spoken, he continued less forcefully, "I'm beat. I'm going to crash for a while." Footsteps sounded on the deck above their heads. Erik looked up, then back at her, his gaze focused on a spot just past her left ear. "Someone's here. Is there any way I can get back upstairs without them seeing me?"

Megan frowned. "Not unless the door to the garage is unlocked." His eyes darkened, taking on a trapped look. His glance flickered to the beach. "Look," she said, "it's probably only your aunt Amy. She'll understand if you're too tired to stay and visit."

"It sounds like a man," Erik informed her.

Megan heard a man's voice, too, one that sent tiny shivers of awareness up and down her spine.

"It's okay, Erik. There's nothing to be afraid of

here.'' Her words were for her own reassurance as much as for his. She didn't hold out her hand because she couldn't bear the thought of him rejecting her touch. She turned and started up the open wooden staircase without waiting to see if he would follow.

Halfway up the flight of stairs Megan knew her suspicion had been correct. She came level with a pair of highly polished black shoes. She kept climbing, directing her gaze past the knife-sharp pleats in the uniform trousers that rose above those mirror-bright shoes, all attention focused on the sound of Erik climbing behind her.

Her mother and father were standing behind and to the left of the tall man at the top of the stairs. Merrick's slight frown and Helene's fluttering hands conveyed their nervousness. ''Megan. We were just coming to look for you,'' Helene began.

''Hello, Megan.''

Megan climbed the last two steps to the deck floor before she answered. ''Hello, Noah,'' she said, raising her eyes to his. He'd changed very little over the last eight years. His face was still as roughly chiseled, his chin like granite, his dark almost charcoal gray—eyes wide-set beneath straight dark eyebrows. His shoulders were just as broad as she remembered, his hips as narrow, his stomach flat and hard. His hair was still as dark as a raven's wing without a hint of gray.

He was a tall man, an inch or two over six feet, his body as well muscled and beautifully proportioned as ever. She darted a quick glance at his chest, noting the new row of ribbons and decorations above his breast pocket. In the military a man wore his résumé on his chest, and Noah's was impressive indeed. And above the rows of ribbons, gold and gleaming was the eagle and trident symbol that proclaimed him a navy SEAL. He stepped back, out of her way, moving with the catlike grace of a man completely at ease with his body.

Megan thought she'd prepared herself for this meeting. She'd thought she could meet her estranged husband face-to-face after eight years and keep her composure. But she was wrong. She had loved Noah Carson passionately, then had come close to hating him with almost equal intensity when their grief over losing their child drove them apart. She could never, never be indifferent to him.

His eyes moved over her face and figure just as she had studied him. She hadn't gained any weight since their separation but she was wearing her hair longer now than eight years ago. He would notice that. Fine and flyaway she'd given up trying to perm some body into it ages ago, and opted for a shoulder-length style that she most often wore, as today, in a soft knot on the top of her head.

"You're wearing your hair longer. I like it."

"Th-thank you," she stuttered, thrown off guard by the compliment. She had expected him to notice her hairstyle, not to mention it.

"It's good to see you, Megan."

"It's good to see you, too, Noah."

"Where is he?"

Megan looked down over her shoulder. Erik had followed her up the stairs but had stopped out of Noah's line of sight. Megan moved out of the way, motioning the boy to join her on the deck.

"Noah," she said, concentrating on keeping the tremors that coursed through her heart and body from transferring themselves to her voice. "This is...Erik. Our son."

Erik stared transfixed for a long moment at the tall imposing figure of his father. Then with a strangled little cry he launched himself into Noah's arms. He whispered a single word as he burrowed into the hard comfort of Noah's chest.

"*Dad!*"

CHAPTER THREE

ONCE SHE FOUND OUT Noah hadn't eaten breakfast or lunch, there was no stopping Helene. He gave up protesting after the third go-round on the subject. His mother-in-law sailed off to the kitchen, taking an un-protesting and obviously shell-shocked Megan with her. Merrick followed them, leaving Noah alone with his son.

"Your mother says that you prefer to be called Erik," he said, suddenly at a loss for words now that they were alone. He had been shaken to the core by the strength of his emotion as he held his son in his arms for the first time in a dozen years.

"Yes, sir," his son replied. Erik had recovered quickly and was now sitting beside Noah on Helene and Merrick's sofa.

"It'll take some getting used to but I think I can manage," Noah said.

"It's what I'm used to being called, sir."

"You called me Dad a few minutes ago," Noah said softly.

"I...I know. But maybe I shouldn't." Erik looked at Noah with anguish in his dark eyes. "I...I told Me...Megan that I would call her Megan, not Mom."

"I see. Is there someone else you call Mom, Erik?"

"Yes. But she died four months ago. Her name was Diana."

"Was she good to you?"

He nodded. "I...I loved her. I couldn't leave her there alone with— Alone." He fell silent once more. He looked down at his hands, then sideways at Noah out of the corner of his eye. "I...I probably upset her. My...Megan, I mean."

"Did you tell her about your other mother?"

"No, I—" His hands dangled between his knees, but Noah saw the tension in the tendons of his bones and wrists. Erik hunched his shoulders, drawing into himself. "I didn't know how."

"That's okay. You can tell her when you're ready. And it's all right to call her Megan. And you can call me Noah if you want to."

"I never called *him* Dad," he said with ferocity. Noah was taken aback, although he allowed nothing of what he was feeling to show on his face.

"Who, Erik? Are you talking about the man who kidnapped you?"

"Yes. I never called him Dad. Never."

"It's okay, son." He reached out and touched Erik on the shoulder. The boy's body stiffened slightly. Noah lifted his hand immediately.

Erik was watching him closely. He took a deep breath and nodded once. "Maybe I'd better call you Noah, okay?"

"Okay. How long did it take you to hitchhike down here?"

"A couple of weeks. I stole our...his...car and I

drove it as far as I could. I didn't have much money. I couldn't afford to spend any of it on gas. I got as far as Ann Arbor—'' He stopped abruptly, as if realizing he was giving away too many details. ''That's when I started hitching. It took a lot longer than I thought to get here. I ran out of money in Mobile. I had to walk for a day or so before a trucker picked me up and bought me a meal. He was going as far as Tallahassee. After that it was easy.''

Noah doubted that. His gut squeezed tight at the thought of what other hardships his son had endured, but he kept his dismay to himself. Erik was close to breaking point. Noah had seen that same state, the same fierce, desperate struggle for control in his SEAL students. The boy needed time to work through the memories of his almost-lifelong ordeal. Noah had no doubt that his son had been through hell. God, what kind of bastard had had Erik in his power all these years? If it was the last thing Noah ever did, he would find the son of a bitch and make him wish that he had never been born.

''Have you always been a SEAL?'' Erik asked abruptly.

Noah pushed away his angry thoughts. ''Since you were just a baby,'' he said.

''Back in Michigan there was an old guy who lived down the road. He'd been in the navy. In Vietnam. Sometimes he'd talk about what it was like. He talked about the SEALs.''

Noah nodded. ''My boss was in 'Nam. He has a lot of tall tales to tell.''

''Tall tales? You mean they're not true?'' Erik's

eyes narrowed, gray eyes, Noah noticed, but not quite as dark as his own.

"Some of them were true," Noah conceded. "Some of them may have gotten a little wilder in the telling."

"Are SEALs really trained to kill a man with their bare hands?"

"SEALs are soldiers, Erik. They are trained to do what soldiers have always had to do." Noah didn't like the turn the conversation was taking. He knew only too well that he could kill a man with his bare hands. Once a long time ago, in a faraway place, he'd had to do that very thing, but it wasn't something he intended to discuss with his son. "Why do you ask that?" His voice must have been harsher than he intended. Erik drew back, putting more distance between them.

"I was just wondering, that's all." He changed the subject. "Are you going to be staying here for a while?"

"In Hurricane Beach, yes," Noah confirmed. "But not here at Sea Haven."

"Why not?" Erik inquired. Noah's acceptance of his change of subject seemed to have satisfied the youngster. He relaxed slightly. The hunted look left his eyes.

"I think it will be easier for everyone if I stay somewhere else. Your mother and I have been apart for a long time. And your grandmother and I haven't always got along. She didn't approve of the fact that Megan and I eloped after only three weeks. Megan was only nineteen and I wasn't much older—a sailor with no prospects. But then you came along, and your grandmother thought the sun rose and set on you.''

Erik managed a half smile. "You won't be far away, will you?"

"Just down the beach. At the Sand Dollar Cabins. Have you seen them?"

Erik shook his head. "I haven't been to town yet."

"Can't miss them. They're just down the boardwalk from your aunt Amy's shop. Cabin C. Lucky for me it's late enough in the season that they had a vacancy, otherwise I'd probably be camping out under the municipal pier.''

"Okay," Erik said, "I think I can find them."

"I think we've given your grandmother…and Megan enough time to prepare whatever it is they're working on in there. Want to join me for a snack?"

Erik glanced toward the back of the house, where the kitchen was located, then shook his head. "No, thanks. All Grandma has done since I got here yesterday is feed me. I'm beat. I guess I'm not used to this much sun. I'm going to go up to my room. Will you tell them for me?"

"Sure, son." Erik stood up and Noah rose with him.

"I'm glad you're here," Erik said.

"I'm glad you're back with us." Noah reached out and after a heartbeat's hesitation ruffled Erik's thick dark hair. Erik didn't flinch, but neither did he smile, just stood there staring up at Noah.

"Did you used to do that when I was little?" he asked.

Noah nodded. The last time he'd done that to his son Erik had been a toddler, today he was almost a man, less than half a foot shorter than Noah. "How about I pick you up tomorrow morning and we go get you a haircut?"

Erik brushed his hair back from his face as Noah dropped his hand. "Yeah. I think that might be a good idea. My mom…Diana," he amended, "always used to cut my hair. I guess it's been a while."

"And I'll bet you could use some threads."

"Yeah. I could."

"How about ten o'clock?"

"Okay. I'll meet you at your cabin."

"Good idea," Noah said. "Ten it is. I'd ask you to breakfast but I doubt you'll get out of here with less than a three-course meal."

"Yeah." Erik smiled.

A real smile. Noah's heart thudded against his breastbone. It was an adolescent, almost grown-up version of the smile on the worn and creased photograph of his four-year-old son that he still kept in his wallet. The picture had been taken only a few weeks before Erik disappeared. It had been waiting for him, along with the devastating news that the little boy had been kidnapped, when he'd returned from a covert operation halfway around the world. An assignment that as far as he knew was still classified Top Secret a dozen years later.

And the old guilt that had plagued Noah all these years surfaced again.

I should have been there to protect my son.

"ERIK? Where are you going?"

Father and son were standing at the bottom of the stairs when Megan walked into the room. Helene was still in the kitchen, searching for fresh nachos to go with Amy's homemade salsa, worrying where Annie, whose day off it was, had hidden the chips. Megan found herself too curious about how Erik and Noah were getting on to be of any help, so she left the kitchen to rejoin her husband and son. When she spoke, Erik looked at her over his shoulder. Noah turned to face her.

"Erik's had a little too much sun. He's going upstairs to rest."

Megan's eyes flew to the teenager. His face and arms and legs were sun-reddened. Professional training and maternal instinct took over. "Are you all right, Erik? You aren't running a fever, are you?"

"No, ma'am."

"Are you sure?" She took a step forward but Noah was blocking her path up the stairs. She stopped, resting her hands on the newel post. She tilted her head up to scan Erik's face. "You're not used to this strong sun. It's easy to get overexposed."

"He's okay, Megan," Noah inserted. "He just needs a little time to himself."

"But the food——"

"Let him go, Megan." There was the slightest hint of command slipping along the edges of Noah's low, rough voice. A subtle warning to her not to push.

Noah was right, little though Megan wanted to admit it. Erik was wary of her. She dared not press too hard for intimacies he wasn't ready to extend. She made herself speak calmly, "Will you be down to join us for dinner, Erik?" she asked as the boy started up the stairs.

"Yes, ma'am," he said. Then to Noah, "I'll be ready at ten tomorrow."

"I'll be waiting."

Megan watched Erik climb the steps. Was there anything familiar about the way Erik walked, the way he climbed the stairs? Nothing that could link the tall lanky adolescent with her lost toddler. Was she going to be able to accept that he was her son? God, she hoped so. But at the moment such a leap of faith was not within her reach.

Noah's voice interrupted her thoughts. "He's had a rough day, Megan. He needs some time to let it all sink in."

"What did he mean he'd be ready at ten tomorrow?" She swiveled to face Noah.

"I'm going to take him to get a haircut and buy some clothes."

"*You're* going to take him?" How had that come about? How had he even known that Erik needed clothes and shoes? They had been alone for barely fifteen minutes.

"Yes."

Megan's head was spinning. Noah had come back into her life almost as suddenly as her son had. Her husband was just as much a stranger. Now he seemed to have made an instant connection with Erik, a bond she hadn't been able to achieve.

"You have no right to do that," she said in a low, strained voice.

Noah's rough-hewn features hardened further at the vehemence of her words. "What do you mean I have no right? I'm his father."

"You were never there for him. He only knew you

from your picture." Megan threaded her hands together where they rested on the newel post, willing away the tremors that coursed through her body. "I don't understand why he came to you and not to me."

"He's had a mother all these years, Megan," Noah said quietly.

Another broadside, another aching blow to her heart and her soul. How many more of these was she expected to absorb today? Abruptly Megan walked away from the stairs, into the cool quiet of Merrick's study. She stared blindly at the walls of built-in bookshelves that held dozens of volumes, old and new, well-read and well-loved, family photographs in gold and silver frames, and mementos of her parents' travels.

"That's why he doesn't know what to call me, isn't it?" Noah had followed her, moving silently and lightly for such a big man. She could feel him behind her although she didn't turn around.

"Yes," he said.

"He wouldn't tell me anything about his life. I...he must not want us to find her, confront her."

"The woman's dead, Megan."

She whirled to face him. "He told you that, too?"

"Yes."

"Did he have another father also?" The words came out sounding mean and petty but she couldn't help herself.

"He had no one but the man who stole him from us."

"He wouldn't tell me anything about them. I think he would have run away rather than tell me who they were." A sob worked its way into her throat. She swallowed hard. "He's protecting them."

"No, Megan. You've got it wrong."

"How can you be so sure?"

"He didn't have a father. He had a captor. He didn't really have a mother. He had a woman who, for whatever reasons, cooperated with her husband to keep Erik with them, and away from us for twelve years. He's exhausted and mixed-up and scared to death."

"Scared to death?"

"He's been abused, Megan."

"No."

"The signs are there," Noah said grimly. Megan had seen them, too, but she didn't want to admit it. Erik didn't want to be touched. He wouldn't make eye contact, as though he was angry, or scared to death, as Noah had said. "Mentally and emotionally for sure, probably physically, too."

She pressed her fingers to her lips to still the scream she felt rising from the very center of her being. "Sexually abused?" she managed to whisper.

Noah shook his head. His features now appeared carved from stone. "I don't know, Megan. It's possible, but there's no way to know if he won't tell us."

"We have to find a doctor. A therapist—"

"I don't think it's a good idea to press him about it now."

"How can you be so sure?" she repeated.

"I work with kids only a few years older than Erik every day. I train them to risk their lives in a hundred different ways, in a hundred different places, Megan. I have to know what makes them tick. It's my job.''

"Oh, God." She looked up at the ceiling as though she might see through the plaster and thick wooden beams into the heart and mind of the young boy above. "He really needs someone to talk to.''

Noah moved closer. The breadth of his shoulders, the hard wall of his chest filled her vision. She could feel the heat of his body, smell his soap and the tangy aroma of his after-shave, the faint pleasantly musky scent of his skin. "He has us, Megan. That's enough for now."

She stepped back, trying to put a little space between them. Every inch of her body remembered the touch and taste and feel of Noah's hands and lips on her skin, the hard strength of his legs tangled with hers.

She took another step backward. *He has us.* A clear hot flame of anger sparked to life inside her. "He has us," she repeated with a hiss. "He never had *us,* Noah. He only had me. You were never there for him. You didn't even come home to me until three endless weeks after he was kidnapped.''

"Megan, we've been over this before.''

"That doesn't make it easier." She flicked her fingertip over the cold metal of the trident badge on his chest. "You were a SEAL first, last and always. Being a husband and a father came in a distant second.''

"You knew what being a SEAL wife meant.''

She spun away. "No, I didn't. I wasn't even twenty years old. I was pregnant. I loved you and I wanted you to be happy in your work. I never knew that I was giving you up to a way of life that demanded everything of you with nothing left for your wife and son.''

"It wasn't like that, Megan.''

She turned back, her anger almost spent. "It was, for me. You were closer to your swim buddy than you were to me. The navy wouldn't even notify you when our baby was kidnapped.'' She bit the inside of her lip hard enough to draw blood. The pain focused her, kept her tears at bay. And kept her from throwing herself into his arms to seek comfort from his strength.

"Megan, I was on a mission—''

"I was alone. Alone.'' She shut her lips tight against other hateful words that bubbled to the surface. "Don't think you can make it all right now. Go back to Coronado, Noah. Leave me with my son.''

He moved so quickly she didn't have time to get out of his way. His face was hard, his eyes flashed dark fire as he towered over her. "I'm his father. I have no intention of going anywhere. You can hate me all you want but you can't keep me from our son, so don't even think of trying to stop him from spending time with me.''

He spun away and was gone from the house before she could gather her shaken wits. Weak in the knees, she sat down heavily on the sofa and dropped her head in her hands.

How had it happened? Even though there was nothing left of her marriage to Noah but a formality of law, they should have been able to find common ground on this the most momentous day of their lives.

A dozen years ago she'd lost her son to a stranger. Now was she going to lose him to his father?

"WHAT IS THE MATTER, Helene?" Merrick rose from the butcher-block table in the kitchen as Helene returned from the living room still carrying the tray she'd taken in moments before. Helene avoided looking directly into his eyes. She hated the wariness, the guarded politeness she saw there so often these days. "Has something happened to Erik?"

"No. I mean I think *he's* all right."

She stared down at the tray of cheese and fruit Merrick had helped her arrange only moments before. After nearly fifty years of marriage, he was still very thoughtful about things like that, as if there was no strain between them. But in the past, they would have talked as they worked. She would have asked him questions, and he would have given her advice. Which she might or might not have taken. And they would have argued a little, laughed a little. Now they were mostly silent. She knew if they were ever going to recapture what they'd had, she was going to have to make the first move. Three months ago she'd talked Merrick into pretending they were contemplating divorce. She'd hoped that Megan, Lisa and Amy, their three estranged daughters, would unite in an effort to save their parents' marriage. But almost immediately her plan had escalated beyond her control. The Pandora's box she'd opened that spring day had exposed long-buried resentments and anger she hadn't even known still existed within her. Merrick had been astounded—and hurt—when she'd accused him of being controlling and overprotective. Finally, Helene had moved out of Sea Haven, and she and

Merrick began to talk of selling the family estate. As a last-ditch effort to save her marriage, Helene had moved back, albeit into a separate bedroom. Now she had to find a way to reach out to her husband.

"Helene." Merrick took the untouched tray from her hands. His voice was sharp, as though he'd spoken her name more than once. "Tell me what's wrong. If Erik's okay, then it must be something else."

Helene forced her thoughts back to the present.

"There is something wrong. I wasn't there for long—they didn't even see me. Megan's in tears in the living room. And Noah stormed out the front door. They've had some kind of fight. A fight over Erik."

"How can you be sure?" Merrick looked past her, as though he could see through the door into the living room.

"What else could it be? They haven't seen each other in years. What else would they have to fight about?"

"You may be right. The three of them haven't gotten off on the best foot."

"I'm certain it has something to do with the way the boy took to Noah so quickly. It hurt her, Merrick."

"What do you suggest we do?" he said.

Helene almost smiled. He was trying hard. She held out her hand to touch his chest, tell him how much she appreciated it, but a flicker of movement behind them caught her eye. She held up her hand in warning. "Erik." She shifted her gaze past Merrick to the doorway of the old servants' staircase that led to the upstairs bedrooms. "What can we do for you, sweetheart?"

"I was wondering if you had any aspirin down here," the boy said. He was wearing shorts but not a shirt. His face and arms and chest were flushed with sunburn, his eyes bright.

"Yes." She hurried over to the cupboard to the left of the sink. "I think there's a bottle here someplace. And I know there's one in the hall bathroom." The medication was on the third shelf, above her reach. A habit left over from when there had been a trio of inquisitive little girls in the house. "Merrick?"

"I've got it," he said, stretching his long arm past her head to snag the aspirin. He handed the bottle to her. "I can never get these childproof things open. Damned arthritis. Will you do it?"

Another small concession. "Of course," she said, and this time she did manage a tiny smile. He didn't smile back, and she wished desperately that he had. She spun on her heel. "Here, Erik. Take these. I'll get you a glass of water."

Merrick had anticipated her words. He handed her a glass. She took it, filled it with tap water without looking at him and passed it to Erik.

"Thank you, ma'am." Erik swallowed the tablets and washed them down with the water.

"Do you think you could call me Grandma?" Helene asked wistfully.

"And Granddad," Merrick added, coming half a step closer.

"Okay." Erik's voice was flat, noncommittal. Helene wished she'd held her tongue.

She touched Erik's shoulder with the tip of her finger. He flinched slightly at the contact. "Oh, dear, you've got a bad burn. Wait a moment. I'll get some vinegar. That's good for sunburn. It takes the sting away."

"No, thanks," he said hastily, walking backward toward the stairs. "It doesn't hurt. Not really. I'll be fine. I'll just go back to my room and rest."

"I'll call you when dinner's ready."

"Is my father going to be here?"

"Well. No." She looked at Merrick, wondering what to say next.

"Actually, he left before we could invite him," Merrick said.

"Yes," Helene said, grateful for Merrick's tactful reply. "He left before we could invite him."

"Oh. I'm not very hungry. I don't think I'll come down, if that's okay."

"If that's what you want. There will be plenty of food. You can come down for a snack anytime."

"Thanks." Erik disappeared back up the stairs.

"Do you think he overheard us?"

"I don't know." Merrick turned back to the counter and closed the open cupboard door. Before, he would have reached out and taken her in his arms, comforted her. But no longer.

"Oh, Merrick," she said wistfully. "This should be one of the happiest days of our lives. We have our grandchild back with us. Megan and Noah have their son." Her next words came straight from the heart, because they spoke to her own pain, as well. "But nothing is the way it should be."

CHAPTER FOUR

THE INTERIOR of Amy's store, Rêve Rags, was pleasantly cool after the blazing heat outside. It smelled good, too, like flowers and spice. A lot different from the smells of wet sand and seawater, and once in a while a whiff of dead fish that had accompanied Erik on his walk into town.

"Let me guess," said a girl's voice, sassy and musical all at the same time. "You must be the Lost Boy I read about in the *Chronicle*."

"Huh?" Erik blinked once or twice, and homed in on a slim dark-haired figure now leaning both forearms on the glass counter near the cash register.

"You read about me in the newspaper?"

She frowned. "Yeah. Yesterday's edition."

"Let me see it."

"I threw it away."

"I've got to find a copy." Who had talked to the newspapers about him? Megan? Helene?

"Hey don't get your shorts in a knot. It's just a little article saying you came back. None of your family would talk to the reporters. Amy told them so. But you're big news around here, so they printed it anyway." He must have still looked shocked because she added, "No one reads that rag except the people here in town and *everybody* knew you were here days ago."

"Yeah. Okay." She was right. No one in Tallahassee or Pensacola cared what went on in Hurricane Beach. And if Byron Fielder ever got this far, he wouldn't need to read the newspaper to find him.

"Hey, I'm sorry. I didn't mean to give you a fit of the vapors or something."

"I haven't got the vapors." Whatever *the vapors* were.

She was quick. "The vapors. Like in *Sense and Sensibility*. You know. Jane Austen. It's a great movie. Have you seen it?" He hadn't seen the movie. But he'd heard of Jane Austen. His moth— Diana had taught Erik to read when he was only five and she'd managed to get him books wherever they were. It was one thing she'd stood up to Byron Fielder about and never backed down, no matter how violent her husband's temper became.

The girl came out from behind the counter. She looked to be about the same age as he was. She wasn't tall but she wasn't short, either. She was wearing pink sandals and a pair of really short cutoffs that made her tanned legs go on forever. On top of that she wore some kind of pale yellow, see-through, lacy shirt over a neon-pink bikini top. The shirttails were tied in a knot just below her breasts. Perched on her short, black hair was a white sailor cap with Hurricane Beach embroidered on it in the same bright pink and yellow as her top. He'd never seen anyone dressed quite that way before.

She stood there tapping her foot for a moment, and Erik realized he was staring at her legs. He lifted his eyes and was dismayed to find them focused on the tanned patch of skin below her breasts. Hurriedly he adjusted his gaze to about the level of the writing on her hat.

"You already know who I am," he blurted out. "Who are you?"

"I'm Kieran Costas. I work here part-time."

"Kieran Costas." He lowered his eyes to her face. Wasn't Costas his aunt Amy's married name? The last few days had passed in a haze. He figured he'd been sleeping at least eighteen hours a day. About all he remembered was waking up long enough to go to the bathroom and eat something once in a while when his grandmother descended on him and demanded that he do so.

There had been other voices and faces, too, he realized. His smiling red-haired aunt Amy with a tall gray-haired man at her side whose dark eyes looked a lot like the ones that belonged to the girl in front of him. His grandfather's gruff voice with its hint of British accent talking to another elderly man he called Doc Yount, who poked and prodded and hmmphed and then, blessedly, let him alone to sleep again.

And his mother and father always there at the edge of his consciousness, one or the other of them, never together, it seemed, but never absent, their voices low and soothing, somehow keeping the familiar nightmares at bay.

"I have a message for Amy," he blurted out, aware he'd been silent too long. "From my grandmother." It was just an invitation to lunch, and having him deliver the message had been Merrick's idea.

He suspected his grandfather knew he needed to get out of Sea Haven, away from Helene's constant hovering.

"She's not here." The girl cocked her head a little to one side. Erik followed the movement with his eyes. She had three glittering earrings in her left ear and two in the right. "She's at her house on the beach. Do you know which one it is?"

"No," he had to admit. "I...I don't. I thought she'd be here." Maybe his dad knew where Amy's place was? He'd seen the Sand Dollar Cabins on his way into town. He'd planned to go back there when he'd delivered his message. Take his dad up on his offer to buy him some clothes and get a haircut, since he'd slept through the outing they'd originally planned.

"Actually, she's with your mother going over the guest lists for your grandparents' anniversary party. Didn't you know that, either?"

"I haven't seen...Megan...yet today. I...slept in." Erik ran his hand through his too-long hair. He did feel a little like one of Peter Pan's Lost Boys suddenly transported out of Never-Never Land. Or maybe it was more like Rip van Winkle waking up after his long enchanted sleep.

"Yeah," the girl said dryly. "For three whole days."

She knew that, too. Erik felt heat crawling up his neck into his cheeks. He'd never spent much time around girls. The Fielder family had never stayed in one place long enough for him to make friends with anyone, really.

"If you want to wait around until Grace—that's

Amy's partner—gets back from the bank, I'll show you where Amy's cottage is. We'll take the scenic route, and I'll show you all the high points of Hurricane Beach.''

Erik's mouth went dry. He was wearing the pair of shorts and T-shirt that Amy had brought for him that first day. His shoes looked as if he'd dragged them out of a Dumpster somewhere—or walked and hitched a thousand miles in them. He really would feel like some kind of freak walking down Gulfview beside Kieran Costas. ''It's okay. I'll ask my da—Noah to help me find it.''

''Your dad.'' Kieran draped herself over a rackful of bathing suits, all sizes and shapes and colors of them, resting her chin on her folded hands, rolling her eyes. ''Steven Seagal in the flesh. I saw him the other day at Amy's place. He's even better-looking than my uncle Jon.'' She screwed up her forehead, considering. ''Actually, he's lots better-looking than Steven Seagal.''

''Who?'' Erik said. Steven Seagal? Who was he? Was she trying to make him look like an even bigger dork because he didn't know this guy?

''Steven Seagal. The movie star. In *Under Siege*. He plays this ex-navy SEAL who has to save a battleship from these crazy wacko, terrorist types... He can do anything. I mean he's indestructible—'' She broke off, straightening up so suddenly that for a split second Erik was left staring at her breasts again. ''Haven't you ever seen that movie?''

Indestructible. That's the way his dad had seemed standing there in his uniform that first day. Tall and strong and safe. Maybe that's why he'd acted like such an idiot and thrown himself into his arms. "I...we lived pretty far away from everything," Erik muttered, realizing she was waiting for an answer to her question.

"Didn't you have a VCR?" Her eyes narrowed. "Didn't you even have a TV?"

Erik shrugged. "The guy I lived with didn't believe in TVs."

Kieran looked at him with disbelief, and he suspected some pity. He held his breath waiting for her to start questioning him about the man who had kidnapped him, but she surprised him. "Bummer," she moaned with real feeling. "What about computers? Did he let you have one of those?"

"No. But—"

"God, how did you survive? I mean, I just don't know what I'd do if I couldn't surf the Net."

"There was—" The bell above the door jangled as someone entered the shop, and Erik ducked a few steps to one side, then swung around.

A tall black woman stopped in her tracks, her eyes widening at Erik's instinctive defensive maneuver. "Hi," she said, swinging a big woven bag off her shoulder and dumping it on the counter with a plop. "I'm Grace Kingsolver, your aunt Amy's partner, and I'll bet my next paycheck that you're Erik Carson." *Erik Carson. Not Erik Fielder.* He liked the sound of that.

"Yes, ma'am."

Grace held out her hand. "Welcome home."

"Thank you, ma'am." Erik took her hand.

"I'm glad to see you're feeling better." Her voice was low and rich and friendly.

"Thanks." Erik relaxed a little. He hoped she hadn't noticed how spooked he'd been when she walked in the door. He couldn't react like that every time someone took him by surprise.

"Erik's looking for Amy," Kieran told Grace. "Is it okay if I walk him down to her cottage? He doesn't know where it is."

"Sure," Grace said. "I'll hold down the fort. It doesn't look as if I'm going to be overrun by customers this morning."

"It's been slow," Kieran agreed. "It's too hot to shop."

"There are supposed to be thunderstorms later today. Maybe that will cool things off."

"Yeah," Kieran said, sounding unconvinced. "It'll take a hurricane to cool things off."

"Bite your tongue, girl," Grace scolded as she opened the cash register and slid a bank bag under the tray. "Let's not tempt the storm gods."

Kieran laughed as she sauntered toward the door. "You know this town's never been hit by a hurricane."

"Praise the Lord."

"The people that founded this town named it Hurricane Beach, like it was a reverse curse," she explained to Erik.

"A what, girl?" Grace demanded, shaking her head.

"You know. They said, 'We'll name it Hurricane Beach and then no hurricane will ever hit the town.' A reverse curse."

"A talisman," Erik said.

"Yeah. A charm. A spell."

"I prefer the story that says they named it Hurri-cane Beach to scare away the developers," Grace said as she hung her bag out of sight in a back room.

"Yeah, well, that's another one. And it worked until Palmer Boyce came to town."

"Who's Palmer Boyce?" Erik wanted to know.

"He's the snake-oil salesman who tried to get your grandparents to sell their land to him so he could build a bunch of high-rise condos. He's the one that's nearly broken up their marriage. Your grandmother even moved out of Sea Haven for a while. My great aunt Aurelia—"

"Kieran," Grace interrupted firmly. "I said you could take the time to go with Erik to Amy's place. But I do need you back here to help log in that ship-ment of accessories that arrived yesterday."

"Okay." Kieran looked momentarily nonplussed. "Let's go."

"Who's Palmer Boyce? What about my grandpar-ents not getting along?" Erik demanded as soon as they left the shop.

"Maybe it would be better if your mom told you everything that's going on. I...I don't know all the details." Kieran looked down at her bright pink san-dals and was silent for a few steps. "Look," she said finally. "I'm sorry I came on so strong back there. About your being a Lost Boy and all. It was mean."

"That's okay." It wasn't okay. But since she was willing to apologize, he could be a gentleman and accept.

She looked up at him, her dark eyes serious, all traces of bravado gone from her voice. "No," she said, "it wasn't okay. You couldn't help what happened to you. You were just a baby. You came back as soon as you could get away. The Lost Boys. They didn't want to leave Never-Never Land. They're like my dad." She swallowed hard. "My dad up and disappeared on me about four months ago."

"Disappeared?"

She clasped her hands behind her back and nodded. "He just took off. He…he's into drugs. He's an addict," she said, stringing the words together in a rush. "We don't know where he is. We don't know *how* he is. So I know a little how you feel. I mean, at least how your mom and dad feel. You know. So I guess, well, I guess maybe thinking about it made me nervous. And when I'm nervous I say things I shouldn't."

"That's okay." This time he meant it. "I took everybody by surprise." So Kieran knew how his mom and dad felt. That was what he wanted to know, too. Maybe she could explain it to him. He was suddenly very glad he'd run into Kieran Costas.

"I'll say you did. It's just like you came back from the dead."

"Yeah." *Dead.* That might just be how he'd end up if Fielder found him again. The thought sent chills up and down his spine. "How much farther is it to Aunt Amy's cottage?" he asked to change the subject. He'd never thought it would be this easy to talk to a girl. She was a good listener. And smart, too. But he had to stay on guard around her. He didn't want to say something he shouldn't, tell her things better kept to himself. Even though she seemed to know everything there was to know about his family.

Kieran gave him a funny look but answered his

question. "Just a couple more blocks down this way. Want to cross over to the boardwalk?"

"Okay. Good idea. It'll be cooler by the water."

"That's Forenza's Café," she said, pointing to a restaurant with colorful red and green and white umbrellas shading white wrought-iron tables on the sidewalk. "Their Italian ices are radical. And over there's a Slice of the Pie. They have the best pizza in Hurricane Beach. All the kids go there on Friday nights. Want to come along with me tonight? Meet some of the kids. School starts the day after Labor Day. That's only two weeks away. You're going to be going to school here, aren't you?"

"I...I don't know. My mom doesn't live here, you know. Or my dad."

"But if you wanted to, I bet you could stay at Sea Haven with your grandparents. I'll be a sophomore. You'll probably be a junior, right?"

He was having trouble keeping up with Kieran's scattergun approach to conversation. "I guess so. I'm sixteen."

"Yeah. I'll be sixteen on my next birthday, too. It's a pretty good school. The football team's awesome."

"I...I'd have to talk to Megan and Noah." She was going too fast for him again. "We haven't talked about where I'll go to school."

"Sorry," she said. "I'm always making plans for everyone else." She was quiet for a little while, then said, "I'd better stick to keeping my own life on track."

"There's something wrong besides your dad being gone?"

Kieran looked at him sharply, then nodded slightly. "I guess there's no way you could know yet, but sooner or later someone's bound to tell you. I did some pretty stupid things last spring. I let this older creep of a guy talk me into using my computer to take money out of other people's bank accounts. We were going to take it and run away. First to New Orleans, then maybe to L.A. Instead I got into a load of trouble. The juvenile court judge put me on kind of like, you know, probation under Uncle Jon's supervision, until I graduate from high school. Lucky for me they recovered the money and ran the creep out of town. But if I get into any more trouble at all, it's off to juvie home. And I have to do community service at the Y and the seniors' center and places like that every summer. And I have to pay back Uncle Jon some of the money it cost for my lawyer. And that's a fortune."

"Bummer," Erik said. He was a little shocked to hear what she had done. Still, he'd stolen a car and driven it hundreds of miles without a license. That was a felony, he was pretty sure. And another thing. Something that he hadn't told anyone. But he didn't want to think about that right now.

"Yeah, bummer," she agreed. "I was pretty stupid." She sighed. "But it's better than being in jail. Which is where Thea Aurelia said I belonged when she first found out what happened. I've been going to see this cool therapist. We talk a lot. I'm starting to figure things out. Like I can't take out my pain over my dad's disappearing act on Uncle Jon and Amy. It's not their fault. And it's not my fault. It's his. You know, stuff like that.''

''Yeah.'' He wondered whether Megan and Noah would want him to see somebody like that. But he couldn't. He didn't dare start talking about Byron Fielder. He might say too much, give away too many clues and then his parents would go looking for Fielder. No. Definitely no talking to a therapist. Or anyone else.

''And don't worry—'' Kieran didn't seem to notice his monosyllabic reply ''—you'll get it all worked out with your family. Well, I guess you could say it's *our* family.'' She smiled again, soft and pretty. ''I'm part of your family now, since Uncle Jon married Amy. Did you know he was married to your aunt Lisa once, too, a long time ago?'' Erik shook his head. ''It's true. It didn't last. I don't know why. But I'm glad he married Amy. She makes him laugh.'' She reached out and poked his arm. ''That makes us shirttail relations. Kissing cousins.''

Kissing cousins. That would take some getting used to. But right now he wasn't going to worry about anything. He'd been in Hurricane Beach five days. He'd been gone from Byron Fielder's tar-paper shack for almost three weeks. So far so good. Maybe he *had* made it safely away. Maybe he really could stop looking over his shoulder every two minutes and start concentrating on making a place for himself in Hurricane Beach, with his family.

''Okay. Here's the guest list so far. And thank the Lord we got the invitations in the mail before Der— before Erik came home.'' Amy gave Megan one of her high-voltage smiles and a pat on the knee before handing her a sheaf of papers with names listed in her sister's untidy scrawl. "I swear I haven't spent a minute thinking of the anniversary party since Mom called me and said he'd come home."

Megan spread her hands to indicate the lists and photographs and scribbled notes that littered Amy's coffee table and had spilled over onto the floor of the screened porch. "I'm awed by how quickly you've put this whole thing together..."

"But?" Amy queried.

"But are you sure it's a good idea? I mean, Mom and Dad still aren't getting along like they used to."

"But they are living under the same roof. And speaking to each other. It's a start."

"And what about Lisa? She still hasn't promised to come home for the party."

"I know." Amy's face clouded over for a moment. "And I understand that she's worried one of the teenagers she counsels is delivering twins that same week. But I can't help thinking that's just an excuse."

"We can't force her to come. You know how uncomfortable she feels around Mom and Dad."

"I know that, too. But surely she realizes they would understand? It was all so long ago. And she and Matt Connell are together now. Maybe we should tell Mom and Dad ourselves..." She sighed. "I really think they should know. It explains so much about Lisa's behavior."

"Yes," Megan said. "So very much." Lisa Hardaway's teenage love affair with Matt Connell had resulted in pregnancy, miscarriage and a broken heart for her baby sister. All of it suffered alone, her pain kept locked away from all of them for more than fifteen years. Matt never even knew she was pregnant. And now, even though Matt and Lisa had fallen in love all over again, the youngest Hardaway sister still refused to tell her parents what had happened so many years before.

"There are still ten days until the party. A lot can happen," Amy said optimistically.

"Ten days. Is that all? I haven't been keeping track."

"You've had other things on your mind. But I figured I'd better give you a call this morning and get you up to speed. Is Erik still sleeping?"

"Yes. At least he was when I left the house."

"Well, I know sleep's the best medicine, but three whole days?"

"He's exhausted, Amy. And Doc Yount says not to worry. He'll wake up and stay awake when he's good and ready."

"Okay. If you say so." She smiled again. "It's a miracle he's come home to us, Megan."

Megan nodded, smiling, too. "I know."

Her sister's smile disappeared. "What's happening with you and Noah?"

"Noah and I are getting along fine." She looked down at the guest list, pretending to study the names. She didn't want to talk about Noah. Having him so close for the past three days had been more unsettling than anything else. There was almost nothing for them to talk about. And since the sound of voices made Erik restless they had remained silent much of the time they were together.

"Okay," Amy said. "I get the hint. Discussions of Noah are as off-limits as they ever were."

"Amy."

The younger woman took heed of the warning tone of voice and changed the subject. "Here's a photo of what the cake will look like," Amy said, picking up from the coffee table an eight-by-ten glossy of a many-tiered wedding cake and passing it to Megan. "What do you think?"

"Godness. It's certainly impressive."

"I know. Three kinds of cake—chocolate, carrot and coconut. And a ton of sugar roses. Not exactly what I had in mind. I wanted something a little more simple, understated. You know, kind of 'beach elegant.' But Jon's mother, Leda, and Thea Aurelia insisted that anything less would be an insult to Mom and Dad and all their guests."

"Then by all means go with this one," Megan said, throwing up her hands in a gesture of surrender. "We wouldn't want to insult any of our friends and neighbors. And of course, the Costas Family Bakery must supply the cake. I doubt if you would ever hear the end of it if we chose someone else."

"Bingo," Amy said with a mischievous grin. "And Quentin Somersby must do the flowers and decorations," she said, referring to the town florist.

"And we are honor bound to hold the reception at the marina."

"Yes. Exactly. Or I'd be drummed out of the merchants' association and ridden out of town on a rail." Amy's grin spread across her face.

"And you wouldn't have it any other way."

Amy laughed out loud this time. "Of course not.

Hurricane Beach is my home. It used to be your home, too. Don't you miss it here at all, Megan?"

"Yes," Megan said truthfully. "I do."

"But not enough to come back."

"I...I don't know. Amy, my whole life has turned upside down again, just as it did the day my son disappeared. Right now I don't want to think about having to rebuild from scratch again."

Amy's sea-green eyes narrowed with what looked like shock for a moment, but she quickly covered her apparent surprise. "But, Megan, you don't have to start from scratch. You have your son back. And your hus—" She broke off and hurriedly bent to shuffle through the sample menus and lists of tentative seating arrangements. "I'm sorry, Megan. That was out of line."

"It's all right, Amy. I do have my son back. It's a miracle, truly it is. But Noah...Noah asked me for a divorce just days before Erik returned." She hadn't meant to mention the divorce papers. She was always uncomfortable discussing personal matters, unlike her volatile middle sister who easily confided in people.

"A divorce? After all these years?"

"Yes." Megan regretted her moment of candor almost immediately.

"Why?" Amy persevered.

"I don't know. Perhaps he's found someone else to love."

"I doubt that," Amy said in a tone of voice that left no room for argument.

For some odd reason, Megan didn't want to think that way, either. "Don't say anything to Mom and

Dad," she begged. "Please. I...I haven't had a chance to discuss any of this with Noah."

"All right. But I'd be surprised if another woman was involved. I never saw anyone more in love than you two were." Amy lifted her chin, daring Megan to deny her words. "It had to have been true love for you—the perfect Miss-Coastal-High-Honor-Society - president - going - off - to - college - to - be - the-next-Florence-Nightingale—to defy Mom and Dad and run off to marry him like you did."

"That was a long, long time ago." Megan changed the subject. "Show me the albums you dug out of the storage closet and let's get started on that montage you wanted to make for the party." The project would keep her mind off Erik. And Noah.

For once Amy took the hint. "Okay. Here's what I've got so far. These are some pictures of Dad in the service, but only one or two. He was a commando, just like Noah. They don't take a lot of snapshots."

"I know."

"And here's Mom touring with the USO show. And, of course, the publicity photos of Dad when he played that doctor on that old TV series."

"Before we were born," Megan said, studying the handsome dark-haired man that her father had been.

"Dad never really enjoyed acting, you know," Amy murmured. "But Mom's always wanted to go back on the stage. She's talking about getting involved with that little-theater group in Panama City."

"Maybe that will be good for her. Take her mind off their troubles."

"Are they still arguing?" Amy wanted to know.

Megan frowned, trying to think back over her parents' interactions the last few days. No," she said, looking at her sister. "But—"

"But not like old times." Amy sighed, sliding a Polaroid from its protective sleeve. The photograph showed the three sisters as very young teenagers on a huge inner tube.

"No, not like old times."

"And it won't be until they reach a decision on whether to sell the land or not?"

"Oh, Amy, let's not start that all over again."

"But it's important."

"Not today, Amy."

Amy scowled, but nodded. "Okay. Not today."

"Truce?" Megan said, trying to coax the return of her sister's smile.

Amy waved the old photo. "Truce."

"Good. Let's get this montage finished. I want to be home before lunch in case Erik decides to wake up and join the living."

"He has," a light, female voice said from the doorway.

Megan hadn't heard anyone coming up the steps to the deck. She swung around, narrowing her eyes against the glare of sunlight beyond the screened porch.

Her son stood there, solemn and silent, alongside Kieran Costas who looked bright and bubbly in an offbeat outfit that only a fifteen-year-old could get away with.

"Erik? Are you okay?" Megan stood up and hurried to the young couple. She reached out, brushed her fingertips across Erik's temple.

He didn't respond to her touch. At least he hadn't flinched, she thought. "Yeah. I got tired of lying in bed," he said, not quite meeting her eyes.

"You're sure you feel okay?"

"I'm fine." A slight wariness tinged his voice.

Don't push, she warned herself. She couldn't push him this way. *Don't try and force your way into his private space.* She took a step backward. "Good. I'm glad. How did you find your way here?"

"Grandma sent me to Rêve Rags looking for Aunt Amy." Erik smiled a little sheepishly, as though trying to make up for his rejection of her hesitant caress. "When she finally let me out of bed, that is. She wants Aunt Amy to come to Sea Haven for lunch. When I couldn't find you at the store, Kieran offered to bring me here."

"Thank you, Kieran," Megan said.

"You're welcome. But I have to get back. Grace wants me to help log a shipment of accessories. If I'm late, I'll really be in the doghouse," Kieran confided. "Hey, what are you doing? Looking at old pictures. Cool. Hey, Erik." She swooped down on the pictures piled on the coffee table. Get a load of this one. That's your grandfather when he was on television. Did you know that? He was like on a prehistoric 'ER' or 'Chicago Hope' or something way back when everything was black-and-white."

"It was called 'Young Dr. Weston,'" Amy said, laughing. "And your grandfather was nominated for an Emmy."

"He was one awesome dude back then," Kieran said. "He's still pretty radical for an old, bald guy."

"Kieran," Amy scolded, but she was smiling.

Kieran made a face and smiled back.

"Cool," Erik said. "I had no idea Granddad was an actor."

"You know what Emmys are, don't you?" Kieran said, then turning to Megan and Amy, "Did you know the guy that had Erik wouldn't let him watch TV?"

"I know what the Emmys are." Erik's voice was gruff. "Are there any pictures of you and...Noah? Are there any pictures of me?" Megan's eyes flew to her son's flushed face.

"I...of course there were pictures of you." She looked helplessly at Amy. She hadn't been able to bear looking at the photographs. She'd told her mother to destroy them. How could she tell Erik that? That she had tried to wipe all trace of him from the face of the earth, as though by denying he had ever been born, she could assuage some of her pain. "But, Erik, I'm sorry—"

"They're not with these pictures, Erik." Amy cast Megan a defiant glance. "After you were kidnapped, your grandmother put those albums away for safe-keeping. All you have to do is ask to see them."

Megan closed her eyes for a moment as her heart sent a quick silent prayer of thanksgiving for her mother's faith. Helene had never given up hope. Helene had believed and had ignored her daughter's heartbroken demands.

"Good." Erik nodded, satisfied. "I'd like that."

"Did the people you were with take any pictures of you?" Kieran asked.

"Not many," Erik said. "I left them behind when I came here."

Kieran picked up the photo of the sisters on the inner tube. "Get a load of this one. That's Amy and your aunt Lisa and your mom. Amy, that bathing suit is seriously retro. I can actually see a whole strip of your stomach." She rolled her eyes. "It's at least three inches wide."

"It was as daring as you could get for a fifteen-year-old back in the Dark Ages," Amy said with a sniff, leaning forward to retrieve the print from Kieran's grasp. Amy made a shooing motion toward the steps. "If all you're going to do is insult my taste in beachwear, you can leave. Go. Tell Grace I'll be there as soon as I can extract myself from lunch with Mom and Dad. And will you stop by the bakery and tell your uncle Jon—"

"You can tell him yourself. Here he comes," Kieran interrupted as Amy's old golden retriever, Sam, shuffled out from under the hammock to inspect the stranger on his porch. Erik held out his hand for Sam to sniff, then straightened abruptly when Kieran announced that her uncle was not alone. "Your dad's with him, Erik. And rats, he's not wearing his uniform," she announced in a penetrating whisper. "I am an absolute pushover for a man in uniform."

Megan closed her eyes on a searing, bittersweet moment of recall. She had only been a few years older than Kieran, with her whole life spread out before her, when she had fallen hopelessly in love with

Noah Carson, even before she'd seen him in uniform. She wondered for a moment how different her life might be today if she had not agreed to go to Pensacola Beach that day, so long ago, with friends.

"Good morning, ladies," Jon Costas said, with the slow smile that warmed and softened his rather austere good looks.

"Good morning, Jon," Megan managed a smile, but in reality she barely gave her new brother-in-law a glance. Her eyes were on his companion.

"Morning, Megan."

"Good morning, Noah."

He was dressed in khaki shorts and a crisp white shirt with a pair of sunglasses dangling from the pocket. It was the kind of outfit a lot of well-to-do businessmen wore on the golf course, or down to the marina. But somehow on Noah the clothes didn't convey the conventional message. To Megan's critical eye he still looked every inch the naval officer, harder, leaner, stronger. The kind of man who always stood out in a crowd.

"I stopped by Sea Haven to check on Erik and found both of you gone. Your mother told me you were here." He gave Erik a quick once-over. "Your grandmother said you were feeling a lot better this morning. I'm glad to hear that."

"Thanks." Erik ducked his head and gave Sam a quick pat on the head.

"I met Noah coming up the driveway," Jon explained. There was a smudge of flour on his chin, and Amy moved forward to brush it away.

"Busy morning?" she asked her new husband.

He smiled again. "Crazy as always." Joh was

helping his parents and aunt and uncle to run the Costas Family Bakery until they could all agree on who to hire to take his place. But soon, Amy had confided to Megan, he'd have to leave the bakery whether his family was ready for him to go or not. Jon was starting a new career with a multinational hotel chain that was setting up corporate headquarters in Hurricane Beach.

"I was just going to have Kieran deliver a message telling you I'm having lunch with Mom and Dad. I thought you might miss me."

"I would have." Jon caught and held Amy's gaze for a few seconds, and Megan noticed her sister's cheeks color slightly. Unbidden memories of when she and Noah were first married and could not get enough of each other came into her mind. It must be hard for Amy and Jon, she thought. Although they had plans to move to a larger place, the newlyweds were still living in Amy's small beach cottage with Kieran, and assorted Costases and Hardaways dropped by at all hours, with little or no advance warning. Megan wasn't the only one to notice the private exchange between the couple.

"Okay. We can take a hint," Kieran said. "We're out of here. C'mon, Erik."

"If you don't mind, Kieran—" Noah's voice was low and polite, but full of command "—I promised to take Erik to buy some clothes and get a haircut. Are we still on?" he asked.

Erik glanced at Megan, his eyes meeting hers for the briefest of seconds. "Is that all right with you? I mean, is it all right if I go with Noah?"

"Of course. Just don't overdo." He didn't suggest

she accompany them, and neither did Noah. The omission hurt more than Megan wanted to admit.

"We'll be back at Sea Haven in plenty of time for dinner," Noah said, smoothing over the small silence that grew after her words.

"Yes. I was thinking perhaps we could have dinner at the marina tonight. Since you're feeling so much better, Erik." Megan took a quick little breath before she lost her nerve. "All three of us."

Noah didn't say anything. A dark stain of color washed into Erik's cheeks. "I...I kind of thought I'd go with Kieran tonight. You know. Meet some of the kids...and all."

"The four-star tour," Kieran said. "I thought I'd show him the sights of Hurricane Beach. And we could try the pizza at Slice of the Pie. It's really awesome."

"Oh," Megan said. "Oh, I see."

"I..." Erik fumbled for words.

"No. It's all right," Megan said. "Really. I'm glad...it's good for you to meet Kieran's friends. Kids your own age. I—" she looked helplessly at Noah.

He didn't miss a beat. "Then it looks like just the two of us for dinner. I'll pick you up at eight."

CHAPTER FIVE

THE RESTAURANT at the Hurricane Beach marina was crowded. It was a favorite with both tourists and natives and always busy on weekends. Megan had picked it for just that reason. So she wouldn't have to dine privately with this stranger who was her husband.

"Great view," Noah remarked before taking a swallow of his whiskey and water. He'd been nursing the same drink all through the meal, she'd noticed.

"Yes, it is." Megan shifted her gaze from a fussy toddler at the next table, who'd been kept up past his bedtime, to the window. The weathered wooden building was perched on pilings at the mouth of Alligator Creek and commanded a panoramic view of the gulf. But it was already well past nine o'clock and storm clouds, piled high in the western sky, had muted the nightly spectacle. And now there was nothing to see but the blinking lights of oil rigs and cargo ships far out to sea.

"Do you miss the ocean, living in Nebraska?"

"No," she said too quickly, too sharply. "I mean. I…yes. I guess, now and then I do." She gestured to include the gentle surf and long expanse of white beach framed by the window. "I suppose this is very different from the Pacific Ocean."

"Yes. But it's still saltwater."

"And you're still a sailor," she said with a twist of her lips that she hoped qualified as a smile.

Noah watched her quietly for a long moment but didn't say anything more. They'd avoided a prolonged silence so far by exchanging bits and pieces of their lives, just skimming the surface with polite small talk. He was no longer an active member of a SEAL team, he'd divulged. His last mission had coincided with the end of the Gulf War. He now "sailed" a desk, he'd confessed with a wry grin that failed to reach his eyes. And he was in danger of being kicked up the ladder so high he wouldn't even have the limited contact with training missions that he had now.

Megan didn't think he sounded happy about his pending promotion but she didn't explore the topic further. Instead, she had let him change the subject to her own career choices and fifteen minutes passed pleasantly enough as she described her work at Graceway Retirement Center.

Noah seemed as disinclined to talk about their son's return as she did. Perhaps he was waiting for her to make the first move. "The view's familiar but I don't think this building was a restaurant when...when we used to visit your parents," he said, when she ran out of stories about Graceway.

"No. It was just a honky-tonk then. It was called the Rusty Nail. Do you remember?"

Noah rubbed his thumb across his chin, his eyes not quite meeting hers. "I remember. I got bombed out of my mind one night on fifty-cent drafts, and ended up throwing up all over your mother's guest bathroom.'' He scanned the large tastefully decorated room. ''It sure doesn't look the same. No peanut shells on the floor. No jukebox blaring in the corner. No drunks arguing at the bar.''

Megan smiled. ''This is the place. The town founders were never so happy to see a business go under as they were when the Rusty Nail closed its doors. Hosannas rang toward the heavens when the yacht club took over the property. This is where we'll hold Mom and Dad's anniversary party. There's a banquet room in the lower level.'' He was watching her closely. She stopped talking.

''I embarrassed the hell out of you that night, didn't I?''

''I was pregnant and I was mortified,'' she admitted. She had tried to get him up off the tile floor and into their bedroom, but he was far too heavy and too drunk. Merrick had come to her rescue and half walked, half carried Noah into the bedroom, and Helene had helped her clean up the mess, her mouth pursed in a straight line of disapproval.

''It wasn't a very auspicious start to our marriage.''

''Eloping wasn't a good idea, either.''

''We should have stayed and faced them.''

He was right. But she had only been nineteen, desperately in love and far more naive than she would ever have admitted to anyone. She hadn't had the strength to stand up to her parents' disapproval. So she had taken the coward's way out and persuaded Noah that running away was their only hope of being together.

''It's over and done with, Noah,'' she said softly.

"We were both so young." And star-crossed. She could see that now. She had made a terrible navy wife, just as she had feared. Noah had probably realized that, too, in the years that they'd been apart. She thought about the divorce papers, still lying beside her telephone in Nebraska. He hadn't mentioned them since he'd arrived in Hurricane Beach. But then again, until tonight, they hadn't been alone.

"God, I was a cocksure young SOB back then. I thought I had life by the tail." His voice was low and honey-smooth. Controlled. Perfectly in keeping with the aura of power tightly reined that was so much a part of him.

"You were a U.S. Navy SEAL, the best of the best and you wanted the whole world to know it."

"No," he said quietly. "I only wanted you to know it."

"Noah, please." She heard the note of desperation in her own voice and knew that he did too. She could skim the surface of their shared past with him, but that was all. She dared go no deeper.

"At least I learned one lesson that night." He leaned back in his chair, broad shoulders straining the fabric of his lightweight black blazer as he twirled his glass between his hands. A shiver of horror snaked down her spine. There were scars across the inside of his left wrist that hadn't been there eight years ago. Long and thin, the kind produced by deep wounds that could sever tendons and ligaments. The kind of scars that could only come from a knife blade. Megan shuddered, curling her hand tightly around her coffee cup as a wave of sympathetic pain jolted through her body.

Where had he been? Who had he been fighting to receive such fearsome wounds? She forced her eyes away from that legacy of violence and stared down at the dregs of her coffee for a moment while she composed herself. "What lesson was that?" she asked, steeling herself to meet his gaze.

"I'm a lousy drunk." He smiled ruefully at her. "I found that out that night."

"And I'm a weepy one," she confessed with a self-mocking smile. "I figured that out a long time ago, too."

Noah's night-dark eyes widened slightly in surprise. "You never used to drink at all." He indicated her unfinished glass of Chardonnay.

"For a while...after we split up...after I went back to nursing school, I drank quite a bit." She lifted her chin a notch. "It didn't help me forget and I found out I'm too maudlin for words when I drink. My roommate in school swore I nearly drove her into a depression crying in my beer—" She broke off, not wanting to discuss further the few disastrous attempts she'd made to drown in alcohol her loss of child and husband. Not even realizing what she was doing, she pushed her half-finished goblet of wine a few inches farther away.

She looked out the window again. A young couple was walking along the beach, a boy and girl, that could have been Erik and Kieran. But wasn't.

Noah's intent gaze followed hers. "Don't worry about him so much, Megan."

She didn't pretend to misunderstand his words. "I can't help it." She fixed her attention on the pulse beating in the shadowed hollow of Noah's throat just inside the open collar of his shirt. She was unable, suddenly, to meet his eyes because for a split second she couldn't control the memory of how much she'd loved to kiss him there.

"He doesn't want to be with us...with *me*. That's why we're here alone, trying to make small talk, and failing miserably." Her voice had risen slightly on the last words, and she was thankful that the table with the noisy toddler was so close by. No one could overhear them.

"Are you ready to leave?" Noah asked. When had he grown so attuned to what others were thinking, so quick to pick up on each nuance of word or gesture?

She nodded, not trusting her voice for the moment. She knew she should be thankful that Erik felt comfortable enough with Kieran Costas to want to go with her to meet her friends. Surely if he had been traumatized too terribly by his life with his kidnappers that wouldn't be the case. But she had hoped tonight he would have wanted to be with her.

Not waiting for the bill, Noah rose from his seat and placed some money on the table. Megan pulled the strap of her small bag over her shoulder and walked ahead of him out of the restaurant. Outside, the lingering heat and humidity of the late-summer evening was an almost-tactile force. The air was as heavy as warmed honey, the breeze off the gulf little more than a whisper of movement against her skin.

"We'll drive down Gulfview on our way back to Sea Haven. Maybe you can spot Erik and Kieran at Slice of the Pie."

Megan shook her head. "No. I don't want him to think we're spying on him."

"It was only a suggestion."

Megan was silent as they descended the stairs to the wooden boardwalk that paralleled Gulfview. Noah pulled the keys to the rental car out of his pocket, but she hung back as he circled the blue sedan to unlock the passenger door. "I think I'll walk to Sea Haven," she said abruptly.

"You're wearing panty hose," Noah said, resting his forearm on the roof of the car.

Megan felt her color rise.

"Slide in here and take them off," he offered, opening the door wide. "I'll stand guard. No one will see you."

"I couldn't possibly."

"Sure you could. I'll turn my back. You might as well be comfortable if you're determined to walk home."

"I..." She caught a glimpse of the smile in his eyes in the glow of a streetlight. She had never been able to refuse him anything when he smiled like that, anything at all. "Okay," she said a little breathlessly. "I will."

She had been foolish to wear panty hose. Just as it had been a mistake to add the ivory cotton jacket to her coral tank top and gathered skirt. She should have known that clothes that were perfectly suitable for dinner in any restaurant in Papillion, Nebraska, would be impractical in Hurricane Beach.

As she scooted onto the seat and kicked off her shoes, Noah politely turned his back. Megan peeled off her panty hose and stuffed them into her purse.

Suddenly, it felt as if she'd peeled off some kind of protective armor. For a moment she sat there stunned, eyes closed, her senses fully alive as they hadn't been in more than a decade. She could feel the soft cotton of her skirt and panties against the sensitive inner skin of her thighs. She fingered the buttery smoothness of the warm leather car seats and remembered the touch of a man's skin on her own. She could smell the hot asphalt of the parking lot, salt on the sultry sea air. And beneath it all the faint tang of Noah's after-shave and the clean smell of soap and warm skin.

She slipped her sandals back on and turned sideways, only to be confronted by the small of Noah's back. She had always loved to touch him there, just above the slight swell of his buttocks. Before she could stop herself, she reached out and touched him lightly.

In the space of a single heartbeat Noah swung around and dropped to a crouch beside her. His hand shot out and hard, strong fingers circled her wrist. Megan stared at him openmouthed. His reflexes had always been remarkably swift, but never could she remember him moving so fast.

Megan gasped in shock. "I'm...I'm sorry. I...I shouldn't have done that."

His aggressive stance and the fierce concentration she glimpsed on his face gave way to an expression of momentary confusion and faint surprise. He blinked, and the confusion was gone, replaced by a mask of calm politeness. He lowered his eyes to her manacled hand, then loosened his grip on her wrist.

"Sorry," he said. "Occupational hazard. I didn't expect you to touch me."

Megan's smile froze on her lips. "No. No, I suppose you didn't." Why should he? For the last year and a half they'd been together, she hadn't let him touch her for fear his pain would breach the defenses she'd erected around her own shattered heart.

He held out his hand, palm up this time, and pulled her out of the car as he rose with powerful grace. "Come on," he said. "I'll walk you home."

"It's over a mile," she protested. "And you'll have to walk back if you leave your car." She shut her mouth, drawing her lips into a firm line as she realized that he could easily travel ten times that far with a hundred and fifty pounds of equipment on his back.

"No arguments. You'll want to be home when Erik gets there." First he'd scared the living daylights out of her grabbing her that way. Now he seemed to have made her angry. Noah wondered how many more mistakes he could make before the evening was over.

Her lips tightened further. "Don't you ever catch yourself slipping up and calling him Derek by mistake?" she asked sharply.

"I try not to." How many times in the last three days had he stopped that name from forming on his lips? He'd lost count. He had failed his son when Erik was small. He wasn't going to fail him again. If it made the boy more comfortable to be called Erik, Noah would do his damnedest to comply with his son's wishes.

"So do I," Megan said with a small sigh, "I try really hard."

The breeze had picked up slightly as a thunder squall moved closer to land. Megan was a half step ahead of him. He was careful not to get too close. The gulf winds stirred loose tendrils of hair at the nape of her neck. How his fingers itched to reach out and touch those curling wisps of moonlight-colored hair. How he longed to caress the smooth curve of her shoulder. He shoved his hands into the pockets of his slacks and picked up the pace. *God, eight years without her, and she still had the ability to make him hard without even a touch.* If he'd thought that by initiating their long-postponed divorce he could break the spell Megan had woven around him since the first day they met, he knew now that he was sadly mistaken.

"A different name is a small price to pay to have him back with us, Megan," he said, to channel his thoughts away from the minefield he'd been traversing. Thunder rumbled closer overhead as they walked.

"I know it should be. But sometimes I wonder. I wonder if he truly *is* Derek." The last sentence tumbled out in a breathless rush. "I hate myself for it, but...how can we be sure?"

He knew how hard it was for her to speak those doubts aloud. Megan had been born to nurture, to be a mother. It must be tearing her apart inside to question, even for a moment, the return of their son. "We can always ask him to have a blood test."

A tiny sob worked its way past her lips. She shook her head vehemently. They had left the boardwalk a few yards back. He reached out and slid his hand under her elbow to help her over the soft sand above the tide line. She stiffened slightly but didn't shake off his touch. "I couldn't do that. He would never forgive us, I'm sure of that."

She was right. The boy would be devastated if he thought they didn't believe him. But Erik had refused to discuss the last twelve years, and Noah had felt compelled to do something. Not only to check Erik's story, but to find the monster who'd destroyed Noah's marriage and stolen his son.

He stopped to pull off his shoes and socks, then shoved his socks into his jacket pocket, tied his shoes together by the laces and slung them over his shoulder. Megan waited, lost in her own thoughts. He might as well tell her. She'd find out what he had done sooner or later.

"I've hired a private investigator," he said as they skirted the edges of the low surf.

"You've what?" She spun around so quickly that her skirt flared around her thighs.

"I hired a private investigator," he repeated. "To try and trace Erik back to where he came from."

"A private detective?" Another low, rumbling peal of thunder underscored her words.

"An ex-SEAL. He left the navy after he busted up his ankle in a skiing accident. He's good and he's thorough. If there's any way to find the man who kidnapped our son, Kyle Jamieson is the man to do it."

"Erik doesn't want us to know where he's been. Or who the people are that have kept him from us all these years."

"It's for his own good, Megan."

"Have you told him this?" He could hear the hurt in her voice as she thought back over the hours he'd spent with his son earlier in the day.

"No. I wanted to wait to see if there are any concrete results."

"I don't know if this is a good idea. If he finds out, he might run off."

"Your father approves."

"My father? You talked to my father about this and not me?" She stumbled as a wave, larger than the rest, washed the sand from beneath her feet.

Noah reached out and steadied her with his hand. She didn't pull away from his touch, but the muscles of her arm were stiff and unyielding beneath his hand. "Yes. This afternoon after I brought Erik back to Sea Haven."

"And he agreed with your decision?"

"Yes. Merrick wants to see the man who stole our son brought to justice as badly as I do."

"He didn't say a word to me."

"I asked him not to." She looked up at him then, but he couldn't read the expression on her face, even though his eyes had adjusted to the near darkness of the stormy summer night.

"I see." Her tone was cool, reserved. He could feel her drawing in on herself, shutting him away, just as she used to do.

They continued in silence until they reached the bottom of the deck staircase. Above them he could hear voices and the sound of ice falling into glasses. He waited to let Megan precede him. She put her foot on the first step and then turned back to him.

The light was better here. He could see the glitter of angry tears in her eyes.

"Don't ever do something like this again without consulting me, Noah Carson. Do you hear me?"

"I'll do what I think best for Erik." She had made him angry, too. Evidently their ability to strike sparks from each other, whether in anger or in passion, was as strong as it had ever been.

"You have no—"

Just then Amy leaned over the railing. "It's Megan and Noah. I thought I heard voices down there."

Megan held his gaze for a second or two longer then turned her face up to her sister. "Amy." Her tone was falsely bright. "What are you doing out here this late in the evening?"

"It's only a little past ten," Amy retorted. "We're delivering Erik back from Slice of the Pie."

Jon Costas's face and shoulders appeared beside his wife. "Speak for yourself, Amy. It's past *my* bedtime. Hello, Megan. Noah."

"Hi, Jon," Megan said as she stepped onto the deck. Noah knew without being able to see her face that her eyes had gone directly to her son. Her fingers tightened on the thin strap of her purse. "Did you have a good time, Erik? Was the pizza good?"

Erik was sitting at the end of Helene's chaise longue. He was holding a soft-drink can in his hand. He was wearing an oversize red-and-blue-striped rugby shirt that he'd picked out that afternoon, and a pair of baggy white shorts that the store clerk had assured him were absolutely radical. A pair of Noah's own regulation issue sunglasses dangled from the placket of Erik's shirt. "Yeah," he said. "It was a carnivore special. Four kinds of meat. It was really good.''

''A lad after my own heart.'' Merrick was leaning against the railing across the deck from Helene's chaise, a glass in his hand.

''Merrick,'' she said, sharply. ''Imagine what your cholesterol count would be if you ate such things.''

''Astronomical,'' he admitted dryly. ''But I would die a happy man.''

''Merrick, don't say such things.''

Merrick glanced at Helene. ''Why not, my dear? If you were widowed it would solve all your problems.''

''Merrick!'' Helene looked shocked.

''Dad.'' Megan and Amy spoke simultaneously.

''I'm sorry,'' Merrick said stiffly. ''That remark was uncalled for. Forgive me, my dear.''

Helene nodded, but didn't speak. Merrick turned his back and looked out over the dark expanse of the gulf.

Noah watched Amy and Megan exchange concerned glances, and realized the rumors he'd heard form his landlady at the Sand Dollar cabins were true. Despite the elaborate celebration planned for their golden wedding anniversary in ten days, Merrick and Helene Hardaway were still having marital difficulties.

''Well, we'd best be getting back.'' Jon wrapped his arm around Amy's shoulders. ''Baker's hours, you know. Five o'clock comes awfully early.''

''Don't even mention getting up at five o'clock,'' Kieran wailed. ''Tomorrow's my day off. I'm planning to sleep until noon.''

"Thank God the bakery doesn't rely on you to get the dough rising in the morning," Amy retorted. "C'mon. We'll see everyone tomorrow."

"Yes. Tomorrow," Helene seconded, twisting her earring nervously with her left hand. "I'll meet you downtown for lunch. All things considered, we really must decide what to do with all this money our friends are including in their cards and letters." She shot a concerned glance at Merrick, then went on, "I can't believe everyone ignored our request not to send gifts. Megan, you come too and we'll decide what charity to donate the money to."

"I thought—" Erik fell silent as everyone's attention turned to him. "Noah said we were going to go—"

"Oh. You and Noah have made plans?" Megan's knuckles turned white on the strap of her bag. "I thought…we…"

"I didn't get a chance to invite Megan to go exploring with us yet," Noah explained. For some reason, he was nearly as nervous as his son, proposing this family outing. Megan looked from one to the other of them.

"Exploring? Where?"

"On down the beach," Erik said. "Kieran told me there are alligators on grandfather's property." He scooted around to face his grandfather. "Is that true?"

"Yes, it's true," Merrick replied. "People do see one now and then, along the creek banks and in the swampy area out by the highway."

"But you don't want to go looking for them,"

Helene said, horrified. "They can be very danger-ous."

"I imagine Noah could handle a gator if need be, my dear," Merrick said.

Helene turned her gaze in Noah's direction. Her scrutiny was clear and direct, but it no longer held the animosity he remembered from the first years of his marriage to Megan. "Yes. I'd forgotten. I imagine he can."

"I think we can manage." Noah ventured a smile.

Helene nodded. "A breakfast picnic would be nice. The thermos and cooler are in the pantry. There's a bowl of fruit in the fridge, and of course the bakery opens at seven."

"Try the almond rolls, they're my favorites," Amy suggested.

"Jelly doughnuts, definitely," Kieran urged.

"What do you say, Megan? I thought we might check out the old pier, if it's still there." The local legend of Crazy Monty, the hermit who'd built a shack on the pier of the long-deserted sawmill on the far edge of the Hardaway land and spent the last years of his life watching for the Nazi U-boat attack that had never come, had always fascinated Noah.

"It's still there," Merrick confirmed. "But we don't encourage people to go out there."

Kieran shuffled her feet. Helene looked down at her hands. Again something passed between the Hardaways. From the look on her face, something that obviously had to do with Kieran Costas.

"Still, I don't see the harm in you three having a look around," Merrick continued. "It'll be your last chance. I'm going to have someone in here before winter to pull the old ruin down. It's too much of a hazard.''

''Amen to that,'' Amy said. ''Well, we're off. Good night, everybody.'' Goodbyes and good-nights were exchanged. Helene and Merrick followed the Costases inside.

''I think I put my foot in my mouth there,'' Noah said.

''It's okay,'' Erik told him. ''Kieran got into some trouble earlier this spring. She…she sort of ran off with this creepy older guy. That old pier, it was sort of her special place. That's where they used to meet. I…I'm glad you asked to see it. I sort of wanted to see it. Because of the crazy old guy and his Nazi U-boats, not because of Kieran. But I didn't have the nerve to ask.''

''You shouldn't be afraid to ask anything of us, Erik,'' Megan said.

''I…I know that. You're coming with us tomorrow, aren't you?'' he asked, rolling his soft-drink can between his palms.

''Yes. I'd like that. Is eight o'clock too early? If we go much later it will be too hot, and any of the gators that are out sunning will head back to their holes.''

''I'll be ready.''

''I'll stop by the bakery and let Jon fix us up a box of pastries,'' Noah offered.

''Great. I'll see you in the morning.'' Erik smiled and ducked his head, but made no move to come closer to either of them. ''Good night.''

''Good night, son.''

Megan took a half step toward him, then stopped. "Good night, Erik," she said softly. "Sleep tight."

"Don't let the bed bugs bite," he said as he closed the French doors behind him, leaving them alone.

"I think that's the longest conversation I've had with him since he arrived," Megan said.

"He's been opening up more every day."

"To you, maybe." She was silent a moment and he could hear the murmur of the surf and the rattle of the wind through the palms at the side of the house. "You're not going to take him away from me, Noah," Megan said unexpectedly. She didn't turn around, but he saw the slight squaring of her shoulders, heard the tiny quaver in her voice that she couldn't quite hide.

"What the devil are you talking about?"

She turned slowly to face him. Her mouth was set in a tight line, her green eyes glittered with suppressed emotion. "Don't think you can make up for all the times you weren't around when we needed you. Presents and picnics and a few days or weeks of your time won't do it. Go away and leave us alone, Noah. I won't share him with you now that I have him back."

CHAPTER SIX

"ARE YOU SURE you won't have this last half of almond roll?" Megan asked. "It seems a shame to throw it away."

"I couldn't eat another bite." Noah's tone was as scrupulously polite as her own. He laced his fingers behind his head and leaned his shoulders back against the sun-bleached wooden siding of the tumbledown shack still perched precariously on the old pier.

"Perhaps Erik?"

"He had three," Noah reminded her, extending his long, tanned legs. He was wearing a navy blue T-shirt that strained across his broad shoulders and clung to the flat hardness of his stomach, and khaki shorts that stretched tight over the rock-hard muscles of his thighs.

Megan shifted her gaze to the bakery box, uncomfortably aware of the increase in her heart rate and breathing. She couldn't deny the effect Noah had on her, but she could do her best to ignore it.

The morning had gone smoothly despite the anger with which they'd parted the night before. Noah had arrived exactly on the dot of eight o'clock. Merrick had offered the use of his black Blazer in place of Noah's rental car, and they'd gone bouncing off down a rutted, overgrown old logging track that wound through scrub pine and palmetto to a marshy area that Merrick promised contained a couple of alligator holes.

And indeed it had. They'd seen two small alligators—barely an arm's length in size—a couple of yards off the road. The reptiles had been sleepy and disinclined to move from their comfortable puddles. All in all, something of a disappointment. But a little farther along they'd come upon one not-so-small specimen that obligingly opened its mouth to reveal two rows of very impressive teeth. Erik took several pictures with the camera Helene had pressed on them. Once the boy had overcome his shyness enough to admit he'd never learned how to use one, Noah had given him a few basic instructions. By the time they reached the pier, Erik was on his second roll of film.

And there, with the help of the camera's automatic timer, against a backdrop of cloud-strewn blue sky and rolling breakers, Megan had her picture taken with her husband and son. A common enough event for most wives and mothers, but far more for a woman who'd never expected that something so wonderfully ordinary would ever happen to her again.

But what would that photograph reveal when it was developed, Megan wondered. A family? Or three strangers drawn together by a twist of fate as random as the one that had torn them apart so many years ago.

"Look," Noah said softly.

Megan looked in the direction he was pointing,

glad to be distracted from her thoughts. Erik was walking toward the end of the pier when a big brown pelican had settled on the railing. In his hand he had the remains of an almond roll. He held out the food, but the big bird made no attempt to take it. After a few minutes Erik laid the offering on the splintered wooden planking and stepped back. The pelican remained on his perch for a few more seconds, then opened his powerful wings and hopped onto the pier. The pastry disappeared into his pouch and with almost the same movement the bird hopped back onto the piling and spread his wings to soar off a few feet above the waves.

"Radical," Erik crowed, sauntering back to where they were sitting. "No wonder Kieran thinks this place is so cool."

Megan recalled what Amy had told her had transpired in the dilapidated shack only a couple of months before. Kieran had been lured here by a drifter known only as Hardball. Fortunately, Amy had found her before she came to any real harm. After that, Merrick had decided to have the pier destroyed.

"Maybe old Crazy Monty wasn't as crazy as he seemed," Noah observed.

"Oh, he was crazy, all right. That's what all the stories about him agree on," Megan responded.

"He sure knew how to pick a spot to live in, though." Erik leaned his elbow on the waist-high railing and scanned the ribbon of sugar-white beach that snaked off into the distance, deserted as far as the eye could see. One of the last undeveloped stretches of gulf beach in the area. Her parents' land—at least for the time being.

As much as she had always loved this place, Megan believed her parents should sell if it would heal the rift that had torn them apart. "I used to dream of living out here, away from the world, with nothing but the sand and the sea—" She stopped abruptly when she looked up to see Noah watching her from intent dark eyes.

"It would be a great place to build a home." He stood up, reaching down a hand to help her to her feet.

Had he chosen the word *home* deliberately over the less personal *house?* Was he trying to tell her something or was she allowing her own long-suppressed dreams to color his words. She thought of the divorce papers waiting for her in Nebraska and hardened her resolve.

"Yes, except that it's really too isolated and inconvenient. And it would cost a fortune to bring utilities way out here. I think Mom and Dad would be better off to sell. It's become a real bone of contention between them." She pulled her hand from Noah's grasp and dusted off the seat of her shorts, rubbing away the unwelcome tingling residue of sensation generated by his touch.

"No way," Erik said. Megan swung around to face him. He colored slightly but didn't look away. "I...I mean I don't think they should sell it to just anybody. I...I've been thinking. I mean, you know, it would be neat to turn it into a conservation area—maybe something like the Nature Conservancy could make it into a park. So the alligators and raccoons and the wildflowers wouldn't get pushed out for a golf course or whatever."

"Yes," Megan agreed. "I know that would be a terrific thing to do. But many of those kinds of organizations can't afford to take over such a large area of land."

"Yeah. I know. They'd need, um…"

"An endowment," Noah supplied. He was standing with his hands thrust into the back pockets of his shorts, his head tilted slightly as he listened to what Erik had to say.

"Yeah. That's the word I was thinking of," Erik said.

Megan was surprised that he knew what an endowment was. Apparently he saw what she was thinking and his neck and cheeks colored once more. "I'm not stupid, you know."

"I know," she said. "I'm sorry. It's just…just that I thought you said…he…wouldn't let you go to school."

"Yeah. That's okay. I told you, Diana taught me at home. And I like to read. I pick up on that kind of stuff."

"What would you do with the property if it was yours, Erik?" Noah asked.

He hesitated a moment, turned to look out over the gulf. "Well, I was thinking that it would be nice to keep some of the beachfront right next to Sea Haven. You know, for houses, well, for the family."

Megan nodded. "I'd like that, too."

"And then Granddad could sell some of it to a developer. Not that Palmer Boyce character, but somebody who would build homes for the people who want to live in Hurricane Beach all year round.''

''I like that idea,'' Noah said.

Erik nodded. ''Kieran says there aren't enough nice affordable places for the people who want to stay here and work and raise families. Especially now that the company her uncle Jon is working for is moving to town,'' he finished in a rush, barely pausing for breath. ''And then you could take the money from the land you sold to the developers and endow the rest of it. And I'll bet Nature Conservancy or the Sierra Club or whoever would jump at the chance to take it over.''

''You've put a lot of thought into this, haven't you, son.''

Erik dropped his gaze to his shoes. He shrugged. ''Yeah. I know it's just kid stuff,'' he said.

''No it's not kid stuff, Erik. I like your plan, too.'' Megan moved to stand beside him at the railing. She looked out over the expanse of blue-green water, restless with whitecaps that had been stirred up by a tropical depression far out at sea.

''I'd like to see people enjoying this peace and beauty like we do.'' She turned toward her son, reached out and laid her hand on his arm. He didn't pull away, and she blinked back a sudden sting of grateful tears. ''I think you should propose it to your grandparents as soon as we get back to Sea Haven.''

''I...''

''It's a good idea, Erik,'' Noah said, coming up behind Megan quietly. His heat radiated through her thin cotton blouse, hotter than the sun.

"Do you really think so?" Erik's eyes went from one to the other of them.

Megan squeezed his arm. "Yes, I do."

"Okay, I'll do it," he said, and smiled at her. The first time he had done so without reservation, and it pierced her heart with joy just as his first baby smile had done sixteen years before.

"We'd better be going," Megan said when she could trust her voice again. "The tide's coming in and we're all going to get pretty wet wading back to shore." Years before, Merrick had had the approach to the old pier torn down and a fence put up to discourage trespassers. Now the only way on and off was to wade through ten yards of surf, and crawl through a hole in the chain-link fence—an exercise that Noah and Erik seemed to enjoy all out of proportion to its charm.

"Yeah." Erik grinned again. "The waves are high enough to boogie board. Kieran said she'd teach me how."

"Can you swim?" Megan asked.

"Sure." His smile disappeared, replaced by an expression that made him look far older than his years. "It doesn't cost anything to learn how to swim. Especially when someone just tosses you in over your head and tells you to figure out how to get back to shore on your own."

"Oh, Erik."

This time he did shrug off her touch, and his voice was as hard as his expression. "It's okay. I told you, I'm a fast learner."

IT WAS COOL and quiet in his grandfather's study. The room, paneled in rich dark wood, was directly below his mother's bedroom. The windows looked out over a pretty little garden and across the road to the pine woods beyond. His grandfather was seated behind his big desk, his computer humming off to the side. But Merrick Hardaway wasn't scrolling through a listing of stock offerings or checking the latest stock-market quotations.

He was listening to his grandson. Erik swallowed hard. Megan had certainly given his idea an enthusiastic buildup. In fact, he was afraid it was a major case of oversell. She was sitting by his grandmother on the leather couch in front of the glass-fronted bookcases, and they were both beaming as though he'd just taken his first step. He glanced across the room at his father who was leaning against the mantel of the fireplace, his arms folded across his chest. Noah hadn't said anything so far, but now he nodded encouragement for Erik to go on.

It seemed, for the moment at least, they'd both forgotten his outburst back there on the pier. But he hadn't. He'd nearly gone and blown it again. He just couldn't help it. Sometimes when he thought about Byron Fielder and the things he'd done to Erik when he was too little to fight back, he couldn't keep himself from blurting it out. He had to stop doing that. He had to be careful or he might say something that Noah or Megan could pick up on, use to trace backward until they came up with a name, and a place. And then his worst enemy would know where to find him.

But he had to quit acting as if what had happened to him over the years still bothered him. He didn't like it when Megan and Noah looked at him as though they were waiting for him to crack and spill his guts. And he didn't like thinking if he told them everything, all about the beatings and the drunken fits of rage, and the just plain mean and petty things Fielder had done to him and to his wife, they'd start to think differently about him.

And he wanted things to be the way they had been this morning. It had been fun. He'd felt like part of a family for the first time that he could remember.

"Go ahead, Erik," his grandmother prompted.

The plan. He had to stop worrying about Byron Fielder and concentrate on what he was going to say. He took a deep breath and launched into his scheme. His grandfather listened attentively, his hands steepled beneath his chin. His grandmother nodded and beamed and clapped her hands when he came to the part about maybe building homes on the beach that ordinary people who wanted to live and work in Hurricane Beach could afford.

"That's it," she said, popping up off the couch. "That's exactly what we should do with the land. Merrick—"

"My dear, I agree. I like the lad's suggestions, but we must look into the plan carefully—"

"Merrick, don't try to put me off." Erik couldn't decide if his grandmother sounded angry or scared.

Merrick was silent a moment. "I wouldn't think of it. But be practical, Helene. Bringing a project like this to a successful conclusion would be a very complicated undertaking."

Helene straightened her spine. She wasn't very tall

but for a second or two she looked fierce as a giant. "Surely you are equal to the task, Merrick."

"Certainly, my dear. But from a business standpoint, selling the property outright to Silver Sands or some other concern would be preferable. The proceeds, even after the government takes more than its fair share, would set up our daughters and their families for life. It *is* what you said you wanted to do—"

"I've changed my mind." His grandmother's eyes flashed and she placed both hands on the desk. "Money isn't everything, Merrick Hardaway. Sometimes I think we were happiest when we had almost nothing."

"I think perhaps we were." A smile quirked up one corner of his mouth beneath the silver mustache.

"I want to do something like this with our land," Helene said. "It's a wonderful solution. No ugly high-rises spoiling the view. No golf courses. There are far too many of them around, as it is." Helene's voice softened in response to his smile. "We wouldn't have to give up Sea Haven," she said, smiling back just a little. "Please, Merrick. Tell me you agree we'll look into the possibilities as soon..." She took a deep breath. The smile disappeared. "No. Not as soon as it's convenient. I meant to say the first thing tomorrow morning."

"It means that much to you, my dear?"

"Yes, Merrick, it does."

"Then we'll set the wheels in motion for a feasibility study right away." Merrick stood up and leaned his hands on the desk, bending toward Helene, his eyes locked with hers. "And does this also mean that I can have our attorneys call Silver Sands Development and tell them—''

''And Mr. Palmer Boyce—'' Helene's eyes were fixed on Merrick's face. Erik was sitting not a foot away from both of them, but he felt as if they'd forgotten he was there.

''To go take a flying—''

The phone rang, interrupting his words. Erik wished it hadn't. His grandfather sounded as if he was just getting started on Mr. Palmer Boyce and Silver Sands Development. The ringing stopped and the fax machine beeped. A sheet of paper began to emerge.

Merrick broke eye contact with his wife. ''Get that fax for me, will you, son?''

''Sure.'' Erik swiveled and reached out for the paper. At the same time, Noah levered himself away from the mantel.

''Erik. Wait.''

Erik didn't hear Noah's voice. His grandparents liked his idea. They were going to look into dividing up the property just the way he'd imagined it. He was on a roll. Maybe his mom and dad would even get back together and they would build a house here, on the beach, close to Sea Haven. And he could go to school at Coastal Senior High and go for pizza at Slice of the Pie with Kieran and the other kids after football games on Friday nights—

Yeah! Maybe he had gotten clean away from Byron Fielder and he wouldn't ever have to look over his shoulder again.

He glanced down at the paper in his hand and felt the blood freeze in his veins. The fax wasn't some kind of stock-market report for his grandfather. It was addressed to Lieutenant Commander Noah Carson, his dad. It was a report from something called SecureTek—and it was about *Erik*.

His dad had hired a private detective to check him out.

He scanned the page, ignoring Noah's outthrust hand, ignoring the sound of his voice. SecureTek had found a car abandoned in Ann Arbor at about the time Noah had informed them that Erik had left Michigan. The Michigan Highway Patrol had tried to notify the owner, one Byron Fielder, but so far they hadn't been able to locate him. Neighbors said they thought he might have left the state, heading south, maybe gone looking for his son who had taken the car and run away from home. SecureTek would keep Noah updated as more information became available.

Now they knew Fielder's name. Knew where he lived.

Byron Fielder was on his way to Florida to get him.

Erik looked up, a terrible roaring noise filling his head. Megan was standing beside Noah.

"You knew about this didn't you?" he heard someone yell. *Him. He was yelling*. God, he sounded as if he was going to start crying any minute. "You hired someone to check up on me. Didn't you believe me? Didn't you believe I am who I said I was?" Somehow that hurt more than anything.

"Erik, it's not like that." Megan was crying again. It seemed as though she was always crying when she was around him. She hardly ever smiled. She probably wished he'd never come back. Noah wasn't crying, but his face was hard and set.

"That terrible man must be found," Megan whispered, attempting to tug the sheet of paper from his hand. He threw it at her.

"No! I told you I didn't want you to go looking for him. Now— It's probably too late already, what with the newspaper article and all. He's probably on his way right here. He'll never let me get away. Oh, hell." He couldn't make them understand. He just couldn't come out and say that even thinking of Byron Fielder made him feel like that terrorized and voiceless four-year-old again. "I've got to get out of here."

He turned and ran out of the room, out of the house. He blinked in the strong sunlight. He didn't have the incredibly cool sunglasses Noah had given him. He didn't have his billfold, but he didn't care. He just had to run. He'd dared to dream his life could be normal, like any other kid. But the dream had lasted only a few hours. Now all the old terror was back, and it was worse than before. Now he knew for certain that Fielder was looking for him.

Merrick's Blazer was sitting in the driveway where Noah had left it. The keys were on the floor, under the mat. He'd seen Noah put them there. Erik didn't stop to think of what he was doing. He only knew he had to get away, lose himself again before Byron Fielder made his way to Hurricane Beach and dragged him back into the hellhole his life had been for the last twelve years.

He twisted the key in the starter and backed out of the driveway spewing sand and gravel from beneath the wheels. God, he was stealing a car again. His grandfather's car. Driving without a license. He didn't have a choice. The panic churning inside him was too strong to fight. He had to get away, somewhere safe. Hide.

He tore down Gulfview, made a right on Cypress and then a left on Second Street. It paralleled Gulfview and he hoped it came out at the two-lane leading to Highway 98 just like Gulfview did. There weren't any traffic lights on the residential street, and he rolled through the four-way stops without encountering any cross traffic. He skidded to a stop at the intersection at the edge of town, his palms sweating and his knuckles white on the steering wheel.

Erik glanced in the rearview mirror and recognized Noah's rental car, and right behind it a police cruiser. They were after him already. His grandfather must have notified the police as soon as he left the driveway. He floored the accelerator and fishtailed onto the county road. He couldn't let them catch him. He couldn't go back. It was too tempting to let himself believe that Sea Haven was the enchanted castle of his protective fantasies, and that his grandparents really were proud of him for thinking up a solution to their problem with the beachfront property. And, the biggest joke of all—that Megan was smart enough, and Noah strong enough to keep him safe from Byron Fielder.

Jeez. Now he *was* starting to cry. Erik took one hand off the wheel and dragged it across his smarting eyes. He risked another glance behind him. Noah was gaining on him. The cop car right on his tailpipe.

Still half blinded by sun, he looked up to see a

logging truck pull out of a stand of pine trees onto the road in front of Erik. His breath caught in his throat. His heart skidded to a stop, then thudded into a jackhammer beat in his ears. He jerked the wheel to the left. There wasn't time to think, no time to slow down. He was going too fast to stop. He had to get past the truck and back into his own lane without hitting another car head-on.

He stepped on the gas and swung around the logging truck. The left front wheel slipped off the pavement onto the sandy berm. Erik fought the wheel, kept on going, a vision of the truck driver's shocked face as he flashed past.

He was going to make it. He cut the wheel to swerve into his own lane before topping a slight rise that loomed ahead of him, but he miscalculated, drifted too far to the right. This time when the tires left the pavement he couldn't fight the drag on the wheel. The Blazer tore through the scrub grass and palmetto, heading straight for the thick stand of pine that lined both sides of the road. There was nothing Erik could do but hold on.

CHAPTER SEVEN

"No!" the denial was torn from Megan's throat as her father's Blazer careened from one side of the road to the other. She couldn't shut her eyes, couldn't look away as the vehicle left the pavement, became airborne, then smashed into the trunk of a pine tree. "Oh, Erik, no," she heard herself cry out. "My God, Noah. Look out!"

"Hang on." Megan braced her hands against the dashboard, the seat belt biting into her breast and stomach. Noah steered the sedan into a bootlegger's turn to avoid rear-ending the logging truck, which had slammed on its brakes after seeing the Blazer crash. Noah pulled off the side of the road, facing back the way they had come, as the police cruiser skidded to a halt just ahead of them.

Megan was out of the car almost before it came to a stop. She ignored the policeman's shouted warning, Noah's voice calling her back. All she knew was that her son was still in the Blazer. At least he hadn't been thrown from the vehicle. But he hadn't been wearing a scat belt, and panic filled her heart.

Smoke rolled out from under the crumpled hood as she ran across the asphalt and plunged through the razor-sharp, waist-high grass that bordered the road. "Erik! Erik, answer me. Are you all right?" she called, struggling to open the door. Branches had penetrated the shattered front windshield. The safety glass of the driver's-side window was cobwebbed with a thousand tiny cracks. She couldn't see inside, couldn't see how badly her child was injured. "Erik!" she gasped, still wrestling with the jammed door. "Please, Erik. Talk to me."

Her only answer was a muffled groan.

At least he was still alive, but how badly injured she couldn't tell. "Erik." Tears clogged her eyes and throat.

A strong brown hand closed over hers. "Let me do it, Megan," Noah said.

Her eyes flew to his face to be greeted with a mask of stoic detachment. A tiny, still-reasoning corner of her brain realized that this is how he must look in combat. "Hurry," she begged. "There's smoke—"

The mask slipped a fraction, and for a moment, a heartbeat only, she saw the fear and worry behind the warrior's guise. "It's only steam, Megan. The radiator's cracked, that's all. There's no fire. Now step aside. I'll open the door."

The patrolman and the truck driver arrived together. The truck driver was white-faced and shaking. He was carrying a crowbar. "I didn't see him coming. I swear. The kid just appeared out of nowhere and next thing I knew he'd swerved in front of me and went right off the side of the road. Megan ignored him. Noah did, too. "Here. Use this," the driver said, thrusting the crowbar in Noah's direction.

Noah waved him off, braced one foot against the frame, wrapped both hands around the door handle and pulled. The muscles in his back and shoulders bunched with the effort. The tendons on his forearms corded with strain. With a screech of twisted hinges the door swung open.

"Lord," the truck driver said reverently. "Where the hell did you learn to do that?"

"The emergency unit is on the way," the patrolman said as Noah hoisted himself onto the Blazer's tilted seat. He gave no indication that he had heard the man.

"Dad? What happened?" It was Erik talking, his voice weak but reasonably steady. "I...my arm." Then a note of suppressed panic. "It's bleeding."

"Noah." Megan couldn't bear standing idle a moment longer.

"Easy, Megan," Noah said, pushing broken glass and pine branches out of the way. "I think the passenger door is free. We can get him out from that side. Take it easy, Erik. I'll be right back." Noah jumped back out of the Blazer. There was blood on his hands. Erik's blood. Megan felt the ground lurch beneath her feet. He reached out, grabbed her, leaving a smear of blood on her arm. "Hang on, Megan. It's a pretty bad cut. Nicked a vein, I think. We need to get him out of there."

"You shouldn't move him until the paramedics get here," the policeman, whom Megan recognized as the youngest brother of a high-school classmate, cautioned.

"He's got a cut on his forehead," Noah said. "There doesn't seem to be any sign of a neck or spinal injury, but he's bleeding heavily. The sooner we get him out of the truck and get a pressure bandage on his arm the better."

He turned around and put both hands on Megan's waist. "I'll lift you inside. He's wedged up against the far door. You steady him while we get it open. You're up to this aren't you, Megan?"

She nodded. He picked her up as though she weighed nothing and set her on the crazily tilted seat. He handed her a clean white handkerchief. "It's not much but it will have to do for a pressure bandage until the ambulance gets here."

"I know what to do." She took a deep breath and scooted carefully around. "Oh, baby." She bit down hard on her lower lip to keep from moaning in anguish. Erik was watching her from pain-filled eyes. The right side of his forehead was scraped raw, blood trickled down the side of his face from a cut that even in her distress Megan's trained eye could tell was only superficial. But the injury to his arm was not as easily dismissed. The gash was long and deep and bleeding profusely. Blood covered his shirt and his shorts, his leg. It dripped off the seat into a puddle on the floor. She closed her eyes and took a long, deep breath. Held it. Let it out.

"Mom? Are you all right?"

Megan shook her head, then attempted a smile. "I'm fine." Then she realized what Erik had said. *Really* said. He was conscious. He was coherent. And he had called her Mom. "I'm just fine, baby." She pressed the folded white handkerchief tight against the cut, watched it turn dark with blood. Erik bit off a cry of pain as she pressed down on the wound. With an effort of will that was almost physical, Megan shut down all her emotions and concentrated on stemming the flow of blood. Somewhere in the distance she heard a siren.

"How is he?" Noah asked, kneeling at the open passenger-side window.

She looked up, her eyes locked with his for a beat of time. "We need to get him to the hospital."

"Erik," Noah said. "I'm going to open the door. "Can you brace your leg against the floor so you don't slide out?"

Erik tried nodding, winced and lost a little more color. "I think I can."

Okay. Here goes." With the same concentrated, controlled strength he'd used before, Noah wrenched open the door and in one smooth motion slid his arm behind Erik's back and under his knees. "Are you ready, Megan?"

"Ready." The flow of blood that stained the compress and dyed her fingers bright red had slowed slightly, but not enough. Any qualms she felt about moving Erik without a neck brace or backboard paled beside her anxiety to get him out of the mangled Blazer and on his way to the hospital.

"Okay. Ready. Here we go." Noah lifted Erik from the Blazer. Megan moved with them. She slid across the seat, ignoring the swift lance of pain as a piece of broken glass sliced her left leg just above the ankle. The siren was louder now. Much closer. She stumbled alongside Noah and Erik as her husband carried their son toward the road. The ambulance pulled up in a shower of gravel and red and blue strobe lights. For a moment longer the siren wailed, then mercifully someone cut the switch.

Noah was on his knees in the short grass by the

side of the road, Erik propped against his shoulder, Megan on his other side, blood staining her blouse and her pale green shorts. One or two cars had stopped, their drivers emerging to offer help. The doors of the rescue unit opened and they were surrounded by jumpsuited paramedics. Questions were asked, answers given. Someone knelt beside her and gently removed her cramped fingers from Erik's arm, replacing her makeshift bandage with a stronger, more efficient one.

She must have whimpered, made some sound of protest at the separation, because Erik opened his eyes and said very clearly, "It's okay, Mom."

Then he was gone, bundled into the ambulance, and the doors closed in her face. "Noah?" She took a step toward the ambulance, but Noah reached out and held her back.

"We'll follow them to the hospital in the car. We'd only be in the way inside the unit."

"Okay." She looked down at her hands and shuddered. It was her worst nightmare come true. She couldn't see anything but her child's blood on her hands, couldn't seem to focus on anything but the terror of how near she'd come to losing him again. Her knees buckled slightly and Noah's other hand shot out, pulled her upright against him.

"C'mon, Megan. Don't pass out on me now."

She lifted her chin. She *wasn't* going to lose Erik. Not to an accident. Not to the man who had stolen him so long ago, and now seemed to be a threat to him again. *Not to her husband.* "I'm not going to pass out on you."

A fleeting grin relieved the dark intensity of his gaze for a heart-stopping moment. "Good."

They beat the ambulance to the doors of Hurricane Beach's small hospital by a good three minutes. Megan wasn't even surprised by Noah's ability to navigate the town's narrow, sandy back streets with a race driver's precision and the apparent familiarity of a lifelong resident.

Amy was there ahead of them. Her face paled at their bloodstained appearance, and she hurried forward to enfold Megan in a fierce, hard hug. "Maida," Amy told her, referring to the art gallery woman. "Maida heard about the accident on her emergency scanner and came down to Rêve Rags to tell me about it," she explained a little breathlessly. "I thought...I thought I'd better come here and see what I could learn before I go out to Sea Haven and tell Mom and Dad. What happened?"

"Oh, Amy...it's all so complicated and so terrible—"

At that moment, the ambulance pulled up to the automatic doors, and Erik was wheeled inside just as Doc Yount came bustling down the hallway, red-faced, white coattails flying out behind him.

"Megan. Commander." The physician, an old navy man himself, greeted Noah with a half salute. "I didn't expect to see the two of you again so soon. And I sure as hell didn't want to see you here."

He stopped the gurney and took a quick look at Erik's injured arm and the scrape on his head, raising the boy's eyelids to peer into his eyes with a pencil flashlight. "Looks clear. That's a good sign," he muttered. Then motioned to the nurse who'd emerged from the swinging doors marked No Entry Without Permission with an imperious wave of his hand. "Get him into number three. I'll be right in."

He turned to the young patrolman who'd followed the gurney into the ER. "You can ask your questions later, Travis. I don't want you hanging over my shoulder, upsetting my patient any more than he is already."

"Yes, Doc," the police officer said as though he'd had this conversation before. "Seeing as how the Blazer belonged to Merrick Hardaway, I'll let Sheriff Ormand handle this one."

"Good call." The physician swung his head toward Megan and Noah. "Megan, you and your husband stay here and fill out the damn paperwork. Then you can come on back."

"Doctor," Megan began to object.

"Rules, Meggie," he said. "You know the drill." He reached out and patted her hand. "Don't worry. He'll be fine. And I can work better without you hovering over my shoulder. Maribelle will help you." He put his hands on Megan's shoulders and turned her toward a kind-faced woman in a pink hospital smock. "Show Megan where to wash up, Maribelle. She'll feel better without all that blood on her hands."

"Will do, Doc."

"And you, Amy Costas, go out to Sea Haven and tell your grandparents what's happened before some Good Samaritan takes it on himself to be the bearer of bad news, and scares them half to death."

"I'm leaving now, Doc."

"Tell them not to worry too much. He's going to be fine."

ALMOST HALF AN HOUR passed before they had dealt with all the paperwork involved in getting Erik treated. Finally, Maribelle buzzed them through the heavy wooden doors and directed them to the brightly lighted, tiled room where Doc Yount and two nurses were clustered around the high bed where Erik lay.

The room was cold and smelled of antiseptic and hospital soap. And faintly detectable beneath the stronger odors, the coppery scent of blood. Noah's stomach muscles tightened. He clamped down on the sudden upsurge of emotion that assaulted his insides, threatened the steely control that had become second nature over the years.

He had been a SEAL for close to twenty years. He had fought and he had bled. He had seen men die; friends he would never forget, enemies he would not let himself remember. But nothing he had seen, nothing he had experienced had prepared him for the sheer horror of watching the Blazer leave the road and slam into the trunk of that pine tree. For a moment it had felt as if his own heart had stopped dead in his breast.

He had come close to losing his son today. For the second time. It had taken every ounce of will-power to allow Erik to be taken from his arms and loaded into the back of the ambulance. It had required a distinct and deliberate act of will to stand patiently beside Megan in the glass-enclosed cubicle answering question after question when he knew Erik was frightened and in pain only yards away. Even now he had to steel himself against the need to be close enough to touch the boy, see for himself that he was getting the best medical care that Hurricane Beach had to offer.

"Megan? Commander? Is that you?" Doc Yount asked without turning around.

"Yes. We're here," Megan replied, taking a half step toward the bed. Catching herself, she moved backward, clasping her arms tightly around her middle as though that restraint might hold her still. Doc Yount and the nurses wore masks and gowns. The top half of the bed was draped with what Noah assumed were sterile sheets, and Megan was obviously keeping her distance in order not to contaminate the field.

"Just about done." Doc Yount continued talking over his shoulder. "Pretty clean laceration. No need for surgery. I'll want to do a CAT scan later this afternoon to make sure there's no damage to that thick Hardaway skull of his. But I don't foresee any problems." He swung his head around to look at Erik. "Hang on a few more minutes, son, and we'll have you back in one piece."

Erik turned his head on the thin hard pillow. His eyes were open but unfocused. A plastic IV pouch of clear liquid was suspended above the bed, feeding into a tube that had been inserted in the back of his left hand. There was a gauze patch over the cut above his eye, and someone had washed the blood from his face. But he was still as pale as death, and Noah ground his teeth against another powerful wave of emotion as he realized once more just how lucky Erik had been.

"C'mon over, Megan," Doc Young instructed. "X ray's on the wall. I know you do all your nursing behind a desk, but you can read an X ray, can't you?"

"Yes," Megan said, her eyes never leaving Erik's face. "I can read an X ray."

"Good. Take a look. It's a nasty cut. Nicked a vein, but there's no tendon or ligament damage. No broken bones. He'll be ready to try out for the basketball team, or I miss my guess. No football, of course. Too soon. But he'll make a better basketball player anyway. Tall. Broad-shouldered. Good hands. I ought to know. Had three boys of my own play the game."

Watch his son play basketball. Shoot hoops together. The words hit Noah with the force of a mine going off under his feet. Play basketball with his son. The image made him smile.

Megan squared her shoulders a little and move forward to study the X ray.

"Mom?" Her head swung around. Noah saw the smile that curved her lips, banished some of the fear from her expression.

"Yes, Erik?"

"I'm sorry, Mom. About the Blazer. I...do the cops think I stole it?" The words were halting and a little slurred around the edges. One of the nurses stepped away from the bed to make room for Megan.

"I don't know. But I'm sure your grandfather will explain."

"I stole *his* car, you know. Fielder's. In Michigan. If they find that out, I'll end up in jail for sure."

Fielder. Noah swung his gaze back to his son's face. It was the first time Erik had spoken his kidnapper's name aloud.

"You're not going to jail," Megan said fiercely. She reached down and curled her fingers around Erik's, avoiding the IV needle inserted into the back of his uninjured hand.

"We'll work it out, son," Noah said, moving to stand behind Megan. "I promise you that." He put his hands on Megan's shoulders, felt her stiffen momentarily and then relax against his chest. He glanced across Erik's body to where Doc Yount was skillfully tying off the last of almost two dozen stitches in Erik's forearm.

A wave of pure homicidal rage arced through his body. Erik had nearly died because of his fear of the man who had stolen him away from them. A man who was probably looking for the boy at that very moment. From now on Noah wasn't going to let Erik—or Megan—out of his sight. As soon as possible he would call Jamieson. Follow up on the fax and make sure the former SEAL kept up the search for Erik's tormentor. And when they found Fielder, Noah would personally make the bastard wish he had never been born.

The turmoil in his soul must have communicated itself to Megan, who turned her head, sensing his anger. She frowned at him.

"I'm sorry," Erik said, his eyelids drooping. "I'm sorry."

"Shh, baby," Megan crooned, bending forward

over the bed railing, distancing herself slightly from Noah and the violence she'd discerned in his touch. "It's all right. Everything's going to be all right. I promise. We'll notify the police."

"No. I don't want him to find us," Erik muttered, frowning in his turn. "If he knows we're looking for him he'd go crazy. He'll do anything to get even. Promise you won't call the police."

"Shh, baby. No police. I promise," Megan whispered.

"I don't—" His eyes closed and his head rolled to one side.

"Doc?" Noah couldn't stop the alarm in his voice.

The elderly physician looked up, peeling off his gloves. "He's just asleep, Commander. Perfectly normal reaction to the combination of pain medication, sedative and general stress. Best thing for him now." He shook his head. "Seems like that's the same thing I told you three days ago. Poor kid. He's been through a hell of a lot."

"My God, Erik! How badly is he hurt?" Helene Hardaway's voice cut through the air.

Noah stepped away from the bed to face Merrick and Helene. Amy was there, too, standing slightly behind her parents. Megan moved with him. But a step away only, her fingers still entwined with her son's. "It's all right, Mom," she said. "He's just sleeping."

"Dozing's more like it, Helene," Doc Yount warned. "He can hear everything we say. Although, I doubt at the moment he's inclined to answer you if you talk to him."

Helene nodded, her fingers pressed to her lips. "Of

course. He…he is going to be all right? We… Merrick and I…just got our grandson back. We're not going to let anything happen to him, are we Merrick?''

Merrick gathered her close to his chest as he looked across the cool, starkly furnished treatment room. ''Doc?''

''Bumps and bruises. Quite a cut on the right arm and a goose egg on his forehead,'' he repeated patiently for the newcomers. ''In two days' time he'll be good as new and in better shape than that black Blazer of yours, Merrick, I dare say. He's one hell of a lucky kid.''

''When can we take him home, Doctor?'' Megan asked as the older of the two nurses began fastening a padded dressing over the stitches with long gauze strips.

''I'm planning on keeping him right where he is for the rest of the day. At least till I get some tests run. Damn insurance regulations just about make it impossible to keep someone any longer than that,'' Doc Yount groused as he dropped his soiled gloves in a container with a foot-operated lid. The metal can clanged shut as he finished speaking, a perfect exclamation point to his words. ''But, like I said, I don't expect to find anything else wrong. And once he sleeps off the sedative and the pain pills, he'll wake up hungry as a bear. Why don't all of you take off and grab a little rest and a bite to eat yourselves?''

''I'm not leaving,'' Megan said stubbornly.

''I think you should, Megan,'' Amy said. ''You

look terrible. There's blood on your blouse and shorts. And on your leg. Are you hurt?''

"No," Megan said shortly, dismissively. "I'm not hurt."

"I gathered up a change of clothes for you and Erik when I went out to Sea Haven," Amy told her. "I...there was so much blood—" Her voice faltered. She held out a plastic bag. "You can come to my place and have a shower and change," she went on, determinedly cheerful again. "I'll fix you a bite to eat."

"No. I'm staying here," Megan insisted.

"Let us stay, Megan," Helene said. "You will stay, won't you, Merrick?"

"I'll be here for as long as you need me, Helene."

She nodded and lifted her hand to his cheek for a brief moment. "Thank you."

"He's my grandson, too, Helene," Merrick said gruffly.

"Our grandson," she said quietly. "Megan, you go with Amy."

"I'm not leaving," Megan said stubbornly.

This was going nowhere. "Then come with me, Megan," Noah said, knowing his tone made the words more of a command than a suggestion. He hadn't been alone with Megan for over eight years. For the sake of his own hard-won peace of mind, he didn't want to be now. But she was as brittle as spun glass, almost at the end of her tether. "My room at the Sand Dollar is closer than Amy and Jon's place. We can be back here in less than five minutes if necessary."

"No," Megan said almost immediately. But Amy overruled her objection.

"Good idea. I'll be back in a couple of hours to spell Mom and Dad. Erik will surely want to be away from here by dinnertime. No one wants to eat hospital food if they can help it."

"Can't feed him here, anyway," Doc Yount mumbled as he bent over a desklike counter, his pen making scratching sounds on the chart he was writing on. "Damn insurance regulations. Not that the food's bad, mind you. I've been eating it for thirty years. But it can't compare to a meal at Sea Haven." He signed his name with a flourish, and handed the chart to one of the nurses.

"Oh, yes. Dinner. He'll be hungry, I'm sure," Helene said, slipping up to the bed. She reached over and pushed Erik's hair from his forehead, careful not to disturb the white bandage over his eye. "When Amy comes to sit with Erik, we'll hurry back to Sea Haven, and Annie and I will make him something wonderful for dinner. What do you think it should be? Soup and a custard, perhaps?"

Merrick had followed her to their grandson's bedside. "Definitely not," he said.

Helene looked up at him. "What do you suggest?"

"How about Annie's fried chicken and mashed potatoes and pan gravy. And some of her Black Forest cheesecake for dessert."

"Certainly not Black Forest cheesecake," Helene said sharply. "Remember your cholesterol." And then relenting, "Fresh fruit for dessert. And cinnamon ice cream?"

"An admirable compromise."

Helene flushed. "Merrick—"

"Grandma?" Erik's eyes were open. He was looking up at Helene as though he wasn't quite certain how she'd got there.

"Yes, love?"

"Tell Granddad…"

"Tell me what, son?" Merrick leaned forward so that Erik could see him.

Erik blinked twice, focused his gaze on the older man. "I'm sorry about the car. I'll…I'll make it right somehow. I promise. Only please—" his head moved restlessly on the pillow "—don't call the police."

"Don't worry about it, lad. It's all taken care of. There'll be no police. You have my word on that. Now just have a good nap and when you wake up we'll take you back home. To Sea Haven. And your grandmother will feed you and fuss over you and everything will be fine."

Erik turned his head away. "No," he said, his eyes closing once more. "Everything won't be fine."

MEGAN LOOKED AROUND the small, clean, one-room cottage with little curiosity. Noah wondered if she was even taking in the sand-colored walls, the brown-painted floor with woven-mat rugs scattered here and there, the inexpensive beach prints on the walls or the king-size bed that dominated the cramped space. On the wall opposite the bed was a closet-size kitchen and a bathroom that was only slightly larger. A couch and chair and cheap wooden coffee table sat in front of the window, at right angles to the big bed. Strong afternoon sunlight filled the room.

Megan took off her sunglasses and winced at the brightness. Noah moved to close the heavy drapes that covered the big window, plunging the room into artificial twilight. "Better?" he asked.

"Yes, thanks. I've got a doozy of a headache."

"It's probably a combination of stress and heat." He'd left the air conditioner running when he left that morning, so the cabin was blessedly cool.

"I've got some aspirin in my purse—" She looked around her, at a loss for a moment. "I came away without it, didn't I?" She pushed a weary hand through her hair. "You don't happen to have any on hand, do you?"

He nodded. "In the bathroom. You can take a couple before you shower and change."

"Shower?" She looked down at her bloody clothes and shuddered. "Yes. I need a shower." She still sounded doubtful. She didn't want to be there. She didn't want to be alone with him. He had no trouble reading her thoughts on that matter. They paralleled his own.

But for different reasons, he imagined.

He knew he had never gotten over loving Megan Hardaway, but he'd learned to live with the empty space inside him where their love had been. But now that they'd been thrown back together, all the fragments, the bits and pieces of his dreams for a family of his own were regenerating with a speed and intensity that shook him to the core.

Megan remained standing in the middle of the room, her back to him. Noah took a step forward, moved to take her in his arms, try to tell her a little of what was going on inside him. She turned around, staring at him as if she wasn't quite certain who he was. He wasn't surprised. After all, before the last week, they hadn't seen each other for over eight years, hadn't spoken more than a few words on the phone. They were almost strangers, thrown together by the unexpected, miraculous return of their son. He had no right to touch her. He had no right to love her again. Noah stopped where he was.

"Go take a shower and some aspirin, Megan. Get a little rest, and then I'll drive you back to the hospital and you and Erik can go home."

CHAPTER EIGHT

MEGAN HUDDLED on the floor of the shower stall in Noah's bathroom and let the lukewarm water pound on her head and shoulders. Let the patter of it on the tiles drown the sounds of her sobs. Once again she was sharing a bathroom with Noah Carson. She was surrounded by his things. His soap. His razor. His scent. Everything she had felt for him so long ago, every suppressed moment of desire, every sensation, every memory that she had forced herself to live without for the last twelve years came flooding back, nearly overwhelming her with their strength.

But she could no more go back and recapture what she had shared with Noah than she could change the past, return to the day Erik disappeared and keep him safe beside her until the unseen danger had passed.

She had shut the mirrored cabinet and stripped off her bloodstained clothes and dumped them in the wastebasket, her movements stiff and slow. She never wanted to see them again. She turned on the taps, stood under the heavy pulse of water, watched Erik's blood mingle with the water.

Erik had nearly died today and it was her fault, just as his kidnapping had been; if not for the same reasons. Twelve years ago she had been angry and lonely and completely and desperately in love with her child's father. She had been focused only on winning Noah away from the navy, away from the SEALs and everything that kept them apart. That single-mindedness had made her shortsighted and careless, and it had cost her her son.

Everything that had happened today, everything that had happened over the last week was her fault as well. But now it was not because she felt too much. But because she felt too little. She had isolated herself too well, insulated her feelings, channeled them so deeply inside that not even she could reach them when it became necessary. She couldn't let go long enough to embrace the joy of having her child back in her arms. She should have insisted that Noah put a stop to the investigation of Erik's past. She should have *known* he was her child—not needed a private eye to tell her. Maybe if she'd accepted Erik—just loved him—none of this would have happened.

The guilt was becoming more than she could bear. She continued to cry. She sat with her arms wrapped around her knees, holding herself tight, trying to choke back the sobs.

Suddenly she wasn't alone.

The glass door slid open with a thump and Noah was there, kneeling beside her. "My God, Megan. What's wrong?"

She couldn't answer. Couldn't get any words past the aching tightness in her throat. She dropped her head on her knees and cried all the harder.

Noah turned off the tepid spray. "Megan. Look at me." It was a quiet entreaty she couldn't refuse. She lifted her face. "Tell me what's wrong."

Water dripped from her hair into her eyes, mingling with her tears. Noah reached up and brushed the wet hair from her cheek. She tried to focus on his face, but all she could see was the bloodstain on his light blue shirt. Sobs tore through her again, harder than before, stealing her voice and her breath. Noah looked down at his chest, following her gaze. "Damn," he swore softly.

He stripped off his shirt, threw it out of her line of sight, then stood up, pulling her with him, dripping wet and naked. He picked her up as though she weighed nothing at all and carried her into the other room. He grabbed a cotton blanket from the foot of the bed and wrapped it around her, then disappeared for a moment, only to return with a towel and an adhesive bandage. He wound the towel around her head and bandaged the cut on her leg with swift efficiency.

"God, Megan. Don't cry," he said in that same soft, dark voice as he gathered her back into the circle of his arms. "I can't stand it when you cry."

"I can't stop," she whispered. "For twelve years I haven't let myself feel anything. And now—" She closed her eyes, shuddering at the image of her father's Blazer slamming into the tree.

"Shh, don't cry, Megan. He's going to be fine."

"I know." But that knowledge did nothing to dispel the horror that gripped her soul.

Noah pulled her close, and she let him. She needed the warmth of another human being. She needed *his* warmth. Noah's touch. Noah's hard strong arms around her. God help her, she needed him and wanted him.

He held her close. She could feel the steady beat of his heart beneath her cheek, and it comforted her. Gradually she brought her emotions under control. "I thought I might die too when I saw Dad's Blazer plow into that tree," she said at last.

"I know. I know." His embrace tightened painfully for a moment.

"It was the same awful knife-sharp pain I felt in my heart when I realized he was gone, really gone, that day in the mall." Putting the old nightmares into words seemed to help calm the turmoil in her soul enough to let her start thinking rationally again.

"I felt as if my heart had stopped," Noah said so quietly she had to strain to hear him over the sound of her own shaky breathing. "I thought this couldn't be happening. That we'd only just found him again. We couldn't be losing him—forever."

She turned her head to look up at him. His face was still set and hard, his eyes bleak with pain, but her hand was resting on his chest and she felt the slow, steady beat of his heart accelerate with the force of his hidden emotion. "You know, when we lost him twelve years ago, you never told me any of what you felt."

"You never let me, Megan," he said quietly. "You shut me out so completely I was never able to tell you how much I hurt. I waited for you to come back to me from that place inside yourself where you'd gone to ground, but you never did."

"I know," she said, feeling new tears well up. "I know. I'm sorry, Noah. I...I turned off everything so that I could survive. Do you understand what I'm trying to say?"

His expression was still guarded, but his voice was gentle. "Yes, Megan. I know exactly what you're trying to say."

"And then today." She waved a hand toward the bathroom. "Just now. It seemed as if everything came flooding back. Everything I'd tried to dam up inside me for all these years. All the joy and the sorrow. The laughter and the tears. The pain..." Suddenly she realized how close they were. That she was naked beneath the concealing folds of the blankets, that he wore only a pair of shorts. She could feel the heat of his body, the roughness of the hair on his chest and the rock hardness of bone and muscle against the side of her breast. And now the beat of his heart had taken on a new, more insistent rhythm.

"What else did you remember, Megan?"

She looked into his face once more, into the ghosts of the past. She remembered the despair in his eyes the day she'd told him she couldn't live with him anymore. But she also remembered the passion they'd shared. She remembered his pride and elation when he'd first held their son in his arms. "I remember the love," she said before she could stop herself.

"So do I, God help me," he said roughly. "So do I." And then he lowered his head and kissed her.

Megan was lost. She knew it the moment his lips touched hers. It had been so long. She had been alone, celibate, for all the years they'd been apart. She had allowed no man to get close enough even to consider a physical relationship. She had closed herself off so completely she'd been sure that she would never feel sexual desire again.

She had been wrong. Very, very wrong. The moment Noah's mouth touched hers, her body responded with a vengeance. She reached up, wrapped her arms around his neck, heedless of the blanket slipping away from her. Her mouth opened to the urging of his.

His hands reached up to cup her breasts. His tongue entered her mouth, and she returned the caress with a hunger that matched his own. She didn't let herself think of the heartache and pain they'd caused each other. She only let herself feel. And knew that Noah was doing the same.

His mouth lifted from hers for a moment. He moved toward the bed, pulling her down beside him. His hands fumbled with the zipper of his shorts. Then they were gone. Noah held her tight against him. He kissed her throat, her collarbone, the curve of her breast before taking one hard nipple into his mouth.

She moaned deep in her throat, pressed herself closer, wanting to keep his mouth tight against her breast. The years and the heartache slipped away as she let herself be transported to a safer more innocent time where loving Noah Carson and being loved by him had been all that she desired.

"Noah, please." Her voice sounded rough and throaty, unfamiliar. "Please." She was suddenly desperate to have him inside her. "Make love to me."

Noah seemed as anxious as she. His breathing was raspy, irregular. He positioned himself above her, rested his weight on his elbows and cupped her face with his hands. The towel he'd wrapped around her head came loose and he threaded his long fingers through her hair. He watched her, their bodies not yet joined. His face was serious, intent as his eyes searched deep into hers.

"Are you sure, Megan?"

She knew what he was asking, but with her blood pounding through her veins it was hard to find the words. "I want to feel alive again. Give me that." She wound her legs around his waist and pulled his mouth down to hers once more.

He entered her slowly, with great restraint, but then his control seemed to crack and he began to move more strongly, more forcefully within her. Megan lifted her hips, meeting thrust for thrust. Then Noah groaned and shuddered, the hot spill of his climax pushing her into her own release.

Slowly Megan came back to herself, aware of a once-familiar feeling of contentment and languor that was an echo of a faraway time and place. Then the weight of Noah's body on hers brought her into the present. She moved beneath him, and he stirred, rolling to his side. His arm lay across her breasts and he shifted his hand, cupping her softness, arousing her with a swiftness that shocked and surprised her.

It also brought an unwelcome awareness of how vulnerable she still was, in body and in spirit.

"Noah, please. Don't do that."

He stilled his movements instantly, raised himself above her, his hand resting heavily on her breast. He studied her face for a long minute. The room had grown darker. Thunder rumbled off in the distance. "Regrets already, Megan?"

Regrets? Yes. So many regrets she couldn't begin to count them all. She nodded, not trusting her voice.

"It shouldn't have happened," she managed to say at last.

He didn't contradict her. "I never could resist you, Megan Marie." No one ever called her by her full name except Noah. And then only when they were alone, intimate. She used to think that she could hear the far-off lilt of Ireland in his voice when he called her that. A trace memory perhaps, a legacy from the parents and family he'd never known. "I'm sorry, Megan. I didn't mean to take advantage of the situation."

"It was my fault as much as yours." She clasped his strong, scarred wrist in both of hers. "But that doesn't change anything. It wasn't wise or prudent."

"And everything you do now is prudent, is it, Megan?"

"Yes," she said, looking at his mouth, remembering his kisses, though she told herself not to. "It has to be."

"Are you still on the Pill?"

She blinked in surprise, and then the meaning of his words sank in. Her eyes flew to his, became trapped by the magnetic darkness of his straightforward gaze. She shook her head. "No," she said, "I'm not taking birth control pills."

"And I never had a vasectomy. There could be consequences from this afternoon, Megan."

"A baby." She closed her eyes. Noah's baby growing inside her again. Her eyes flew open. She couldn't allow that dream to take root. "I don't think that's likely, Noah," she said tightly. "I'm thirty-six, not nineteen." She knew he was remembering how easily she'd gotten pregnant with Erik. "I...I don't think you have to worry. I know it's a complication you don't want to deal with in your life right now." Her voice broke on the last word.

He twisted his wrist from her grasp and cupped her face with both hands, resting his weight on his elbows. "It's a complication I'd gladly deal with."

His answer surprised her. "But the divorce papers? I thought—"

"What did you think, Megan?"

"I assumed there was someone else in your life."

He shook his head, absently stroking her hair as he did so. "No, Megan Marie," he said softly. "There's no one else. There's never been anyone else."

"Are you telling me there haven't been any women in your life these past eight years?"

He frowned, and for a moment his face assumed the hard contours of his warrior's mask. "We're still married, Megan."

"I didn't think that would keep you from...from finding someone else to love."

"There's been no one, Megan," he repeated.

"Then why did you ask for a divorce now, after all this time?"

He kept on stroking her hair, but he turned his head slightly so that her eyes were no longer captive to his. "I thought it was time you were free."

"I didn't want to be free," she said quietly.

"I know. Married, but not married. Safe and cloistered as a nun."

"It wasn't like that," she said heatedly.

"Wasn't it? Have there been other men in your life, Megan?"

Her face flamed and her heart skipped a painful beat. "No," she said, lifting her chin. "There's been no one else."

"Why were you faithful to vows you no longer believed in?"

She wasn't going to answer him. She couldn't answer him because there was only one answer possible. That she was still in love with Noah Carson.

"I...I have to get back to the hospital. Please, Noah. Let me go." She was breathing in short little gasps. He hadn't realized he was leaning that heavily on her, pinning her to the bed as though he could keep her with him by sheer physical force.

He rolled off her, didn't try to stop her when she sat up, pulling the thin cotton blanket around her once more. He reached out and circled her wrist with his hand. "We can't pretend this never happened, Megan," he said gruffly.

She shook her head. "You're wrong, Noah. We have to pretend it never happened, because it can never happen again. When I get back to Nebraska I'm going to get in touch with my attorney, go ahead with the divorce proceedings, just as you wanted."

"No." He rose to his knees, pulling her around to face him so quickly she lost her balance on the too-soft mattress and fell against him. "I don't want that."

"I do," she said, pushing away from him, sliding from the bed. He still held her wrist imprisoned in his hand and there was nowhere for her to go. "I have to think of Erik from now on."

Noah stood up, too, towering over her. He knew his naked powerful body intimidated her and he didn't care. "Dammit, Megan. You're not making any sense." His heart was hammering in his chest. She wasn't looking at him. She was looking through him. He'd seen that look before, too often in the months after Erik's kidnapping. She had shut him out, concentrating on her own inner pain. He could feel her turning inward again, sealing away the most caring and vulnerable pieces of her heart and soul. He gave her arm a shake, trying to bring her back.

Megan blinked, looked down at her manacled wrist and then up into his eyes. "It's my fault, what happened today," she whispered brokenly. "I couldn't let myself believe my son—"

"*Our* son, Megan," he said more sharply than he had intended.

She flinched slightly, then nodded. "Our son was really back."

"What are you saying? Don't you believe that Erik is our son?"

"I didn't say that—"

He put his knee on the bed and leaned toward her. "Megan, there is one way to be sure. We could do blood tests. You'll have to give Doc Yount a sample for that. But it will be easy enough to get Erik's blood for testing after today. I'm willing—"

"No." She tried to jerk her hand free. He didn't let her go. She raised her chin, anger flaring in her eyes to match his own. "Let me finish. I don't want blood tests. I don't need them. Today—" She swallowed hard but kept on talking, "Today, when he was hurt, he called me Mom." Her breath sifted out in a sigh. She was silent a moment. "He's never called me that before. In my heart, I knew from the first moment I saw him that he was our son.

"But I've been afraid for so long. Losing him hurt so much. For so long I've been afraid to hope, to let myself feel strongly again. I held back from him and kept a space between us. We nearly lost him again today because I didn't put a stop to your investigation. I can't let that happen again. I have to keep him safe. I'm his mother and he must be my first concern. That's why I've decided I'm going to take Erik away as soon as possible. Back to Nebraska."

"No." The denial was torn from the very center of his soul. She cried out in pain as he tightened his grip involuntarily. He released her immediately and she took a step backward. "You're not going anywhere," Noah said firmly, keeping his voice low and even.

"What are you talking about? We can't stay here. It's more than likely a madman is stalking our child. If Fielder gets this far, no one will tell him where we've gone. We'll be safe in Nebraska."

"You won't be safe anywhere if the bastard really wants to get Erik back again."

Megan drew in a deep breath. She sat down on the bed with a thump, as though her legs were too weak to hold her upright. Two crystal tears rolled down her cheeks. She stared at the far wall and when she spoke her voice trembled with emotion. "Then he should go with you. To Coronado. You can keep him safe." Noah knew how much it had cost her to say those words. He wanted to take her in his arms, soothe her fears, pull her close and reignite the passion that had burned so hotly between them just minutes before. But instead, he let her go, reached for his shorts and pulled them on while she watched with wary, tear-bright eyes.

"I'm not taking Erik to Coronado," he said, jerking up the zipper. "And you're not taking him to Nebraska. We're staying here where I can keep an eye on both of you."

"No. It's too risky. I think we should notify the police."

"It's a risk we have to take. Erik's just beginning to trust us. If we go to the authorities now, we'll lose his trust." He hunkered down, reached out, took her by the shoulders so that she had to look at him, had to acknowledge him. "Hurricane Beach is a small town. We'll both be here to keep an eye on Erik. I'm going to talk to your parents about my moving into Sea Haven. From this minute on our son will never be alone."

"I...can't—" Her eyes flickered to the rumpled sheets of his bed.

"I promise I won't touch you again, Megan," he said through clenched teeth. "But get the idea of a divorce out of your head. From now on we're a family. We're going to do this my way. I failed Erik all those years ago just as badly as you think you did. This time I intend to keep him safe and no one—not even you—is going to stand in my way."

SO THE KID had gotten this far before he ran out of gas. Byron Fielder squinted against the strong sunlight pouring into the impound lot at the suburban Ann Arbor garage where the cops had towed his car, and surveyed the nondescript sedan. Pretty good mileage for the old gas guzzler.

"It'll cost you two hundred and fifty bucks to drive her away," the attendant said, leaning against the chain-link fence. "That's towing charges and the fine for leaving it abandoned on the highway."

Fielder grunted. He had no intention of paying to get the car back. It wasn't worth two hundred and fifty bucks. They could have it. But the garage attendant was a burly man who didn't look as if he took kindly to being told to take the heap and shove it where the sun didn't shine. "Will you take a personal check?"

The attendant looked him over carefully and shook his head. "Cash, money order, Visa or MasterCard," he said, fishing a toothpick out of his coverall pocket and sticking it between his teeth.

"I don't have a credit card." Fielder attempted a smile. "And I don't have that much cash. I'll have to go to a post office and get a money order."

"Suit yourself," the man responded. "We're open until four."

"Yeah. I'll be back." He turned and the attendant slammed the gate shut, locking it behind them. Fielder ventured another smile. "Say, you don't happen to know anything about the guy who stole my car, do you? The police won't tell me anything."

"Nope." The man shook his bald head. "Just that there was some PI type, ex-military, if you ask me, snoopin' around here a few days ago. Wantin' to know the same thing. He ain't been in touch with you, huh?"

"Nope." So someone else was looking for the

brat, too. He hadn't expected that. Did it mean Erik had found his way home? He scanned the half-empty lot with a wary eye. Were the cops hiding out somewhere here, waiting to take him in?

"Dammit, Diana!" he fumed, crawling back behind the wheel of the battered Jeep he'd bought from a neighbor. "Why'd you have to go and die on me, woman?"

Diana would remember the address the kid kept babbling about before he'd tanned his hide often enough to make him forget it.

After all, he'd only taken the brat to please her. To make her stop crying after their own little angel was taken from them and they found out they couldn't have any more. She'd cried so much and so long that he was afraid she'd waste away to nothing and he'd lose her, too.

Kidnapping. It wasn't something he'd planned to do. It had just happened, like a gift from God. The little dark-haired boy, so like his lost Reggie, had come wandering down the aisle in the department store at that mall in Tallahassee, and he'd been alone. All alone with no one around. Fielder had just picked him up in his arms, held him tight and taken him back to the fleabag motel where they were living while he looked for work. He'd thought his wife could play with the little guy, hold him, hug him and kiss him like she kept praying she could do with Reggie again. After a couple of hours he'd figured he'd take him back to the mall and turn him loose for his folks or the security cops to find.

But Diana—she wanted to keep the little tyke. convinced herself he was lost and God had led him to them. He hadn't told her otherwise. They'd just packed up their old truck that same day and left town. Since then he'd lost count of all the places they'd lived, all the jobs he'd been fired from or laid off from, until they'd finally ended up on the twenty acres of scrubland up past Cheboygan, Michigan, his old man had left him.

Now it was going to take every last cent he could scrape together to go after the ungrateful pup.

Diana had taken to the boy right off, but he never could. The kid didn't like him. And the older the boy got the more it showed. Diana had gotten funny, too, as the years went by, siding with the boy more and more, taking Erik's side every time the brat sassed him or didn't do what he was told. It had gotten so bad he'd started having to use his belt on her as well as the kid to show them who was boss.

But he'd never thought the boy would run off like that. Never thought he had the spirit or the guts. Fielder had wasted a week waiting for Erik to show up back at the cabin, like a whipped pup with his tail between his legs, but that hadn't happened. And now he figured Erik had to be headed back to Florida. Back to his folks if he could find them. And that was bad news.

Fielder wasn't crazy. He knew what he'd done that day twelve years ago. There was no statute of limitations on kidnapping. And Florida had the death penalty, as far as he knew. No, there was no way he could let Erik get back to where he came from. If he could just remember where the hell that was.

He started the cantankerous old Jeep and headed it south toward the Ohio border and Intersta

He'd follow it all the way to Valdosta and then head west for Tallahassee. All he figured he had to do then was walk into any library and ask to see some old back copies of the newspaper. There would surely be reports of the kidnapping, complete with names and addresses.

And then he'd know exactly where to go looking for that ungrateful young whelp. And exactly what he had to do when he found him.

CHAPTER NINE

THUNDER, muted by the thick stucco walls of Sea Haven, growled and grumbled overhead, rattling the windowpanes as if to gain attention. Megan turned her head to look out the window of her father's study. "Is it raining again?" she asked Kieran and Erik. The teens were seated behind Merrick's desk, heads bent over a project that had kept them entertained for the better part of an hour.

"I don't want to hear about it if it is," Amy pronounced. She had brought Kieran to Sea Haven to keep Erik company for a few hours. He was still a little stiff and sore from the accident the day before, a little unsteady on his feet from loss of blood.

"No," Kieran said, scanning the sky, as well. "It's not raining now. But it's supposed to, off and on, all day, according to the weather lady on the radio. It's because Fred's turning out to be such a whopper." "Fred" was a new hurricane, the sixth of the season. The storm had blown up fast, and it was big and dangerous. The latest satellite forecasts predicted that Fred would stay to the south of Hurricane Beach, coming ashore in Texas or Mexico. But there were no guarantees that the Florida Panhandle would be spared, and the whole town kept a close eye on the weather.

"No more hurricane talk," Amy warned from her seat on the leather sofa in front of the flower-filled fireplace. "I will not hear of bad weather spoiling the party."

"The Storm Spirits hear and obey, Oh Goddess of the Universe," Kieran replied in ringing tones, raising outstretched hands above her head in mock tribute.

"You're weird," Erik remarked, not looking up from what he was doing.

"You, my dear nephew, are wise beyond your years." Amy made a face at Kieran. Megan giggled behind her hand at the girl's impertinence and earned a sharp look from her sister. "Don't encourage her."

"I'm sorry," Megan said contritely, but she was still smiling.

"What are you two doing over there, anyway?"

"Nothing," Kieran said too quickly.

"That sounds ominous." Megan rose from her chair and crossed the room. She put her arms on the back of Merrick's big leather chair where her son was sitting. Erik had his back to her, fiddling with a pencil. Both arms rested on the paper in front of him, obscuring the details of what he'd been working on. Megan leaned closer. "May I see?"

The back of Erik's neck colored slightly, but he didn't flinch or lean away. "It's nothing," he said, turning his head to look up at her. He'd dispensed with the bandage but the skin above his eye was red and abraded. She offered a little prayer of thanks, reminded yet again of how close she'd come to losing him. "Just some doodling. I'm not very good."

"That's not true. He's real good. Helene bought

him a drawing pad and colored pencils this morning. Real ones," Kieran offered. "Like artists use, not kid toys."

"I didn't know you liked to draw."

"I've never had any lessons or anything like that. But Grandma saw me messing around the other day, so she bought this stuff for me," he finished in a rush, as though he wasn't quite certain Megan wouldn't take the pencils and pad away from him.

"He did a lot of drawing because the guy who took him wouldn't let him have a TV or a computer or anything else," Kieran supplied. "What a dork."

Erik stiffened slightly but made no direct reply to Kieran's remark. "There wasn't much else to do where we lived. And drawing stuff doesn't cost much."

Megan fought to hide the surge of outrage that lanced through her every time Erik's kidnapper was mentioned. Noah was right—the man must be found and punished. But putting Erik at risk by staying at Sea Haven was not the way she wanted to accomplish that. "I can't draw a straight line," she said. "But your father's very good at it."

Erik's eyes lit up at her mention of Noah's ability. "Really? He likes to draw?"

"Yes." She had thought at one time that Noah might leave the navy, go to college, become an architect. One night after they made love she had told him of that dream. He had laughed at her fantasy, pulling her into his arms, kissing her until she could barely breathe, let alone defend her position. "I might want to build houses someday," he had told her. "But I don't want to sit behind a desk and design them."

Megan crossed her arms under her breasts, holding back the memories and sensations of the past. Both the long-ago past that was beyond mending and the very-near past, when Noah had held her in his arms, and she had dreamed again, and felt desire again, if only for a short time.

"I remember that," Amy said from across the room. "Noah did a caricature of me once when you were a baby, Erik. It was very good." She shrugged and laughed a little. "For a caricature, that is. He gave me huge ears, I remember, and the braces on my teeth were as big as fence posts."

Megan remembered the caricature, too. "I don't know if he's still interested in drawing or not. You must ask him about it sometime."

"I will." Erik was smiling. She hoped he hadn't heard the sharpness in her voice. "I'll ask him when he gets back. Maybe he can help me with the perspective on some of these buildings."

"What are you working on?" Megan prompted.

Erik hesitated just a fraction of a second. No longer than any teenager would, when faced with having to expose something precious to possible criticism, Megan told herself. Then he smiled again, and her heart lightened. "Sure," he said. "It's…it's a gift for Grandma and Granddad. For their anniversary."

"It's sort of our idea for what Erik's plans for the Sea Haven property would look like," Kieran said. "I think it's great."

"Like I told you, it's not very good," Erik said.

"It's a good thing you're left-handed or you couldn't get it done in time for the party. Not with those stitches in your arm," Kieran observed.

Left-handed. Like Helene. Every time she looked at Erik now she saw more and more little things that told her he was her son. The way he tilted his head when he smiled; the same way Noah sometimes did. His laugh, like Merrick's years ago, Helene insisted. She didn't need blood tests or DNA analysis or anything else to convince her who he was. She'd known that the moment he looked at her across the width of the smashed Blazer and called her Mom.

"No, Erik," Megan said, her throat tightening a little with pride and love. "It's very good. You have real talent." The perspective was slightly skewed, the scale a little off, but even she, who knew nothing about the mechanics of drawing, could see the potential in the work.

Sea Haven was there, at the edge of the sheet, and three small Victorian-style houses, raised on stilts, beside it. A little farther down the beach were low-rise condos, also with Victorian elements. There was a swimming pool and a play area between the two buildings. Patios with tiny gardens filled with red and pink flowering plants were located behind each unit.

A fence, and rows of trees and shrubs, separated the housing units from the main bulk of her parents' property. Sea Haven Wildlife Preserve was neatly lettered in the middle of the page. There were parking lots, and trailheads, stairs across the dunes, even a bathhouse and picnic area in the vicinity of the old pier. "It's great, Erik." Megan patted his shoulder. "Amy, come see."

"What? Yes. In a minute. I have a few more cards to look through," Amy said a trifle absently.

"The playground between the condos was my idea," Kieran said importantly as Erik began shading in waves and seabirds in the gulf. Megan was barely listening. He hadn't shaken off her hand. Such a small thing for any other woman, but a wonderful step forward for Megan. "We want them to be for families who want to live here all year, remember," Kieran went on. "Not just snowbirds and retired people who will only want to be here in the winter."

"Yes," Megan said, lightly touching a rendering of two tiny crocodiles basking by the side of one of the hiking trails Erik had included in the sketch. "For families. And these three houses here?" she asked, pointing to the buildings next to Sea Haven.

Erik stopped drawing. A sea monster was taking shape beneath his pencil. A fantastical beast, Megan noted fleetingly. A snakelike dragon figure with fire coming from its nostrils, like the creatures shown on old, old maps.

"They're for you," Kieran said when Erik didn't answer. "You and your sisters. One house for Lisa and Matt. One house for Amy and Uncle Jon with a bedroom for me. She touched the middle one with the tip of her fingernail. It was shell pink with blue trim. From the corner of her eye Megan saw her glance quickly at Erik. "And this one's for you and Noah and Erik," she finished in a rush.

"For us?" Their house was sketched in only, not colored as the other two were.

"Yes," Erik said quietly, looking up at her once more. "I thought. Maybe we could—"

"Good Lord, Megan," Amy yelped in an awe-struck voice as she waved an embossed anniversary card in front of her. "This can't be. Do you know who this card is from? The governor."

"What? In a moment, Amy." The tenuous connection between mother and son was broken by the sound of Amy's voice. Megan wanted that connection back. "Erik, what were you about to say?"

But the moment had passed. He bent over his sea monster once more. "Oh, nothing. Just that I... wondered what color you'd like...our house to be?"

"Green," Megan said, giving his shoulder a brief squeeze. "Sea green with ivory trim. Can you manage that?"

"Sure." He picked up the green pencil immediately. "One sea green house coming up."

"Megan. There's a hand-written note and everything. Do you think if we sent an invitation to the party, the governor would come?"

Megan wanted to stay by Erik's side, watch him work, but she wasn't certain he wanted her to remain there despite his acceptance of her hand on his shoulder, so she returned to her seat in the chair by the sofa. Amy pushed the card into Megan's hand. "He and his wife have made a very generous donation to Mom and Dad's favorite charity."

"That's nice." She gave a cursory glance to the card and the note signed with the governor's scrawled signature before handing it back to her sister. "Be sure to add their names to the thank-you list."

"Already done." Amy tapped the spiral notebook

on her lap with the tip of her pencil. "I would make a perfect social secretary to some rich and famous globe-trotting superstar."

"Which might be difficult since you never want to leave Hurricane Beach," Megan observed.

"True. Are you all right?" Amy asked, lowering her voice slightly as she glanced at the amiably arguing teens across the room.

"I'm fine," Megan assured her. She was regaining her equilibrium. She hadn't missed a once-in-a-lifetime opportunity to learn what was on Erik's mind. They would talk about his dreams for their future again. She would explain to him in just the right words why the two of them would be returning to Nebraska as soon as possible. Without Noah. She had all the time in the world to make him understand that was the way it had to be, to forge new and stronger bonds with her son. *Thank God, all the time in the world.*

"You don't look fine," Amy said bluntly. She shuffled the stack of cards and letters into a neat pile.

"Well, I am fine. There's nothing wrong with me."

Amy lowered her voice again. "But there is something wrong between you and Noah."

Megan knew she should have been expecting this. By now, Helene would certainly have told Amy that Noah had moved into his own room at Sea Haven. She had thought her mother would also have explained why. "There has been something wrong between Noah and me for almost twelve years."

"I'd hoped when Mom said he was coming here

to stay that you'd reconciled. But that's not the case, is it?''

Megan cast a glance across the room from the corner of her eye, but Kieran and Erik seemed to be busy estimating the cost of having Erik's drawing matted and framed, and appeared completely uninterested in what she and Amy were talking about.

"No. We haven't reconciled. Noah is here to watch over our son, that's all. We have reason to believe that the man who kidnapped Erik is looking for him again. I thought you knew that."

Amy nodded, unusually subdued. "Mom told me everything the other day at the hospital. But after you and Noah left together...and didn't come back for so long. I...well, I just hoped—"

Megan felt herself flush, but she couldn't let Amy go on hoping for a happy-ever-after ending to their separation that wasn't going to occur. "Noah and I are still estranged, Amy. Our marriage is over. It has been for a long time now."

Amy never gave up easily. "I like Noah. I always have."

"We've grown too far apart. There's too much old pain between us to start again," Megan said softly.

"I'm sorry about that," Amy said.

Megan was surprised to see a faint sheen of tears in her sister's eyes.

"I had thought we might all be a family again," Amy went on. "Now that we have Erik back and Lisa has Matt. And I have Jon and Kieran—"

"You were hoping that Noah and I would reconcile."

"Yes," she said, giving her head a toss, looking

stubborn and determined, as only Amy, the peace-maker, could.

"It's not going to happen, Amy," Megan said, aware the words sounded cold and flat but unable to help herself. "I'm sorry."

"You're telling me to mind my own business?"

"I'm telling you it's over between me and Noah. Not even having Erik returned to us will make a difference."

"I'm sorry," Amy said, sadness in her eyes.

"Don't be," Megan replied, sorry herself that she had hurt her sister's feelings. Amy only wanted all of them, all of the Hardaway girls, to be one big happy family again. "I'm sorry for snapping at you. Let's just concentrate on the anniversary party and let the rest take care of itself."

"I don't like letting things take care of themselves," Amy said in what Megan considered the understatement of the decade. "I think—"

Just then the phone on the table beside the sofa rang. Amy picked it up on the second peal. "Sea Haven," she said into the mouthpiece.

"Lisa? It's Amy." She lifted the receiver away from her ear. "It's Lisa," she repeated unnecessarily for Megan's benefit.

"I gathered as much." Megan laughed, relieved that Amy's attention was diverted from her failed marriage to another subject near and dear to her heart—ensuring Lisa's attendance at their parents' party.

"Where's Mom?" Amy repeated Lisa's question, waving a hand at Kieran, gesturing for her to bring Merrick's portable desk phone to Megan so that she could listen in on the conversation. "She and Dad are taking a drive together," she told Lisa. "She asked him to go at lunch. That's a good sign, don't you think?" Amy nodded her head as she made the statement. "I think so, too. I'm keeping my fingers crossed," she said as she suited actions to words. "I'm glad I was here when you called, Lisa. I drove Kieran out to visit with Erik. Megan and I were just going through today's batch of cards and letters. There's one from the governor and his wife... Yes. Really. Isn't that nice?" She picked up the card and waved it in the air as though Lisa were there to see it. "Yes, it's boiling hot and the humidity is beastly. We're right in the middle of a thundershower and there's a new hurricane brewing, you know. Fred, they call this one."

"Don't let her get started on the party," Kieran whispered to Megan, rolling her eyes as she handed her the portable unit. "Or it will be round six of the Amy and Lisa Grand-Slam Super-Mega Battle of Wills."

Megan hid her smile, but couldn't keep it out of her eyes. Kieran gave her a wicked little grin and sauntered back to her chair behind the desk. "Hi, Lisa," she said into the mouthpiece. "It's Megan."

"How are you?" Lisa said. "How is Erik? Mom called and told me about the accident. You're sure he wasn't badly injured?" Lisa's voice sounded cool and composed as always, but Megan could detect the undercurrent of real concern that threaded through the words.

"He's fine. And very lucky. He came away with only a bad cut on his arm."

"Twenty-eight stitches," Amy interrupted.

"And a bump on the head. But by Mom and Dad's party he'll be fine."

Amy shot her a grateful look for mentioning the party, giving her the opening Megan had no doubt she would have soon made for herself, anyway. "Speaking of the party, Lisa. Have you got your plane tickets booked yet? Do you know the flight number so someone can meet you at the airport?"

"Not exactly," Lisa's voice came back. "Actually, that's why I'm calling. Matt has to be in Hurricane Beach this weekend to sign some papers regarding his grandmother's estate. We're flying down Friday for the Labor Day weekend. We're staying at Bea's house."

"If you're coming this weekend, will you be able to fly back the following weekend, as well?" Amy probed.

Lisa's voice grew a little cooler, a little more distant. "We'll talk about it this weekend, Amy."

Amy ricocheted onto another subject. "I'm going to call Ian Medford, the photographer, and set up an appointment for a family portrait," she said out of the blue.

"What?" Lisa said.

Megan raised her eyebrows. "I didn't know you were planning to do that," she said.

"I just got the idea," Amy said. "It's great. We're all going to be here. Nothing too fancy. But bring a nice dress, Lisa, and tell Matt to pack a suit and tie. We'll do it right here at Sea Haven. Right here in Dad's study. I've always loved this room."

"I...I don't know, Amy. Matt and I are going to

be so busy. I won't have much time to spend at Sea Haven. There are all of Bea's things to go through and start packing—''

"We'll help you. That way you can spare an hour for a family portrait," Amy said firmly. There was a tiny frown between her eyebrows. Her mouth was set in a stubborn line. "It's going to be our gift to Mom and Dad. I'll let you know when Ian can work us in as soon as you get into town."

"All right," Lisa said with what sounded like a sigh. "If that's what you want."

"That's not *all* I want."

"Do you want someone to meet you at the airport?" Megan interrupted before Amy could begin hounding Lisa about the party.

"No. We'll rent a car. Matt will need it to get back and forth to the Brassworks. Tell Mom and Dad we'll be in Friday evening."

"But Lisa," Amy began again.

"I have to go, Amy. One of my girls' obstetricians is on the other line. It's Julie, remember I told you about her? She's expecting twins and her blood pressure's up. I have to take the call. Bye, you two. I'm looking forward to meeting Erik. And seeing Noah again," she added after a slight pause. "Bye now. I really have to go." She broke the connection.

"Lisa's so stubborn," Amy fumed. "If she'd only tell Mom and Dad what hap—''

"Amy," Megan said warningly, inclining her head slightly toward the teenagers. "We've discussed this before. It's Lisa's decision, not ours."

"Okay." Amy looked subdued, suddenly close to tears.

Megan segued into a safer subject. "I didn't know you wanted a family portrait taken. I like the idea. But heavens, I didn't bring anything to wear."

"I don't even own a tie," Erik said, proof that he and Kieran had been listening to their conversation from across the room. "Or a suit."

"What's this about needing a suit?"

Megan and Amy turned toward the sound of a male voice in the doorway. Jon Costas stood there in running shorts and a sweat-stained T-shirt. Noah was behind him, also in running shorts. His tank top was old and faded and fit him like a second skin. The SEAL emblem, trident and eagle, was dull gold against the blue, barely visible beneath the white towel he had draped over his shoulder.

"I didn't hear you come in," Amy said, her face brightening at the sight of her husband. "Hi, Noah," she said, waving her fingers.

Noah raised his hand in salute. The left one, and for a moment the scars on the inside of his wrist and forearm were visible. Amy's smile faded away. She looked at Megan with horror in her eye, but she said nothing.

"Hello, Megan," he said quietly. If he'd noticed Amy's reaction to his scars, he didn't acknowledge it.

"Where have you been?" She hadn't seen him that day. He'd promised not to leave Erik alone, and he hadn't, to be truthful, until this morning.

"I told Erik I was going for a run," he said, his voice all steel and velvet.

"It's okay, Mom," Erik said quickly, defensively. "I knew he was going. It's okay. Nothing happened.'' Megan looked from Erik to her husband and realized whatever new bond had grown between mother and son, the one he'd forged with his father was, at the moment, even stronger.

"I see." She didn't look at Noah again.

"I was jogging on the beach and met up with Noah," Jon explained into the charged silence. Jon Costas was in pretty good shape, Megan had noted. But his face was red and his prematurely gray hair was plastered to his head with sweat. He looked as if he'd been exercising in ninety-degree heat and humidity. Noah, although his skin was covered with a fine sheen of perspiration, wasn't even breathing hard.

"How did you know I was here?" Amy cast her husband an affectionate look.

Jon grinned. "Your car is parked in the driveway."

She laughed, slightly embarrassed. "How stupid of me. Of course it is. I drove Kieran out to visit Erik and help catalog the cards and letters Mom and Dad have received for their anniversary," Amy said. "They're taking a drive. *Together.* I think that's a hopeful sign, don't you?"

"It would seem so."

Amy smiled. "And guess what? Lisa called. She and Matt are coming down for Labor Day weekend. They'll be here Friday night."

"That's good, too." Jon and Lisa's short-lived marriage had ended amicably. And, while his marriage to Amy had caused some friction between the two sisters, things were much better now. "But that doesn't explain those ominous words—need a suit."

"We're going to have a family portrait taken. I'm going to call Ian Medford's studio and set up an appointment as soon as I get back to Rêve Rags."

"A family portrait?"

"Yes," she said, jumping up off the couch to slip her hand into Jon's. "All of us. Mom and Dad. Megan's family. Lisa and Matt. You and me, and Kieran if she wants to be included."

"Me?" Kieran looked surprised, then flushed with pleasure. "Yeah. I'd like that."

"And when he's through with all of us, the photographer can take Megan and Noah and Erik, together," Amy prattled on delightedly. "Then we'll each have a remembrance of Erik's being returned to us. Megan and her family together again." Her voice faltered a little on the last words as she obviously recalled Megan's assertions of a few minutes earlier. "Please, Megan. For my sake."

Megan glanced at Noah. His expression was noncommittal, there was no emotion evident in his storm-dark eyes. Then she turned her head and saw Erik watching her, watching both of them, with a frown creasing his forehead, and she made her decision, made herself smile. "Of course we'd like a family portrait. I'm so glad you thought of it. The three of us. Together again."

"OH DEAR. There seems to be something wrong with the air-conditioning." Helene touched the button that rolled down the driver's-side window of her little silver sportscar.

"That's okay," Merrick said. He looked hot and uncomfortable. He was jackknifed into the low-slung seat, his knees nearly touching his chin. "Once we get out on the highway it will be cooler."

He hadn't asked where they were going. She was glad, because she had no set destination in mind. Now inspiration struck. "Let's stop for an ice at Forenza's." She swung the car into the parking lot a few doors down from the café.

"I'm not really hungry," Merrick said. "We just finished lunch."

She touched the back of his hand where it rested on his knee. "Please, Merrick. We need to talk."

He looked at her a long few seconds, his expression unreadable, and then nodded. "Whatever you say, my dear."

Helene got out of the car, straightened her skirt, then reached inside and took her straw hat out of the tiny back seat. She looked up at the sky. The sun had gone under, dark clouds rolled overhead, promising rain before much longer. She threw the hat back onto the seat and slammed the door.

They walked the few doors to Forenza's Café in silence, chose a table from the half-dozen placed outside on the sidewalk and gave their orders to the waitress, the college-aged granddaughter of one of Helene's bridge-club members.

"Iced coffee for me," Merrick said. "Two sugars. None of the artificial stuff, mind you. I want the real thing." He gave Helene another long measuring look.

She closed her mouth on her automatic caution about too much sugar and caffeine. "I'll have a lemon ice, Cathy," she said, smiling at the girl.

"Coming right up, Mrs. Hardaway."

Gulfview was almost devoid of pedestrian traffic this stormy afternoon. There were only two other couples seated beneath the umbrellas at Forenza's, and only one table was occupied at Java Joe's across the street. A low roll of thunder vibrated through the air. "I hate hurricane season," Helene said, tracing the outline of the restaurant's logo on the cardboard coasters Cathy had placed in front of each of them.

"Is that all you wanted to discuss today, Helene? The weather? We could have done that in the comfort of our own home."

Helene picked up the coaster and tapped it against the metal tabletop. She'd thought that if she and Merrick were alone for a little while they might be able to start talking to each other again. It was so busy at Sea Haven these days, the house full of people. It seemed as if she could never find him alone. Except at night. And so far, she hadn't had the courage to confront him in his bedroom. "No. I don't want to talk about the weather. I want to talk about us. I don't want to go on like this, Merrick."

His jaw tightened. "Are you asking me for a divorce," he said quietly.

"No."

Cathy appeared at Helene's shoulder with the ice and the coffee. "Anything else?" she asked when they'd been served.

"No, thank you," Merrick said with a polite smile. "We're fine."

"Okay." She walked over to one of the other occupied tables. Helene watched her go.

"We're not fine," Helene said a moment later. "That's the problem."

"What *do* you want, Helene?" he asked wearily.

"I want..." How to say it? She had to find just the right words. *Be strong,* she told herself. *Be in control. You know what you want. Go after it.* "I want us to be together again. I'm trying to find a way, Merrick."

"Helene, I have to tell you I still don't fully understand what happened. When did we go from pretending our marriage was in trouble to actually putting it in jeopardy?"

She sat up a little straighter. "I'm sorry that I asked you to go along with my idea of a faux divorce."

"Helene, I know you hoped your plan would bring our daughters together. What I didn't know was that you really felt I had ruined your life, stifled you. Manipulated you for half a century."

"Merrick," she said, calling on all the dignity she could muster. "I'm sorry for using those words. I guess I panicked."

"I frightened you that badly?"

"No." She shook her head. "Let me speak my mind, Merrick."

"I am all ears."

"I got to thinking. Fifty years of my life. What had I to show for it? My acting career over. My daughters estranged. My world revolving around you and Sea Haven and the bridge club and the community center. Nothing I did made any impact, I thought. Nothing I did mattered. I...I just started to feel old and...and useless."

"And I contributed to your unhappiness by trying

to make everything perfect for you, to take all the worry on myself and keep you safe and happy.''

''Yes,'' she said, trying to smile. ''That's exactly what you did. And I let you.''

''I'm a very old tiger to be changing my stripes,'' Merrick said, stirring his coffee but leaving it untasted. ''But I'm willing to try.''

''I know.'' She reached over and covered her hand with his. ''And I appreciate that. And I've been doing a great deal of soul-searching. Especially since Erik was hurt. We came so close to losing him again, Merrick. And we'd only just gotten him back. There in the hospital, when you took me in your arms again, after so long, and held me and comforted me...I saw it all so clearly. Independence doesn't have to mean being alone. It doesn't have to mean doing it all myself. I want us to be together again, Merrick. A couple. Partners. Can you give me that?''

He looked past her, remained silent, then returned his gaze to her face. ''I would give you the moon and stars if that would make you happy.''

''I only want your love and your respect.''

''You have always had them, my love.''

''Oh, Merrick. Then maybe this wasn't all for nothing. I had time to think and I feel so much better about myself. I know myself better now. I know my life hasn't been wasted. I gave birth to three wonderful daughters who have grown into strong independent women. I...we've built a wonderful home for them. I have friends and a place in the community. I can act again if I want. I can stay home and tend my garden and walk on the beach. And perhaps more than all that, I know how very much I love you."

"And I love you," Merrick answered. "And since we're talking about things you can do, how about taking over the administration of the Hardaway Conservancy Trust?"

"Yes," she said, smiling more broadly. "I can do that. I'm so glad we decided to follow Erik's plan. And I do want to be a part, a very big part, of what we leave to Hurricane Beach."

"It's settled then?" he asked, one silver eyebrow lifting.

"What's settled then?" she asked, her heart beating fast.

"Our reconciliation."

"Yes, my dear, I guess it is."

He turned her hand over and traced a fingertip across her wedding band, thin now with age and wear, but still gleaming softly in the gray rainy light. He was quiet for a little while, gazing down at her hand. Then he looked up and all her anxiety melted away as the first raindrops of the summer storm pelted down on their sheltering umbrella. Neither Merrick nor Helene paid any attention.

"I have always loved you, Helene. I will always love you. I have honored you every day of the last fifty years. I will spend the next fifty years striving to make you happy."

"Oh, Merrick." Helene raised her hand to caress his cheek.

It was raining harder. Merrick placed a bill under his glass and took her hand in his. "Let's go home, Helene."

She laughed, feeling light and free and very young again. "Why are you in such a hurry?"

"Have you forgotten?" he asked, folding her hand into his. "Today's our golden anniversary."

"Today? Not today," Helene responded, flustered as much by his touch as by his words. "Our anniversary is ten days away."

"Not our wedding anniversary." He watched her so intently she couldn't breathe. "Surely you haven't forgotten what happened fifty years ago today?"

She searched her memory for the date. Then recognition dawned. "This is the day you arrived in New York from England," she said triumphantly. "I took the train all the way from Tallahassee to meet you when the ship docked."

Lightning struck somewhere nearby. Neither of them noticed. Thunder grumbled and growled above their heads. The rain came down harder, driving the other diners inside. Helene and Merrick stayed where they were. "Yes. And what happened fifty years ago tonight?"

Helene felt a blush steal across her throat and up to her cheeks, even though the rain had cooled the air around her. Fifty years ago this night they had made love for the first time. "I...I didn't think you would remember."

He stood up. "How could you think I would ever forget? Let's go home, Helene."

"Yes," she said. "Let's go home to Sea Haven."

CHAPTER TEN

MEGAN AND LISA, the youngest Hardaway sister, descended the stairway of the late Bea Connell's house Saturday morning. "This really is a lovely house," Megan said. "It's a shame to see it sitting empty this way. I hope Jon and Amy decide to move in for the winter." From upstairs she could hear Helene and Amy arguing the merits and drawbacks of the five bedrooms and outdated plumbing. Matt was at the Connell Brassworks discussing business with his cousin, Joanne. Matt and Joanne co-owned the Brassworks, with Joanne running the company's day-to-day activities, and Matt acting as silent partner. Noah, Erik and Merrick had gone to Toomey's Garage to hear the mechanic's verdict on the future of Merrick's Blazer. Megan hadn't been able to bring herself to join them for that venture, or listen to her mother and Amy chatter on about bathroom makeovers or cross ventilation in the bedrooms. So, for the moment, she and Lisa were alone in Bea's quiet living room.

"It would be the perfect solution," Lisa said. "Matt won't have to worry about it sitting empty. And Amy and Jon will have all the extra space they need."

"With Kieran around, they'll need lots of room,"

Megan remarked, peeking into the kitchen. "Having a teenager underfoot all day is exhausting."

"As you're learning yourself." Lisa's voice held none of the sarcastic bite it had so often in the past.

Lisa was not yet thirty-two—almost five years younger than Megan. She had the slightest build of the three sisters. Her eyes were the same brown as Merrick's. Her hair was golden, the color of a wheat field in sunlight, somewhere between Megan's cool ash tones and Amy's vibrant strawberry blond. Megan's little sister, the one she'd always tried to protect when they were small.

Lisa was still quiet and introspective around Helene and Merrick, but she had opened to her sisters. She'd allowed them to see her pain, the pain of a lost child. Pain she and Megan had unknowingly shared for twelve years. But Megan's prayers had been answered. Her lost child had been returned to her. For Lisa, that could never happen. Megan could only hope her sister and Matt Connell would soon have another child to love and cherish.

Megan turned around and smiled. "Right. As I'm learning."

"How did the shopping trip go yesterday?"

"Very well. He's very easy to buy for. Clothes fit him well." She and Erik had driven to Pensacola to buy him a sport coat and tie for the family picture Amy had arranged for Sunday afternoon. At first it had seemed Noah would insist on going with them. But then he had decided that it would be safe enough for just the two of them, since no one suspicious had been seen in Hurricane Beach. And, in any case, Byron Fielder was not likely to be looking for Erik two hundred miles west of where he had taken him.

"He's a good-looking boy," Lisa remarked.

"Yes." The compliment pleased Megan. "Last night Noah taught him to tie a Windsor knot." Another small miracle she'd thought never to experience, watching Noah's big strong hands curiously gentle as he taught their son to tie a necktie.

"I understand from Mom you bought a lot more than a sport coat and tie."

"Yes," Megan confessed, laughing, eager to relegate personal thoughts of Noah's touch to a seldom-visited corner of her mind. "I bought him a boom box, and a Walkman and a pair of Rollerblades. I..." She felt herself blush. "I think I got carried away."

"You have every right in the world to got carried away. You've missed out on a dozen Christmas mornings and a dozen birthdays." Lisa turned away from the screen door where she'd been standing. She smiled gently. "We all did. I can't imagine how I'll get all the presents I plan to buy for him on the plane come Christmastime."

"Amy's determined you're going to be back here sooner. The party's coming up."

"I know." Lisa's brown eyes refused to meet Megan's. "And I'm glad Mom and Dad have reconciled." Megan had reported that Merrick had moved back into the master bedroom with Helene. "But I can't guarantee I'll be back next week, I told you that."

"Yes, I know."

"I'm very worried about Julie."

"The girl who is carrying twins?"

"Yes. Her blood pressure was up again yesterday. I very nearly stayed behind."

"I'm glad you didn't. You'd just worry yourself and Julie, too. From what you've told me, your partner is very competent. She'll take good care of her."

Lisa nodded, but didn't say anything, as though she didn't quite trust her voice. She walked over to a small side table and began arranging and rearranging a trio of millefleur paperweights. "Dena's great with the girls. She connects with all of them. Better than I do sometimes."

"But this girl, Julie, is different?"

Lisa set down the paperweight she'd been turning over and over in her hands. "Yes, she's different. She's brave and determined, and it breaks my heart watching her grieve for the babies she's giving up for adoption."

"Do you see something of yourself in her at that age, Lisa?"

Her sister didn't answer for a moment, walking instead to the window that overlooked Bea Connell's beloved garden. "Yes, I suppose I do. I also see how much she wants to keep her babies."

"Is there any way to make that possible?"

Lisa turned away from the table, a sad little smile playing around the corners of her lips. "I don't see how, short of Matt and I taking her to live with us."

"Why *don't* you arrange for Julie to live with you?"

Lisa folded her arms beneath her breasts as though holding herself close, holding her emotions in check, as Megan herself sometimes did. She shook her head. "I can't do that. Julie has decided on adoption. I can't influence her decision by offering her a home with me and Matt.''

"It sounds to me as if Julie hasn't made a decision. She's accepted the only option available to her at this point in her pregnancy. She's only what? Seventeen? Her mother tried to force her into marrying the babies' father, didn't she? And she's washed her hands of the girl, according to Amy.''

"Right on all counts. But still. It's not professional—''

"Lisa, sometimes being professional isn't enough. If you care for this girl as deeply as you say you do, then maybe it's time to break your own rules.''

"I do care for her.'' Lisa took a deep breath. "It's just that *I* want a baby so badly I'm not sure I'm being clear-sighted about this. Oh, Damn. Forget I said that.'' There were tears in her eyes that she brushed away with a furious hand. "I can't start crying. If Mom sees me—''

Megan walked to the bottom of the stairs. "It's all right,'' she assured her distraught sister. "I can hear Mom talking away a mile a minute. They won't be down any time soon. Lisa, I had no idea you wanted a baby so badly.''

"I do. Matt and I haven't used any kind of birth control and I'm still not pregnant.''

"But you've only been together a short time.''

Lisa's chin came up a fraction of an inch. She was in control of herself once more. "I know, but I can't help being afraid.''

"You must see a doctor,'' Megan said firmly. "Get a thorough checkup. That will put your mind at rest.''

"I have seen a doctor. She wants a complete family history. If I ask Mom all those kinds of personal questions, she's going to have a whole flock of them to ask in return—"

"And you still don't feel you can tell her and Dad about your miscarriage? Oh, Lisa."

Her sister held up a restraining hand. "I know. They'll understand. I just can't. Maybe it's because I've kept the secret for so long. I never told anyone but you and Amy. I...I just don't want to talk about it."

"But Lisa—"

Lisa's eyes flashed. "When Erik was taken from you, you didn't want us to talk about him."

"Because it hurt so much," Megan whispered.

"Because it hurts too much. It still hurts too much."

Megan nodded. She couldn't force her baby sister to release the pain inside her until she was ready. "And because you're so worried about not being pregnant, you suspect your professional judgment is being clouded where Julie is concerned."

"Yes. Maybe I should simply encourage her to give up her babies. It's the conventional wisdom." Lisa went back to the table with the paperweights, picked one up and began turning it over and over in her hand again.

"Screw conventional wisdom and your professional judgment," Megan said inelegantly. "What does your heart say?"

Lisa's eyes grew big as saucers. "Trust you to get to the heart of the matter," she said with a faint smile. "My heart says that Matt and I should have

Julie and her babies live with us. Julie dreams of being able to go to college and then law school. If she moves in with us, she'll be able to do that."

"And in the fullness of time you'll have babies of your own."

"You don't think I'll become overly attached to Julie's babies?"

"You might," Megan admitted. "But isn't it worth the risk?" Megan felt like a hypocrite urging Lisa to take risks with her heart, when she was far too cowardly to do the same thing.

"Yes," Lisa said, "I think it might be."

"And when the time comes for Julie and her babies to strike out on their own, you'll do what's right for them again."

"That's exactly what Matt said."

"A very intelligent man, your Matt." Megan smiled.

Lisa smiled back. "You didn't always think so."

Megan felt her face color even more than the hot room warranted. She had slapped Matt Connell's face at Amy's wedding reception after Lisa had told her he was the father of the baby she had lost so long ago. "I know better now. Especially if he agrees with me that you should ask Julie and her babies to come and live with the two of you."

Lisa nodded. Her smile was strained, a little sad. "I wonder what Mom and Amy are doing up there?"

"If I know Mom, she's probably measuring for new curtains," Megan replied, accepting her sister's change of subject. "She always liked Mrs. Connell, but she said more than once that all Bea's artistic abilities were in her green thumb."

"Yes. I didn't get the chance to know Matt's grandmother very well, but everyone in town knows how she loved to work in her garden." She lowered her voice. "But some of this furniture really has to go."

Megan looked around the crowded living room with its overstuffed, outdated furniture and wallpaper. Nothing appeared to have been touched since Bea died. There were framed photographs of the Connell family—sadly all deceased now, except Matt and his cousin, Joanne—in one corner packed full of bric-a-brac, and a gateleg table with a cut-crystal vase of potpourri beneath the window. A spectacularly ugly crocheted afghan in shades of fuchsia and blue and purple was folded over the back of the couch, and a silver bowl of butterscotch candies rested on the coffee table in front of the sofa. Butterscotch candy, Lisa had told her, had been Bea's favorite.

"Well, yes," Megan said tactfully. "I think you might donate some of these things to charity with a clear conscience. But it must be a hard decision for Matt to make. Selling off his family home."

"Yes." Lisa ran her fingertip across the top of a piecrust table, a lovely piece Megan hoped Lisa intended to keep. "He doesn't want to sell. As a matter of fact, he wants me to consider opening a home for pregnant girls here."

"In this house?"

"Yes."

"Do you mean you'd move back here from Connecticut?" Megan asked. Amy would be pleased to hear that.

"No. No, of course not. Dena's family all live in the Northeast. I couldn't ask that of her."

"Lisa, you can't be considering trying to commute between Brennan House in Connecticut and this place?"

"That would be one solution, wouldn't it?"

"I suppose it would," Megan said doubtfully. "But very difficult. And, I imagine, very expensive."

"Yes. Mom or Amy probably told you Matt insisted on endowing the group home with some of his own money. But with two facilities in Danfield... And then there's the question of staffing. I wouldn't even consider such a thing if I couldn't have a top-notch team of counselors. And a really first-rate administrator that I trusted, well, as much as I trust you."

"What are you trying to say, Lisa?"

"Well...I...it's just an idea I had. Would you consider being administrator?"

"Lisa? I'm not qualified to work with troubled teenagers." It was tempting. Not just the possibility of a job in Hurricane Beach, but a job that involved beginnings and not endings. She loved her work at Graceway, but there was no denying that the residents there, no matter how hard she worked to make their days happy and fulfilled, were waiting to end their lives. Teenagers, no matter how difficult their present circumstances, were waiting to begin theirs.

"That's easily remedied, Megan, you're one of the most competent and intelligent women I've ever met. You'd be wonderful working with young people. I know I couldn't pay you anywhere near what you're making at your present position. And the benefits..."

Lisa smiled ruefully. "There aren't any benefits. But you'd be here in Hurricane Beach. It will be much easier on Erik living here. I mean, once this business of the kidnapper is settled. And I'm sure Noah—" She looked at Megan, her brown eyes narrowing. "Perhaps I'm out of line. Are you planning on returning to California with Noah?"

Megan curled her fingers around the back of a wing chair. "No," she said too quickly and too loudly. "Lisa, I've already had this conversation with Amy. Noah and I are not going to reconcile, not even for Erik's sake." Lisa didn't look convinced. Megan couldn't blame her. The words sounded hollow to her own ears. "I...I'll consider your offer—" A new life for her and Erik. Here in Hurricane Beach. It was tempting. So tempting...

Footsteps on the stairs and the sound of Helene's and Amy's voices drifting into the room caused her to leave the sentence, and the thought, unfinished.

"I don't know, Mom. This house is so big. Even if Kieran does come to live with us, that leaves three empty bedrooms. And I could never sell the beach cottage—"

"Whoever said you had to sell your beach cottage?" Helene challenged, fanning herself with a magazine she'd picked up from somewhere. "Lisa, you do intend to have air-conditioning installed, don't you? I know Bea's circulation was not good at the end. But this house is stifling. I do wish you'd come to stay with us at Sea Haven. It would be much more comfortable."

"Yes, we're going to have air-conditioning seen to as soon as possible," Lisa said sharply, sidestepping her mother's invitation. Helene looked hurt. Lisa softened her tone. "I would have opened the windows for you, Mom. But some of them are painted shut. And besides, it's going to storm."

Helene cast a glance through the living-room window at the thunderclouds piling up out over the water. "Another thunderstorm? I swear it would almost be a relief if that dratted hurricane did come this way. At least the suspense would be over."

"Mother, bite your tongue," Amy chided. "Fred's just sitting out there in the gulf getting bigger and meaner every day."

Helene sighed. "I know and that's what worries me. Someday our luck will run out. But God willing, not this time." She ran her hand over the ugly afghan on the back of the overstuffed couch. "Poor Bea. Her flowers were beautiful, but then, God chose the colors for them." She gave the afghan a loving pat. "I miss her."

"So does Matt," Lisa said, smiling at their mother.

Helene smiled back, tentatively at first, then more broadly. "Will he be joining us for lunch?"

"No. He'll be busy at the Brassworks the rest of the afternoon. Well, Amy what do you think? Would you and Jon consider living here this winter?"

"It's such a big house," Amy hedged. Megan thought her sister looked a little pale, tired, as if she'd been working too hard, or getting too little sleep. Probably both, Megan decided, and promised herself she'd do everything possible to make last-minute party preparations easier for Amy in the week ahead.

"A house this size needs a big family to make it feel like a home," Helene agreed. "Have you and Matt made a decision on whether or not to use it as another group home?"

Lisa cast Megan a quick glance from the corner of her eye. "Not yet, Mom. It's a big decision. I couldn't be here all of the time. And I couldn't think of expanding our services if I didn't have a staff and an administrator that I trusted implicitly."

Helene frowned, then nodded. "Of course, dear. You're absolutely right. I agree wholeheartedly. But, alas, Hurricane Beach, just like a lot of other places, needs a facility like yours."

"I know, Mom. And I'm considering it. But in the meantime, Amy and Jon could have a whole houseful of babies and fill up those empty bedrooms themselves," Lisa said.

Megan thought Amy turned a shade paler. Was it because she'd picked up on the slight edge to Lisa's tone and didn't recognize it—as Megan now did— as a thin protective shell cocooning still unhealed wounds? Or maybe it was only the heat. The living room *was* stifling.

"Sure. Maybe," Amy murmured, avoiding eye contact. "But look, I've got to get back to Rêve Rags. And don't forget to be at Mom and Dad's for the family photos tomorrow. One o'clock sharp. Be there. Or else." She smiled and tossed her head, the old Amy. Megan glanced quickly at her mother and youngest sister, but neither seemed to have taken Amy's statement at anything but face value. And Megan wondered if she was, once more, the only one who noticed the strain in Amy's voice, and the worry in her sister's sea-green eyes.

DAMMIT. The library was closed. He'd had car trouble in Georgia and hadn't made it into Tallahassee until late Saturday night. And now with the holiday on Monday, he'd have to wait until Tuesday to try to track down where Erik had come from. Byron Fielder headed off toward a Waffle House restaurant to get himself some breakfast. Sunday morning. He hated Sunday mornings. His little boy. His Reggie had died on a Sunday morning, and to this day he couldn't hear the sound of church bells without wanting to howl and scream like a madman.

Tallahassee was a big town. He'd had trouble even finding the library. And now he was going to have to wait. He racked his brain—as he had for the last two days—trying to remember the address the kid had kept repeating in that irritating singsong voice. Something about a hurricane? Or a beach? Was it a town? Or a street? Or an apartment complex? Hell, he couldn't remember. He'd just have to wait until Tuesday. And he was a man who didn't like to wait.

A row of newspaper racks were lined up outside the door of the Waffle House. There was the Tallahassee *Democrat* and the weekend edition of *USA Today,* and two or three smaller papers. At the end of the row was a rack with a single beat-up copy of the *Hurricane Beach Chronicle.*

Hurricane Beach. Fielder dragged the paper out of the rack. That was it. That was the name of the town. Erik's little-boy voice came back to him demanding to be taken home to his mother, home to Sea Haven, Gulfview Road, Hurricane Beach, Florida.

So the kid hadn't forgotten where he came from. He'd found his way home. Fielder swerved away from the restaurant and headed for the gas station next door. Now all he needed was a map. Once he found his way to Hurricane Beach, the rest would be easy.

CHAPTER ELEVEN

MERRICK HARDAWAY folded the Sunday edition of the newspaper and looked toward the study door. "I believe I hear voices in the hallway. Helene and Megan must have returned from church."

Noah had heard voices, too. Megan's voice, in particular, low and musical, as she answered a question Helene had posed. But he kept his eyes, and his attention, focused on the fax in his hand. Harrison Mannley wanted him back in California. Although his CO knew the reasons for his being in Hurricane Beach, and understood their importance to him, appropriation hearings were looming on the horizon, and he wanted Noah to return ASAP. The latest round of Pentagon budget cuts had hit the teams hard. They were going to have to fight for every last dime, and his commanding officer wanted him there to fend off the bean counters.

Noah saw the next ten years of his life being spent waging just such battles, and not for the first time he found the prospect less than appealing. He was a SEAL, a warrior, a soldier, not a bureaucrat. He didn't have the stomach for paper wars. Maybe he should find a new career when his tour was up. But where would he go? And what would he do? There was no guarantee he could win back Megan's love and reunite their splintered family. He could very well end up alone—no wife and son, no naval family.

Helene entered the study looking like summer in a pale pink dress and a wide-brimmed straw hat with roses on it. She crossed the room and placed a quick kiss on the top of Merrick's head. "Good morning, Merrick," she said softly.

"Good morning, my love."

"Good morning, Noah. Erik," she said.

"Good morning, Helene."

"Hi, Grandma. Where's Mom?" Erik asked. He was seated behind Merrick's desk looking through one of the leather-bound photo albums that Helene had unearthed for him.

"She's changing. Then she's going to help me with brunch. Are you hungry?"

"I could eat a bear. Who is this guy?" he asked, pointing to one of the photos in the album. "Is that Doc Yount holding me? It looks like some kind of picnic or something. Maybe the Fourth of July?" Helene glided over and looked at the photo in question.

"That's him and you," she said. "And it's probably the Spring Break celebration. Doc's legs are white as snow. Definitely not the Fourth of July."

"Doc was a lot skinnier then. And he had a lot more hair."

"That was the case with many of us fifteen years ago," Merrick said. "There's an ad in the newspaper for a used Saturn," he announced to the room in general. "It would make a good car for you, son."

"For me?"

"Yes," Merrick said. "I'm thinking if you have

a car of your own, you won't be inclined to...borrow...my vehicles."

Erik's face reddened, but Merrick was smiling and he soon regained his composure. "I don't have a license."

"That's easily remedied. There's a good driving school in Hurricane Beach."

"But I..." Erik flicked a quick glance in Noah's direction. "I don't know how much longer we'll be staying here."

Merrick frowned slightly, then nodded. "You're right about that, but it will be at least a couple of weeks..." He paused for a few seconds, choosing his words carefully, "Before anything is settled on that score. And you'll need wheels wherever you're living. Your grandmother and I have missed out on giving you a lot of things over the years."

"But we're *not* going to give you a car," Helene announced.

"What?" Merrick's silvery eyebrows snapped together in a frown.

"It isn't our place to be buying a car for Erik," she said firmly. "That's a decision for Noah and Megan to make."

"But," Merrick sputtered. "I...I only—"

"I know, my love," she said, her voice softening. "But you are wrong." Their eyes met and held.

Merrick pursed his lips and let out his breath in a snort. "You're right, of course." He turned his gaze on Noah and smiled sheepishly. "I apologize. I was out of line not consulting you first. However, I would still like to give Erik a car. If you and Megan agree."

"Dad?"

Noah switched his gaze to his son's face. He could see excitement in Erik's eyes. But a frown creased his son's forehead and the boy had begun nervously tapping a pencil on the desk blotter.

"It's very generous of you, Merrick," Noah said at last. "I have no objection. If Megan agrees."

"Thank you," his father-in-law replied. "I know buying a first car is something most men look forward to doing with their sons. I thought...hoped maybe this time it could be with a doting grandfather tagging along, too."

"I'd like that," Noah said. "What do you say, Erik?"

"Great. Thanks, Granddad." Erik's smile was strained. He rubbed the back of his neck with his uninjured hand.

"We can get the ball rolling Tuesday. Directly after Labor Day. Get you signed up for classes. Check with the Motor Vehicle Department about getting a learner's permit and all that."

"I...I can't even prove I am who I say I am. How can I get a learner's permit?" Erik burst out.

"Your birth certificate is right here in the safe," Helene informed him.

"Behind that set of Dickens." Merrick pointed to the third row of books to the left of the desk. "Would you like to see it?"

Erik nodded. "Yes," he said, his voice a little hollow-sounding. "I would."

Merrick unfolded himself from the depths of his chair and crossed the room to the bookshelves. "Your grandmother and I put it here for safekeeping years ago." He removed the books, worked the combination of the recessed safe, pulled on the door and nothing happened. "Damn arthritis," he said, rubbing his fingers. "Would you open this dratted thing for me, Erik?"

"Yes, sir." Erik stood up and walked to his grandfather's side.

"The combination's my birth date," Merrick explained. "Nine, left. Thirty, right. Twenty-three, left. Good," he said, slapping Erik on the shoulder when the safe door swung open. Merrick removed a small stack of documents, and began sorting through them. "Ah, here it is."

Erik took the birth certificate and stared down at the embossed document. He ran his fingertip over the tiny inked footprints and read the vital statistics of his birth. Length: *twenty-two inches,* Noah recalled. Weight: *seven pounds, thirteen ounces.* Long and skinny, red-faced and bald. A small monkey-faced scrap of humanity that had been the most beautiful thing he'd ever seen.

"April twenty-fourth," Erik said softly. "That's my birthday?"

Merrick frowned. "Yes, son. Don't you remember?"

"I...I wasn't sure. I thought I remembered."

"Did you celebrate another birthday?" Noah asked.

Erik's voice hardened, became a man's voice. "Yes. Diana always told me I remembered wrong. January seventeenth. That's the day she picked. I thought maybe that was the day I was...kidnapped?"

"No," Merrick answered for Noah. "You were stolen from us in August."

"I thought I remembered it was real hot. Anyway, after Diana died, Fielder told me the truth. It was their real kid's birthday. He was four when he died." He handed the birth certificate back to Merrick. "I...I think I'll wait a while to get my license. Thanks anyway, Granddad."

"But son—"

"I'm...I'm just not ready to drive yet, okay? The accident and all," Erik explained unconvincingly. He held his injured arm just above the elbow. "You know."

Merrick nodded, and returned the birth certificate to the safe, unable to hide his disappointment. "Of course. If that's what you want. We'll wait." He shut the safe door without further comment.

"Thanks." Erik went back to the desk and sat down. He picked up a sheet of paper and began to draw. Helene moved to the desk and patted Erik on the shoulder.

"What are you drawing?" she asked, bending a little closer. "Why, I recognize it. It's the old pier. You really are very good."

"I'm glad you like it."

She touched the bandage on his arm. "Is it feeling better?" she asked.

"It's okay. It's starting to itch a little bit."

"That's a good sign. Means it's healing."

Helene looked up and noticed the sheet of paper Noah was still holding. Her voice acquired a slight edge. "Is that a fax you're holding?"

"Yes, ma'am."

Helene steepled her fingers and raised them to her lips. "It isn't from that...from that private detective, is it? It's not more bad news about that terrible Fielder man?''

''No, it's from my boss in Coronado. Captain Mannley. He wants me to come back.''

''Are you going?''

Noah folded the fax and shoved it into his pocket. ''No, ma'am. I'm not leaving.''

''Good.'' She nodded briskly. ''I think it's a good idea for you to stay until that awful man is behind bars. Now, I must go and change so that I can help Megan get brunch on the table.''

''I'll help you, my dear,'' Merrick offered.

Her smile softened, turned private, and she led the way out of the room.

Noah was alone with his son. He got up and went to stand by the flower-filled fireplace.

''I think Grandma and Granddad aren't fighting anymore,'' Erik said thoughtfully.

''I've noticed that too.''

''I'm glad.''

''So am I.''

Erik bent his head to his drawing once more.

''Erik, why did you change your mind about getting a driver's license?'' Noah asked.

The teenager didn't answer. He continued to draw, adding details to his sketch with short, quick strokes of his pencil that revealed his agitation.

''Erik, I asked you a question.''

More silence. Finally Erik laid the pencil down and crossed the room to where Noah was standing. ''I do want a driver's license,'' he said at last. ''But I can't get one.''

''Why not?''

"If I get a license, it will be registered with the government, right?"

"Yes," Noah agreed.

"Fielder hates the government but that doesn't mean he's so crazy he wouldn't use it to find me. If I get a license, he could trace me here. Right to this house. I can't take a chance on that happening. I can't let him find me. Or any of you." His voice cracked. He ran his hand over the bandage on his arm. Then his chin jutted out, the same way Megan's did when she was ready to do battle for something she believed in. "I can take care of myself. But I can't let him find me because I don't know what he might do to you or Mom and Granddad and Grandma."

Noah wanted to reach out and pull his son into his arms, but the hard, set look on Erik's face stopped him.

"I understand what you're trying to say," Noah said carefully. "But if Fielder is looking for you, I don't think it will be your driver's license that draws him here."

"Why not?" Erik leaned forward, one hand on the back of the couch, gripping it so tightly that his fingers bit into the soft leather. "How do you know that? How can you be sure? Has that guy, that other SEAL, contacted you again?"

Noah shook his head. "I haven't heard from Jamieson since the day of your accident," he told him truthfully. "But I expect to before too long."

"Will you tell me when that happens?"

"Yes," he said. "I'll tell you."

"Good." Erik picked at the hem of his green-and-yellow-striped T-shirt. His shorts were long and baggy and his running shoes weren't tied. He looked like a typical teenager, except for his eyes. His eyes were old and wise beyond his years. "I'd like to know. I don't want him surprising me. Us."

"I'll do my best not to let that happen."

Erik nodded once, still holding his gaze. "I know that. Thanks."

Noah swallowed hard. "You have to help me, too. No taking off without telling one of us where you're going. As a matter of fact, I'd appreciate it if you'd stick pretty close to Sea Haven for the next few days."

"Okay." Erik's chin came up again. "Do you really think your friend can find him first?"

Noah had promised never to lie. "I don't know, Erik. It depends. But if Jamieson has proof Fielder is headed for Hurricane Beach, or even Tallahassee, he's going to recommend going to the authorities."

"Like the police?"

"And the FBI," Noah said. "Kidnapping is a federal offense."

Erik turned away, took two steps back toward the desk and the window, then spun around again. "I don't know. I—"

"Erik, it won't be enough for us to track Fielder and keep him away from you. He has to be punished for what he did to you."

"You don't understand," Erik pleaded. "I think Fielder's crazy." He made a whirling motion at his temple with his left hand. "Not right." He took a deep breath. "I know he's dangerous."

"All the more reason to call in the authorities."

But Erik didn't give up easily. "You and this Jamieson guy. You're SEALs. There isn't anyone better. I know...I've been reading up. Everything I can find. You're the best."

God how he wanted that to be true. "I'm still only one man, Erik. We need help on this, do you understand?"

The boy's eyes fell. "I suppose you're right. It's just that..." Noah saw Erik's shoulder rise and fall in a slight shrug.

"What, son?"

"I just wish he'd disappear forever and I'd never have to think about him again."

"I know. That's what I want, too. But it's not likely that's going to happen, no matter how hard you wish."

"I wish he was dead," Erik said angrily. "I wish I'd had the nerve to kill him before I left Michigan. I could have, too," he continued defiantly. "There were guns everywhere in our house. I could have. One night I even tr-tried." He stuttered slightly in his haste to unburden himself. "I got a shotgun and I loaded it and I took it to his room. He was passed-out drunk on the bed."

God, that a child of his, that any man's child, should have been driven to such extremes.

Erik's voice fell. "But I couldn't. I was too scared. Just as scared as when I was a little kid, and he yelled at me, and beat the crap out of me and Diana and I couldn't do anything to stop him." His hands curled into fists. He looked down at them, wincing as the action pulled at torn muscles and flesh. "I couldn't do it," he whispered brokenly. "I couldn't do it."

"Because you knew it was wrong," Noah said, pulling him close for a heartbeat, then stepping back so he could look directly into Erik's eyes. "Your heart and your conscience told you it was wrong to hurt another human being, even a man who had caused you so much pain. That's what your mother and I would have wanted to teach you if you'd been with us."

"But you could have done it. You could have killed him."

Noah shook his head. "Not when there's a legal recourse. And never in cold blood," he said, choosing his words very carefully. "That's the difference between a soldier doing his duty and a murderer. That's the difference between you and me and a monster like Fielder."

"You don't think I'm a coward?"

"I know you're not a coward. I'm proud of you. I know your mother would be proud of you, too. But maybe she's not ready to hear this part of your story quite yet."

Erik bit down on his bottom lip, then nodded. "Yeah. Not yet. I...I want to think about it some more myself. Thanks, Dad. I feel a little better about it now."

"Good." Noah ruffled his hair. One step at a time. Slow but sure. He didn't care what it took now, he was going to stay with his son. His career be damned. Erik needed him more than Harrison Mannley and the United States Navy SEALs. Now he only had to convince Erik's mother of that same thing.

"You'll do what you said," Erik repeated.

"You'll tell me everything that's going on with Fielder as soon as you hear anything?"

Noah held out his hand. "You have my word."

Erik gave his hand a shake. "Okay," he said, managing a smile. "I guess I can deal with that. I guess I can even deal with the FBI if I have to."

"Sure you can."

"And I'll stay close to Sea Haven. "You have *my* word on that." His smile disappeared. "And I'll watch my back."

"HERE YOU ARE." Megan was relieved to hear her voice sounded almost normal. She didn't want Erik to know she'd overheard his conversation with his father. "The quiche is getting cold. Mom wants all of us at the table, pronto."

"Quiche?" Erik's nose wrinkled in distaste.

"Have you ever eaten quiche?"

"No," Erik revealed. "Never." The last word was spoken with great vehemence.

"It's not that bad," Noah said with a chuckle.

"Actually, it's very good. Sort of an egg pie," she explained. "Annie made this one with bacon and ham, and cheese and mushrooms. I think you'll like it if you give it a try."

"Okay," Erik said. "I'm game. Besides, I'm starved to death. Lead me to it."

"Go ahead, Erik," Noah said. "Your mother and I will be right behind you."

He looked at Noah, then Megan, not quite meeting her eyes. "I'll tell Grandma you're on your way," he said, and left the room.

"You overheard what he was telling me, didn't you." It was a statement, not a question.

"Yes, I heard." She laced her fingers together in front of her. "You handled it very well."

Noah took two quick strides toward her. His voice was low and sandpaper rough. "He needed to get that out of his system, Megan. It was eating away at him."

"He wouldn't tell me." Her voice caught on a tiny sob.

"He thought he *couldn't* tell you, Megan. There's a difference."

"I don't understand." She took a step backward. He'd made no move to touch her, but she couldn't take the chance that he might, and that she would give in to her need to be held and comforted in his strong arms.

"Look around you, Megan. This is where you come from. This is where you belong. You eat quiche on Sunday morning. You know the difference between Pavarotti and Paganini."

"What are you getting at, Noah?"

"Erik has been shuffled from one backwater town, one tar-paper shack to another almost his whole life. He had no one to fight his battles but a sick woman who was, in her own way, as responsible for keeping him from us as Fielder was. He had no one to rely on but himself. He had no one to tell him what was right or wrong."

"I could understand," she whispered, no longer quite able to control her voice. "I would have told him exactly what you did."

He looked skeptical. "Exactly?"

Megan's lips firmed. She ignored the sting of tears on her cheeks. She cried so easily these days. And so often. "All right. I don't know how it feels to kill. I have never killed. But I feel the same *rage* you do, Noah. I really think I *could* kill Byron Fielder if I got the chance. So don't tell me I can't relate to Erik's feelings. To our son's pain."

"I'm not trying to come between you, Megan. I love him as much as you do." A muscle jerked along the straight, hard line of his jaw. "I feel as responsible for what happened to him that day as you do."

A red haze of fury flooded her vision, colored the man and the room around him. "Don't say that," she snapped. She wrapped her arms around her middle in a familiar gesture to hold in the anger, the rage that had festered in her heart for so many years. "Don't patronize me, Noah Carson. *I* was the only one responsible for Erik's being taken. It was my fault. *I* didn't pay enough attention to him that day. *I* let him wander away." Her throat tightened, her voice died away to a whisper once more. "*I* let him wander off while I mooned over what was happening to our marriage and daydreamed that a blue dress with spaghetti straps and a short, short skirt would seduce you away from your missions and your team. I was thinking only of myself. And of you. And I let him be snatched into a nightmare that still hasn't ended."

"Megan." He was beside her in an instant, in the blink of an eye. She couldn't move quickly enough to avoid him taking her in his arms. "God, is this what you've been doing to yourself all these years?"

"Yes," she said, breathing hard. She lifted her

chin, stared him straight in the eye. "This is what I've faced every day of my life. This is what I'll go on atoning for until the day I die."

"For God's sake. It was an accident, Megan—"

"Hey, you two." Amy's face peered around the doorjamb. "Mom's having a cow in the dining room. Come—" She stopped talking. The rest of her appeared in the doorway. She looked from Megan's tear-streaked face to Noah's dark one. "I—I'm sorry," she stammered. "I didn't mean to interrupt."

Noah's arms fell away, leaving Megan free...and bereft. "It's all right. We...we were just discussing—" She stopped talking abruptly. Her voice was shaking, her hands were shaking, her whole body was shaking. It was no use denying that something was wrong. Amy had eyes in her head. She could see they had been arguing. "I didn't hear you come in. Is Jon with you? I...is it time for the photographer already?"

"Mom invited us for brunch. Ian will be here in an hour."

"I'm not hungry," Noah said. "Would you make my excuses to Helene?"

Amy nodded. "You'll be here for the pictures, won't you? Like I said. Ian will be here in an hour."

Noah remained silent for a telling moment. He looked at Megan. She avoided his eyes, looking down at the toes of her shoes instead.

"Megan?" There was a note of pleading in Amy's voice.

For Erik's sake, Megan lifted her eyes and looked into her husband's set face. "Please, Noah. I—"

"I'll be in my room. Just give me a holler."

CHAPTER TWELVE

"OKAY. Great. Let's get settled, everyone. People! Let's get settled here." Ian Medford, Hurricane Beach's only professional photographer, was a five-foot-three-inch tyrant with a bald pate and a ponytail. If Merrick resembled Sean Connery with his silvery mustache and eyebrows, Ian looked like a middle-aged Mickey Rooney, with a boyishly youthful face and thirty extra pounds around the middle. The owner of Medford's Fine Photography ruled over every major social occasion in Hurricane Beach with an iron hand, and had chronicled the lives and loves of most of its residents.

Twenty-five years ago, he'd taken the anniversary portrait of Merrick and Helene that hung above the fireplace. He'd recorded for posterity all three of the Hardaway girls' high school sports careers, their graduations and their souvenir snapshots of Coastal High senior prom nights. Amy with her date, the class clown, now a Catholic priest. Megan with hers, the class valedictorian, now a tenured professor at Florida State. And Lisa, who had turned down the star quarterback of the football team as well as the drum major of the marching band, to go with a trio of girlfriends. Megan had always wondered why. Now she knew.

And, of course, Ian had taken all of Erik's baby pictures. The last one only weeks before he disappeared.

"Merrick. Helene. On the couch, please. We'll just bunch your lovely daughters and their families around you like petals around a flower."

Merrick snorted.

Amy giggled.

Ian popped up from his viewfinder, looking a little sheepish. "Sorry, people. I do have a tendency to get carried away with my work, don't I."

"It's all right, Ian. We appreciate your coming out here on Sunday afternoon to do this for us," Helene said soothingly. Her voice broke slightly. "It's a wonderful occasion for us, having our family together again after all these years. It's what I've hoped and prayed for." She squeezed Merrick's hand.

"Okay," the photographer said briskly. "Megan and young Erik and Commander Carson. I'll want you right here." He framed an area with his hands. "Thank goodness you didn't wear your uniform, Commander. They just simply overpower a composition."

"I wish he had," Kieran said in a penetrating whisper. "I'm telling you, he looks just like Steven Seagal."

Ian narrowed pale blue eyes in Noah's direction. "Yes, dear. I see the resemblance, but that doesn't change anything. Uniforms are simply too strong an element to blend into the whole."

Noah leaned slightly forward and whispered to Megan, "Good Lord, I'd forgotten about this guy.

He's the same one who took our wedding picture, isn't he?"

"Yes," she whispered back. "The very one."

Helene had insisted they have a wedding photo taken even though they had eloped. Megan had worn her high school graduation dress. And Noah his uniform. Ian had fussed and fumed about it then, too. If she closed her eyes, she could see that image now in its silver frame. See them as they once were. She, young and a little overwhelmed by what they had done. Noah, protective and defiant. They had been so much in love. And had had so little idea what life held in store for them.

Noah rolled his eyes. "I thought so." He gave Ian a once-over, taking in the loud Hawaiian print-shirt, the wrinkled khakis and sandals, the ponytail. One dark eyebrow rose slightly. "Stuck in the sixties, are we?"

"Shh," Megan whispered, trying not to smile. "He'll hear you." Automatically she lifted her fingers to brush a speck of lint from his lapel.

"That's it, Megan. Step in a little closer," Ian directed. "Commander, put your arm behind her. And close the distance between you. There are a lot of people to squeeze into this shot."

Megan suddenly found herself trembling all over. She'd managed to put the ugly scene out of her mind for a little while, but now the anger and hurt returned full force. The smile that had been tickling the corners of her mouth froze. Noah saw her response and his expression hardened, as well. Megan dropped her hand and turned away, her whole body suddenly cold, but at the same time acutely aware of his steel-hard body touching her from shoulder to knee.

"Let's see. Erik, that's your name, isn't it?"

"Yes, sir."

"Good. You look good right where you are. Just turn a little to the right so that nasty bruise doesn't show. No. No. Your right, not mine. Yes. That's it. Great profile. Good. Now straighten your tie."

The tips of Erik's ears were bright red. He tugged at the knot of his tie with his good left hand. "This guy is weird," he whispered as Megan reached up and straightened the knot.

She forced a smile for her son's sake. Everything she was doing today was for her son's sake, she reminded herself. "Shh, he'll hear you. And he is good. He's very talented. And a perfectionist. Bear with it."

"Megan, I told you, closer to your husband. Commander, please return your arm to your wife's back, as I requested.

Noah did as he was bid but now his hand was a lead weight at her waist. Ian moved to adjust the light umbrella by the bookcase. Helene twisted on her seat and looked up at them from the corner of her eye. "Megan, are you all right?"

"I'm fine, Mom. It's just…I hate to have my picture taken, you know that." She widened her smile. "How's this?"

"Better." Helene didn't look convinced, but Ian was berating her for wrinkling the skirt of her dress, as he fiddled with the lights behind the tripod. She looked down at her lap and began smoothing the silken folds.

"Okay. Amy. Jon. Kieran. You three on this side of Merrick and Helene. "Good. Good, Amy dear. You're looking a trifle pale, and I do believe you've added a few pounds. Forgive me for saying so, but the camera never lies, you know.''

Megan turned her head just in time to see her sister pale a little more, open her mouth as if to refute Ian's tactless remark and then think better of it.

"Lisa and Matt, isn't it?'' the photographer asked.

"Yes, sir,'' Matt replied.

"You two right here in the middle.'' Lisa and Matt moved into their designated places. Ian dropped his head to his viewfinder yet again. "Yes. You have the look of young grandfather Mathias,'' he said after a moment's fiddling with the aperture adjustment. He lifted his round face; his inquisitive eyes softened slightly. "Bea Connell was a good woman. She'll be missed in this town.''

"Thank you,'' Matt said. "I miss her, too.''

"Okay. We're just about ready.''

Ian took his place behind the tripod. Kieran fidgeted slightly and tugged at the waistband on her broomstick pleated skirt.

"Kieran, be still. Just another second. Merrick, turn your shoulder a little to the left. Helene, that glorious smile of yours, please. Drat! The light's accentuating the shadows under your eyes, Lisa.''

"I'm sorry,'' Lisa said.

"No. No. I'll take care of it. It's not your fault really. But you should try to get more sleep, you know. That will take care of it.'' He bounded over to the light umbrella and began moving it in increments of a quarter of an inch.

"Jeez, he's really nosy," Erik whispered, barely moving his lips. "Does he boss everyone around like that?"

Megan answered just as quietly. "Ian doesn't have any family of his own so he treats everyone in Hurricane Beach as if they were his family. He doesn't mean to be rude. It's just his way."

Erik watched the photographer from the corner of his eye. "I know how he feels. It's hard not to have a family. There's something inside you. Inside all of us, I think, that makes you want to be part of one. Even if the people you're with aren't who you want them to be."

"Erik—"

"Do you suppose—" Erik twisted his head a little, trying to settle the tie more comfortably over his Adam's apple "—that he might give me a few photography lessons? I mean, if we stay around Hurricane Beach—" His color heightened a little once more. "I don't—"

"I know, Erik," she replied. She knew it wasn't fair to keep him hanging like this. She had to decide on their future. She only wished she knew herself what she wanted to do, where she wanted to be.

Ian was back behind his camera. "Wonderful!" He clapped his hands. "This is it. Let's see everyone smile. Oh, excellent. A most handsome family." The phone on Merrick's desk began to ring. "Don't anyone move a muscle," Ian barked in a tone that would have done Noah's SEAL instructors proud. The motor of the camera whirred. The shutter clicked, once, twice. The phone kept on ringing. Ian took two more shots and then Merrick stood up.

"Hell and damnation," Merrick muttered.

Ian groaned and slapped his hand to his forehead.

"He never could let a ringing phone go unanswered," Helene explained apologetically.

Ian waved her words aside. "Then by all means answer it. But none of the rest of you move. I'm not finished yet."

Megan's cheeks hurt from smiling. A dull ache throbbed in her temples from the stress of standing so near Noah. She closed her eyes and let her expression go blank. Ian noticed immediately. "Megan. No. No. No more sadness. This is a wonderful day. All you Hardaway girls have your mother's smile. Let's see it." Quickly, before she could protest, he focused on Megan's small family grouping as she unconsciously responded to his imperious order. The camera's motor whirred once more. The shutter clicked. "There. Wonderful. Reunion. I love it," Ian crowed.

He swung the camera to Amy and Jon, caught her smiling down at Kieran while Jon's arm rested across her shoulders. "If guerrilla photography is what it takes to get you Hardaways on film, then Ian Medford is up to the challenge. Amy! Jon!" They looked up, clearly startled to hear the snap of the shutter. Ian caught the trio again, Kieran smiling into the lens this time, too.

Then it was Lisa's turn. The volatile photographer was zeroing in on Matt and their youngest sister when Merrick spoke.

"It's for you, Lisa. It's Dena. You're needed back in Danfield."

Lisa turned at the sound of his voice just as Ian

pressed the shutter and the photograph was ruined. Ian gave a theatrical groan. Megan made not a sound, but a small, superstitious burst of unease assailed her.

Once more Lisa was not included in the family unit. She cast a glance in Amy's direction and saw by the stricken look on her face that she felt the same. As if something far more significant than a photograph had been missed when Lisa walked away from the rest of them to answer a summons from her life in Connecticut.

Noah stepped back, away from Megan, and she felt the cool air-conditioned air swirl between them like the breath of winter.

"What about you and Merrick, Helene?" Ian prompted as Merrick returned to his seat on the couch. "Do you want a head-and-shoulders shot of the two of you? Or do you want to come into the studio for a more formal session?"

"I don't know," Helene said, looking into her husband's eyes. "It would be nice, I suppose. But—"

Merrick leaned forward and took her hands in both of his. "But we're more interested in having a portrait of our family around us, am I right, my love?"

Helene's breath sifted out in a sigh. "Yes. All of us together."

For a moment they might have been alone in the room.

Merrick cleared his throat. "You heard my wife, Ian. We'll be replacing the portrait above the mantel with one of the entire family. If you think you need any more shots, you'd better get them while you have the chance."

Ian cast a glance at the large portrait in its ornate frame above the mantelpiece. "Yes," he said, his eyes narrowing as he watched his subjects begin to stray from their assigned positions. "I'll want a lot more shots."

"I'm sorry. I can't stay," Lisa said, replacing the phone in its holder. "I have to return to Danfield right away."

"Oh, Lisa. No," Amy wailed.

"What's up, Lisa?" Matt wanted to know. "Is it Julie?"

Lisa nodded. "Her blood pressure is dangerously high. The doctor has decided to perform a cesarean section tomorrow morning."

"But you'll be back for Saturday," Amy insisted.

Lisa shrugged, looking both worried and trapped by her sister's single-mindedness. "I don't know, Amy. The babies aren't due for three weeks. They're small. There might be complications."

"Lisa, this is important to me. It's not only Mom and Dad's anniversary. It's…I…"

"Amy, what is it?" Lisa asked impatiently.

"I'm pregnant," Amy blurted out. "I'm going to have a baby. I wanted it to be a surprise. I wanted everyone to be there when I…we…" She looked appealingly at her husband. "When we made the announcement."

"I knew it," Ian Medford crowed. "I knew it. The camera never lies." Everyone ignored him.

"A baby?" Jon grabbed his wife by the shoulders and spun her around.

"I'm pregnant," Amy said, and started to cry.

"We're going to have a baby. I just found out. I'm pregnant and I don't know how it happened."

Kieran giggled and threw her arms around Amy's neck. "What do you mean you don't know how it happened? Do we need to go off and have a little girl-to-girl talk?" She giggled again. "Oh, Amy. This is great! I love babies. I've always wanted a baby brother or sister. But a new little cousin is almost as good."

Amy sniffed. "Is it?" She looked up into Jon's shell-shocked face. "I'm sorry. This isn't the way I intended to tell you. I...I know we'd planned to wait to start a family. It...it just happened."

"It's wonderful news," he said, sweeping her into his arms. "In the Costas family babies are always good news."

Amy held him tight for a long moment, then leaned back in his arms. "I was worried you might think it was too soon, with your new job and all."

"It's just a job, Amy," he said quietly. "This is our baby." He kissed her. "I love you."

"I love you," she whispered back.

Helene reached up and took Amy's hand between her own. "How long have you known?"

"Since Friday," Amy revealed, smiling through her tears. "Two days. The longest two days of my life."

"Is that why you were acting so oddly at Bea's yesterday?" Megan asked, giving her a hug.

"Yes. I...I kept trying to picture myself living there. A baby in the nursery. A swing set in the yard..."

"How wonderful," Helene said. "It's been ages

since we've had a baby in the house. Isn't it wonderful, Merrick?''

"It certainly is." Merrick stood up, leaned over the couch and gave Amy a peck on the cheek. "Congratulations, sweetheart." He turned and slapped Jon on the shoulder. "Congratulations, son."

"Thank you."

Amy twisted in her husband's arms. "I wanted to make the announcement next week. But that's not the only reason I wanted you here, Lisa."

Lisa's hands were locked together in front of her, her expression guarded. "Amy, I'm very happy for both of you." She moved stiffly across the room and gave Amy a quick hard hug. "Congratulations, Jon," she said over Amy's shoulder. She smiled, and Megan knew how much that smile had cost her. "I'm so happy for both of you."

"Thanks, Lisa."

Matt put his arm around her shoulders. "We'd better go, Lisa, if we want to catch the last flight out of Tallahassee."

Amy grabbed her hand. "Lisa, please. Try to get back for Saturday."

"I...I don't know. It all depends. Julie. The babies..." Her voice cracked slightly. "I'll let you know."

IT WAS LONG after midnight but Megan couldn't sleep. She couldn't blame the heat or humidity; the air in her bedroom was cool and dry. But beyond the window the night was alive with wind and rain. Fred had started to move late Sunday afternoon, the hurricane's course erratic. The storm surge and deadly tornado-spawning thunderstorms kicked up ahead of the giant, threatening communities all along the Florida Panhandle. Lisa and Matt had barely made it out of Tallahassee before the airport was shut down.

Along with her anxiety about the weather, Megan's own demons had made her sleep restless, and her dreams disturbed. Every time she drifted off, she'd find herself back in the mall in Tallahassee with Erik—only then he was Derek—tugging on her hand, his face screwed up into a pout, stubbornly pulling her in the direction he wanted to go. Away from danger, away from what she wanted, the blue dress with the spaghetti straps that she'd so desperately and foolishly believed would save her marriage.

She'd had this dream almost every night for months after Derek was taken. So often she had willed herself to change the ending, turn away from the blue dress and the shadowy figure of a stranger moving toward her unsuspecting baby, scoop Derek up into her arms and hurry out of the store to safety.

And when she finally made herself accept that Derek wasn't coming home, that version of the dream had become as painful as the reality of his kidnapping, and she'd willed herself not to have it at all. But tonight it was back. The shadowy figure was more menacing than ever. Closer. And when she turned to look at the little boy tugging on her hand, she found herself staring at Erik as he was today. A teenager with the dark, haunted eyes of a boy grown into a man before his time. Her gaze moved past his face, past the bandages on his right arm, to his hand. He was holding a gun.

Megan sat up, her heart pounding with fear. She

tried to tell herself to go back to sleep, that everything was fine, but she could not make herself believe
it. Another flash of the nightmare image of Erik's
shadowy abductor coincided with the flicker of lightning outside, filling her with renewed dread.

Erik. She had to be certain he was all right.

She pushed her hair behind her ears, slipped out
of her room and hurried across the hall, barefoot.
Erik's door was slightly ajar. She put her hand on
the knob and stood there listening to the sound of his
breathing, heavy, relaxed, not quite a snore. She
wasn't going to wake him. She just needed to see
him sleeping, safe, unharmed.

The hallway was dark, only a night-light burning
at the top of the stairs, and the dull glow of a streetlight struggling through the window at the far end.
The house was quiet. Even the flashes of lightning
were not accompanied by thunder. The silence closed
in around Megan. Suddenly she sensed more than
heard a figure, large but soundless, coming up behind
her. She whirled in panic, but even before she could
draw in her breath to scream, Noah was beside her.

"Shh. It's okay. I heard you come out of your
room," he whispered, his voice black velvet in the
night.

"How?" she whispered back. "I didn't make a
sound."

"Yes, you did."

"Nothing loud enough to wake someone sleeping
behind an inch-thick mahogany door."

"I heard you." Even in a whisper his tone of voice
left no room for argument. He had promised to pro-

tect Erik. He had given his word. No one would get past him in the night. Not even her.

"I couldn't sleep. I…I wanted to see if Erik was okay."

"Bad dreams, Megan?" he asked, reaching out to tuck a stray wisp of hair back behind her ear. Could he read her mind, or was the residue of her nightmare still visible on her face? Considering the darkness she doubted even his night-sensitive eyes could see her expression.

"Yes," she replied. "Familiar ones."

"He's okay, Megan."

"I want to be sure," she said.

A glimmer of lightning illuminated the hallway for a brief moment. Megan blinked, then shut her eyes against the brightness, but not before Noah's image was imprinted on her mind. He was barefoot also, wearing nothing but pajama bottoms riding low on his lean hips. The sight of him brought another image to mind—disturbing in its own way—the two of them making love in his bed at the Sand Dollar.

Noah leaned forward and pushed open Erik's door. His chest brushed against her bare arm, the coarse hair abrading her skin, making her breath catch in her throat. She rubbed away the sensation before the chance touch could awaken the sensual awareness of him that always lurked just beneath the surface of her thoughts.

In her desperation to check on her son, she hadn't stopped to pull on her robe. Now, with Noah so close behind her she was very much aware that she was naked beneath the gathered folds of her cotton night-gown. She forced her arms to remain at her sides, didn't lift them to cover her breasts, or wrap them around her middle in the self-comforting gesture that had become second nature over the long years alone.

Instead, she concentrated on her son. Erik was lying on his stomach, his long, lean body relaxed in sleep. His right arm was flung over his head, the bandage pale in the darkness, his left foot hanging over the edge of the mattress. His face was hidden in the crook of his elbow, but his breathing remained deep and regular. He was oblivious, and if he dreamed, the dreams weren't disturbing his rest.

She had missed so much with him. All the nights she could have come into his room to watch him sleep. All the Christmas Eves she could have tucked him in before going off to fill his stocking. All the birthdays she never celebrated with him. *His first lost tooth. She* should have been the one to put the quarter under his pillow. Noah should have been by her side. But it hadn't happened that way. And it never would.

Megan reached down, ran her fingertips over the softness of Erik's hair. The skin on the back of his neck was cool to her touch. She lifted the sheet that he'd pushed down to his waist and pulled it over his shoulders. She stood quietly for another long moment, watching her child sleep, very aware of her son's father, Noah, the intimate stranger, standing just behind her.

"Come on, Megan." Noah's words were more sensation than sound. "He's fine. You can go back to bed."

She whirled to face him. "He's not fine," she whispered fiercely. Erik stirred at the sound of her voice. Noah glanced at him, then took Megan by the arm and led her from the room.

"He's not fine," she repeated when they once more stood in the hallway. "He'll never be fine. Not the way he should be."

"He's strong and he's intelligent. He'll work through all this."

"How can you be sure of that? He confessed he considered murdering the man who took him. I'm scared."

"You're scared of our son?"

She couldn't speak. She shook her head. "I'm not afraid *of* him," she whispered. "I'm afraid *for* him."

He could feel her eyes searching his face in the darkness. "I know how you feel. We're both flying blind. But we have to trust that our son will be okay." Noah pulled her into his arms. He felt her breasts against his chest, felt the softness of her belly against his and steeled himself not to respond physically. She had been sealing herself off from him bit by bit ever since they'd made love three days ago. He could see it happening in her every move and gesture, and there wasn't a damn thing he could do about it.

"Noah, we have to get him help. Now. Right away." She let him hold her, but she was stiff and unresponsive in his arms. "I want to take him away, back to Nebraska. I have friends there. People who can suggest the best therapist possible."

"You can't go now, Megan." He wanted to crush her close, hold her until she responded to him, but he kept the pressure of his arms light, unthreatening.

"Jamieson's on his way here. So is Fielder, or I miss my guess."

She lifted her head from his chest, and looked at him in horror. "All the more reason to leave at once."

"No." He wasn't going to budge on this. He couldn't. Erik's life was at risk. All their futures were at stake. "You're not leaving here. I can't guarantee your safety in Omaha. And I think it's time to talk to Erik about calling in the authorities."

"Can you guarantee our son's safety in Hurricane Beach, Noah?"

"A hell of a lot better than I can anywhere else."

"That's not the answer I wanted to hear."

"I've never lied to you, Megan."

She closed her eyes and spoke softly, "No. You've never lied to me. But I can't go on like this, Noah."

She tried to step away, but he tightened his hold, and she didn't struggle to be free. She didn't have to, physically she might be in his arms, emotionally she was a thousand miles away. Panic tightened like iron bands around his chest. He fought it off. Over-powering her physically to try to prove how much he still loved her would only drive the final wedge between them, seal his fate and doom him to a future of sharing only fragments of his son's life, and Megan's.

"You don't have to go on alone, Megan," he said, hating himself for equivocating, for not having the guts to come right out and say what was in his heart. *Megan, I love you. I've always loved you, that's why*

I never asked for a divorce earlier. That's why I want us together again, a family again.

She refused to meet his eyes. "No, Noah," she whispered, her breath warm against his throat. "Don't say any more." He reached down and tilted her chin up, made her look at him. Her eyes were as blank as her expression. "I tried to tell you before...when...when we were together in your cabin. I don't have enough love for both of you."

"That's a damn lie."

She reached up and touched his cheek. Her face was a smooth, beautiful mask, nothing more. "Shh, you'll wake him."

"Megan, don't do this to yourself. Don't do this to us. I love you." There, he'd said it. Somehow he'd found the courage and now he couldn't stop. "God, I've always loved you. I never stopped loving you. And you love me. I know you do. You proved it the other day in my bed. You prove it again every time you tremble at my touch—"

She lifted her hand to his lips. "Don't, Noah. Don't say any more. I have no choice. I made a terrible mistake twelve years ago." She shook her head as though bewildered by her own thoughts. "I wanted that blue dress so badly."

"What are you talking about?" Anger and desperation boiled up inside him.

She smiled, a sad, wistful smile that tore at his heart. "I wanted it all so badly." A single crystal teardrop traced down her cheek. "But I'm never going to take a chance on trying for the moon and the stars again. I have my miracle. Our son. I can't ask for more. I can't ask for love."

"Don't talk like that," he said, and she winced at the harshness of his tone. "There are different kinds of love. You can love Erik with a mother's love. You can love me with a wife's."

"I can't," she said simply.

"You won't, you mean. You're afraid to love. You're afraid of life. Even your work is preparing for death. But you won't admit that, will you?" He shook her , trying to force a response. "Do you hear me, Megan Marie? You're afraid, that's all. Come back to me. I'll never let you be afraid again, I promise."

She lifted her hand to his cheek. "It's too late for promises, Noah. It's too late for us. Everything I have to give from now on must be for Erik. Not me."

"Megan."

She pulled free of his grip before he could stop her. "No more, Noah. Please. I won't change my mind. I can't." She held out her hand to stop him as he took a step toward her. "Let me go. It's late and I have to be up early to help Amy with her sale at the store tomorrow." She turned on her heel and disappeared into the shadows.

ERIK DIDN'T MOVE a muscle but he knew he was awake. His arm throbbed from being elevated on his pillow, and his heart pounded with the shock of what he'd just heard. He rolled over and looked at the door, still standing slightly ajar. The hallway was quiet now. But he hadn't been dreaming. Their standing beside his bed had been real. And so had the argument that followed.

It had seemed like a wonderful dream at first, hearing Megan's voice, the light touch of her fingers in his hair, the softness of the sheet as she pulled it over his back. He'd liked hearing the quiet murmur of her voice and the low rumble of Noah's replies. The dream was so vivid he'd even smelled the lemony scent of her perfume, and felt the air stir as she moved across the room. It was just as he'd read about in books, the way he knew in his heart it should be. His parents—his real parents—checking on him, keeping him safe.

And then they'd left the room and gone back out into the hallway and the dream had turned scary. That's when he'd realized it wasn't a dream at all. He was awake, and his parents were arguing. About him. He couldn't make out everything they said. But he did hear his mother say she was afraid of him. Scared he'd go crazy and do something awful. But he wouldn't. He couldn't then. He couldn't now. Or ever. Didn't that count for anything? She was crying and arguing with Noah, telling him she couldn't love him. Because of *Erik*.

He wished he could hear more, but he was too much of a coward to get off the bed and listen at the door. He might hear something even worse than he already had, and he didn't think he could stand that. So he'd lain there without moving for a long time.

At last he sat up, watching the heat lightning in the sky for a minute and then stood up. He knew what he had to do. He couldn't stay here anymore. He was causing too much trouble for everyone.

It had all been too good to be true. He'd really begun to think everything would be all right. They'd be a real family again. They'd made him think it could happen. And they were good at it. Family picnics and pictures and everything. But it was all a lie, a sham. Because of him, none of it would ever happen.

Unless he went away. Maybe without him Megan and Noah could sort things out. And then he would come back and they'd be a family again. It wasn't going to happen while he was here, that was for sure. He was just too much trouble for both of them.

This time he wasn't going to steal a car. He'd take the bus. Of course, that meant that he was going to have to get some money somewhere. And he couldn't ask anyone for it. They would suspect right away what he was up to. So he was going to have to steal some money, he didn't see any other way to get out of town. There was a lot of cash in the safe, he'd seen it when the door had swung open. Merrick wouldn't miss it for days. Erik remembered the combination—Merrick's birthday. He'd take just enough for a bus ticket and some food. Not a cent more. And he'd pay it back as soon as he was able.

As soon as he came back…if he came back.

CHAPTER THIRTEEN

"WE'RE NOT OPEN for business today," Amy hollered, making shooing motions with her hands to discourage the pair of matronly women jiggling the doorknob of Rêve Rags.

"But your sign says Labor Day Sale," one of the women hollered back. "The last time I looked at the calendar, today was Labor Day."

"'All Summer Merchandise Fifty Percent Off,'" her companion quoted from the flyer she waved in her hand.

"That was before Fred." Amy turned her back on the women and returned to packing away accessories in a large waterproof plastic storage box.

"Other stores in town are open," Grace said, catching Megan's eye and frowning at her partner's unusually brusque response to potential customers. "There are no plans to evacuate this part of the coastline. As a matter of fact, the town's full of people. It *is* a holiday, you know."

"Well, they shouldn't be here," Amy insisted, dropping a cardboard display stand of ruffled organdy hair clips into the storage box. "They're just asking for trouble. Haven't they been listening to the weather reports?"

"The latest reports said Fred would probably

come ashore in Louisiana,'' Megan reminded her. She'd arrived at Rêve Rags soon after Amy's frantic phone call at 7:00 a.m. asking her to come and help move the inventory upstairs, in case the storm flooded Gulfview.

Amy sounded so unlike herself that Megan had left the house at once. She had planned to spend the day at the store helping to deal with an onslaught of holiday bargain hunters, not preparing for Armageddon. But anything was preferable to lying sleepless in her bed at Sea Haven, regretting what had happened between her and Noah last night.

By the time Grace Kingsolver arrived to open the store at 10:00 a.m., Amy and Megan had removed all the merchandise from the front windows and packed up half the jewelry and accessories displayed in the glass counters along one wall of the store.

"Girl, what are you up to?" Grace had demanded, standing in the doorway, hands on hips, a look of disbelief on her face.

"I don't want to see my life's work washed away in a hurricane," Amy insisted. "I'm taking precautions, that's all."

"You're losing us a thousand-dollar sales day, that's what you're doing." Amy kept right on piling merchandise into the big blue box on the counter. "You're acting like you've lost your mind." Then Grace's beautiful dark eyes narrowed. She chewed on her lower lip for a moment and made a pronouncement. "I don't think you've lost your mind. You seemed normal enough the last time I saw you and that was only sixteen hours ago. Amy Costas, are you pregnant?"

"Yes." Amy avoided Grace's eyes as she ripped off a length of bubble wrap and laid it over a tray of rhinestone pins and earrings before she sealed the lid of the box. "I'm pregnant. But that's got nothing to do with Fred coming, and I don't know how you figured that out from the way I'm acting. I'm acting like any normal person whose livelihood is being threatened by a natural disaster."

The menace of Fred was momentarily forgotten. "Go on," Grace said, a glorious smile banishing the frown from her eyes. "Pregnant. I knew it. That explains why you've been moping around here every morning. I don't think I've seen you take more than a bite of your almond roll for the last two weeks."

"Don't mention almond rolls," Amy muttered. "I can't stand the sight of them."

"How long have you known, girl?" Grace demanded, leaning over the counter to give Amy a hug, which Amy returned, blinking hard to hold back quick tears.

"Just a few days. Oh dear, why did this all have to happen now?"

"What do you mean? Megan?"

Megan lifted her shoulders in a shrug.

"The hurricane. The party. The baby," Amy whispered. "Now Lisa will never come home."

Grace twisted her head around, still holding Amy around the shoulders, and looked to Megan. "What's she talking about?"

Megan hadn't wanted to tell Amy what Lisa had confided to her in Bea's house Saturday afternoon, but Amy was nobody's fool and had guessed from Lisa's reaction to the announcement of her pregnancy at the photo session that something was wrong. She'd eventually worn Megan down and learned about Lisa's fear that she couldn't become pregnant. Now Amy was more upset than ever.

"I'll explain later," Megan said. "Amy, I think Grace is right. Let's open the store. We'll have plenty of warning and plenty of help if Fred changes course again and, God forbid, heads back this way."

"I…I don't know. Do you agree, Grace? Do you think Megan's right? I don't know what's the matter with me." Amy sniffed. "I can't make up my mind about anything. It's like I don't know myself anymore."

"Hormones," Megan said. "It'll get easier as you go along."

"I hope so," Amy said. "I hate feeling like this."

"C'mon, girl. What's a little wind and rain when there's a sale on and a baby coming," Grace coaxed, lifting the rhinestone jewelry out of the plastic box. "Let's get this stuff back in the case and open the door. We'll show Fred who's boss around here. And then I want all the down-and-dirty details of this baby business. When can we expect the little darling? And what do you want—a boy or a girl?"

"Okay," Amy said, dragging the back of her hand across her cheeks. "You're right. Who cares about eighty-mile-an-hour winds and fifteen-foot tides. Piece of cake. I'll get the hang of this pregnancy thing. You see if I don't."

Megan laughed and went to unlock the front door.

AN HOUR LATER Fred changed direction again and headed back to the east, putting Hurricane Beach on course to be battered by the strong wind and rain on the fringes of the storm.

Amy took the news well this time. At least as far as Rêve Rags was concerned. Their parents' anniversary party was another matter. She started crying again as she and Megan stood on the covered walkway that surrounded the marina and watched as volunteers sandbagged the lower floor—where the party was to be held.

Already the rising winds had driven the level of Alligator Creek over its banks. The Costas Brothers' fishing boats, as well as several yachts and a number of smaller craft, had been moved up the creek as far as the Connell Brassworks to ride out the storm.

"It's all my fault," Amy wailed. "Everything's going to be ruined and it's all my fault."

"It's not your fault," Megan said patiently. Dealing with Amy's moodiness had at least kept her own bleak thoughts at bay during the busy afternoon.

Amy threw up her hands indicating the stormy waves beyond the breakwater and the lowering sky overhead. "I know the hurricane isn't my fault. But Lisa's not coming back is. Oh why couldn't I keep my mouth shut about the baby a few weeks longer?"

Megan took her sister by the shoulders and spun her around. "Don't ever say such a thing. Your being pregnant is the most wonderful thing that's happened to this family since—"

"Since Erik came back?" Amy said, smiling through her tears, sunshine through storm clouds, mirroring the day.

"Yes," Megan said, smiling, too. "Since Erik returned. Lisa will feel that way too, once she gets used to the idea.''

Amy leaned her elbows on the railing and watched as the last of the Costas fishing boats, the *Leda C*, chugged upstream to the relative safety of the Brassworks pier. ''At least that girl, Julie, and her babies are okay.''

''Yes,'' Megan agreed, moving toward the staircase leading to the boardwalk. Lisa had called Rêve Rags just a short while before to announce that Julie's babies, a boy and a girl, both small but healthy had been safely delivered. Julie's blood pressure was coming down, and it looked as though all three of them would be okay.

''She still wouldn't commit to Saturday.'' Amy gave the sandbagging crew—the waiters and busboys from the restaurant—one last glance.

''She didn't say no,'' Megan hedged. ''She just said it would depend on the storm. And the babies.''

''Of course, the way things are going there won't be any place to have a party for her to miss on Saturday,'' Amy said bitterly.

''Amy,'' Megan said in a warning tone. ''Enough.''

''Yes, big sister,'' Amy said in a long-suffering tone.

Megan held out her hand. ''C'mon. We've been gone long enough, Grace will notice.''

''Do you think we should still move everything upstairs?''

''I don't know,'' Megan admitted, raising her voice to carry over the sound of the surf and the wind as they left the shelter of the marina complex and headed onto the boardwalk.

Wind tugged at Megan's hair, wrapped her skirt around her knees. She could taste salt spray on her lips. Even the birds were grounded, a trio of large white gulls strutted along ahead of them searching for windblown scraps. A few hardy souls stood at the edge of the dunes, watching the storm-driven waves break far up on the beach. The police had set a seven o'clock deadline for evacuating the beach area, and most people had already obeyed. A great many of the holiday day-trippers had left town hours ago, the blowing sand and heavy rain squalls driving them away even before the threat of Fred's return became certain The hurricane had held steady on its course for the last four hours. The eye of the storm would pass well to the west of the town, but winds and tides would be high and dangerous, the threat of flooding possible, for the next twenty-four hours.

"Do you need help packing up things at the beach cottage?" Megan asked.

"I'm going to finish up at the store first," Amy said, linking her arm through Megan's. "I know Jon and Kieran can manage on their own..."

"But it's your house," Megan said.

"Yes," Amy said. "I'm kinda partial to that little shack." She used her free hand to push her hair out of her eyes as they turned onto Gulfview, and the buildings blocked some of the wind. "I wonder if we shouldn't have boarded up the windows instead of just taping them? If the wind gusts any harder it could really start knocking things around."

Ike Forenza had taken in his sidewalk tables and

chairs, Megan noticed, and closed the big glass doors that were almost always opened to the sun and sea breezes. The windows of Quentin Somersby's flower shop were protected with X-shapes of gray tape. Beside the flower shop, Maida was supervising the installation of plywood covers over the huge plate-glass windows that showcased many of her gallery's valuable pieces.

"See what I mean," Amy continued to fuss. "Maida's boarding over her windows. She didn't do that for Opal and that came as close to Hurricane Beach as any storm I can remember." She bit her lip. "Do you suppose she's heard something we haven't?"

"Why don't you ask her," Megan said, her gaze skipping past Maida and the little dog she carried strapped to her ample bosom in a baby carrier. Ordinarily, Megan would have taken the time to watch the flamboyant gallery owner direct the two burly workmen wrestling the plywood sheets into place with expansive gestures of her plump, beringed hands. But today Megan only had eyes for her husband and son.

Erik was halfway up the ladder propped against the second floor of Amy's shop and Noah was beneath him. Working together they were applying the same heavy gray tape that adorned the storefronts of merchants up and down the street. Kieran and Grace watched from the sidewalk. Kieran held another roll of tape.

"Good job," Amy said, surveying the heavily taped windows with a critical eye. "Do you think we should bring a load of sandbags back from city hall?

The water's never come this far over the dunes before—''

"Quit borrowing trouble. We're not going to need sandbags," Grace said. "And if we do, there's plenty of time to get them."

"You're right," Amy said, but she was frowning as she splayed her hand over her flat stomach. She caught Grace's eye, looked down and dropped her hand, coloring slightly. "I know. I know. Hormones. But I'm getting better. I'm not insisting on the sandbags."

"And you didn't burst into tears." Grace laughed, and Amy giggled.

"What's so funny?" Kieran demanded, looking from Grace to Amy.

"Never mind," Amy told her. "Where's Jon?"

"We loaded the car with everything we could fit inside," Kieran reported. "Then we came back into town to unload it at Grandma's, and she asked Jon to stay there and help tape up her bay window, so I came down here to see what's going on. Is that the phone?" Kieran tilted her head in a listening attitude.

"Oh, damn, I left the portable on the counter. A lot of good it does me in there," Grace grumbled, and headed into the shop.

"You've done a good job," Megan called up to Erik, pushing strands of hair out of her eyes that the wind had loosened form the knot on the top of her head.

"Yeah. It looks okay." He didn't meet her eye or return her smile as he started down the ladder.

"Is everything battened down out at Sea Haven?" she asked next.

Erik made a great show of moving the ladder away from the window. Finally, Noah stepped in and answered her question. "All squared away. We closed all the storm shutters and cleared the deck and patio of everything that wasn't nailed down."

She barely registered Noah's words. Megan was puzzled by Erik's attitude. Had something happened? Had some new information come to light? Information about Fielder? She felt a cold hard knot of fear begin to grow in the pit of her stomach.

"I'll take the ladder around back," Erik said, picking it up with his uninjured hand.

"I'll help." Kieran took one end of the wooden ladder and they disappeared down the narrow walkway that Rêve Rags shared with the gift shop on the other side.

"Noah, what's the matter with him? He seems...I don't know...distracted. Has there been some news of Fielder's whereabouts?"

Noah slid back the blade of the utility knife he'd been using to cut the strips of tape. "Let's go inside," he said. "The wind's getting fierce out here."

Megan reached out and grabbed his shirtsleeve. "Tell me. You've had some news."

"Jamieson tracked Fielder to a motel in Tallahassee," Noah said. "He checked out yesterday morning and disappeared again."

"He's on his way here, isn't he?" Megan looked around, the knot of fear expanding with each breath she took. Amy stepped over and put her arm around Megan's shoulders.

"Megan, it's all right. Erik's right around the corner. He's fine."

"Fielder might already be here." She thought of all the people who'd walked past the store that day. Maybe Erik's abductor had been one of them. "We don't even know what he looks like."

"Erik's promised to draw a sketch of the man. He doesn't want to do it, but he promised. I'll get him to work on it this evening, when all the storm preparation has been done."

"Yes." Megan wrapped her arms around her waist and then made herself stop, dropped her hands to her sides. "We have to know what he looks like."

"Jamieson's spending the rest of the day in Tallahassee," Noah continued. "He's tracking down a couple of leads the motel clerk gave him, but so far they're all dead ends."

"You've told Erik this already."

"Yes," he said simply. "I told him I would let him know what's going on."

"We need to notify the police. We need to get some help to keep him safe."

"Jamieson will be here by midnight. We'll take turns keeping watch tonight."

"Sea Haven's like a fortress," Amy reminded her.

Noah nodded his agreement. He'd made no move to touch Megan. She didn't want him to, she reminded herself. She'd told him that in no uncertain terms.

"We'll be fine tonight. Now that the sheriff's notified the FBI, they'll have someone here tomorrow afternoon or Wednesday morning at the latest," he said.

"Wednesday. That's too far away. Anything—" Megan broke off what she'd been going to say as

Kieran and Erik reappeared at the same time Grace came out of the shop.

"Grace, what's wrong?" Amy demanded the moment she saw her friend. Grace's flawless coffee-colored skin was pasty with shock. Her eyes were wide and there was a pinched look to her mouth.

"It's Nick," she said, staring down at the portable phone in her hand. "It's Nick. He's alive. And he's on the phone."

"My dad?" Kieran asked in a strangled voice.

"Yes, sweetie. He's been in a rehab center in Tampa. He's got a three-day pass. He wants to see you. He wants to come home to Hurricane Beach." She held out the phone.

"No," Kieran said, slapping the phone out of Grace's hand. "I never want to see him again." She watched it tumble to the sidewalk in horror, and then turned around and began to run as if the devil himself were on her heels.

"Kieran, come back!" Amy called.

Grace picked up the phone. Her hands were trembling. Megan knew that Grace and Nick Costas had been very close to falling in love when he disappeared. His out-of-the-blue return would be as traumatic for her as it was for Kieran.

"I'm going after her," Erik annunced, pounding off down the street after Jon's niece.

"Erik, no. Come back!" Megan was suddenly frantic not to lose sight of him. She had already taken two steps after him when Noah reached out and circled her wrist with his long, strong fingers.

"Let him go, Megan."

"But Fielder…"

"Stay here with Amy and Grace. I'll keep him in sight. Kieran's the only friend he's got right now and she's hurting. He wants to help. We have to let him. He'll be okay, Megan. I promise."

"KIERAN. Wait." She didn't slow down, just kept running, fighting her way forward against the strong gusts of wind. "Wait. I can't keep up. My arm—" She slowed down half a step, holding on to the railing of the municipal pier to keep her balance, and turned around. He grabbed his arm just above the elbow to give credence to his white lie. "Thanks."

"Did you hurt yourself again? Is it all right?" she asked quickly.

He felt like a rat. "It's okay," he said. "It just hurts when I have to run to keep up with you."

Kieran stayed where she was, her hands still wrapped around the railing. "He's not dead," Kieran said as Erik came up beside her. The wind had teased her dark hair into a riot of curls. There were tears on her cheeks and her nose was red from crying. "My dad's alive. I just got used to the idea he wasn't coming back and now—bam!—out of nowhere he calls and says he's been in Tampa, for God's sake. And he wants to come home. Just like nothing's happened."

"Just like me," Erik said.

She turned away from him, watching the angry surf pound against the pilings of the pier. "Not just like you. You didn't go away on purpose. Your coming home was a miracle. Everyone says so."

"Yeah, that's what everyone says, but it still turned everyone's life upside down."

Kieran turned to him, turned her back to the wind and the advancing storm clouds. "Like I said, you couldn't help what happened to you. My dad could. Now he wants to come back, and he wants me and Grace and Grandpa and Grandma and Uncle Jon to forget it ever happened. Just like that," she repeated bitterly. "Just like he might not do it again. Well, I'm not going to get hurt again. I want to stay with Amy and Jon. I want things to be like they've been this summer. Not the way they were."

Erik wished he could say something reassuring but he couldn't think of anything that would help. "Are you going to see him when he comes home?"

"Not if I can help it," Kieran said bitterly. "Can I come out to Sea Haven and stay with you?"

"I..." He pushed his hip against the railing and felt the roll of bills he'd filched from Merrick's safe press against his thigh. A thought struck him. Maybe he wouldn't have to leave Hurricane Beach alone. Kieran was a good sport, and smart as a whip. She was the only friend he had right now. They could make it together somewhere. He knew they could. He would have enough money for both of them if he worked it right. "Are you thinking of running away?" he asked.

Kieran shook her head, at the same time he realized he couldn't be that selfish, couldn't ask her to go with him, or even tell her what he was planning to do. It was too dangerous.

"I tried that once," she said. "It didn't work. I just don't want to see him." She looked at him and blinked back new tears. "I don't want to start loving him again."

THE TOWN WAS FULL of cops. He hadn't counted on that. Damn hurricane was making a mess of everything—including his plans to get Erik back. He'd have to wait until things settled down. Probably spend the night out in the swamp at the end of some abandoned logging road. He could stay in the cab of the beat-up pickup he'd stolen from the parking lot of a roadhouse back down the highway early that morning. Even if he found the kid today, chances were that there'd be a cop of some kind close enough for Erik to holler bloody murder, and get Fielder thrown into jail for the rest of his life.

Ungrateful brat. After all he'd done for him, too. Treated him like his own son for a dozen years.

He was taking a chance driving through town, but he wasn't too worried. There were plenty of cops, sure, but they were busy keeping tourists off the beach and the main drag so he figured he was safe enough taking a look around.

He hadn't seen the kid. Hadn't really expected to be that lucky. But now that it looked like the damn hurricane was going to blow itself out somewhere over Louisiana he had all the time in the world. He'd just wait for Erik to come out of hiding. This time he'd make sure the kid never got away again.

CHAPTER FOURTEEN

"THERE IS A MAN sleeping on the deck," Helene said, pushing open the swinging door leading to the kitchen with such force it missed hitting the wall by no more than inches. "A very large man. Dressed in black."

Noah finished pouring coffee into the second of the two mugs he'd placed on the counter. "That would be Jamieson," he said, turning to his mother-in-law.

It was only a few minutes past eight o'clock on a blustery Tuesday morning, but Helene looked rested and alert, far younger than her years. Far younger and happier than she had looked when he arrived in Hurricane Beach a week ago.

"Has he been there all night?"

"Since he relieved me at 3:00 a.m."

"Well, I hope that coffee's for him," she said, eyeing the two mugs Noah was holding.

"Yes, ma'am."

"Good. I don't want him to think Sea Haven is lacking in hospitality."

"No, ma'am."

"Invite him inside for breakfast."

"Thank you, ma'am."

"You don't have to keep ma'am-ing me, Noah Carson."

"Yes, ma'am," he said, and smiled. After a moment so did Helene.

"Noah." He remained silent, merely lifting an eyebrow in response, and her smile grew. "We haven't had much time to talk these past few days. And there is a great deal I'd like to say to you. Some of it not very flattering to myself."

"You don't owe me any—"

She cut him off with a flick of her hand. "I've owed you an apology for fifteen years. I'm sorry I made it so hard on you and Megan when you were first married. I know you thought I was a snob. But my objections were not because I thought you weren't good enough to marry my daughter. I didn't want you to marry Megan not because of *who* you were but because of *what* you were. What you were trained to do. Because you were like Merrick."

"A soldier."

"Yes." She looked relieved that he understood. "They called them commandos in our war. But the breed of man is the same. Trained to do the most terrible jobs, in the most terrible places. And dedicated enough to give up their lives doing it. I didn't want Megan to suffer the terrors I did waiting for Merrick to come home safe from the war. But then she did suffer. And I feel more than a little responsible that she wouldn't let you help her share her grief, and move beyond it." She sighed. "I owe Megan an apology, too. I didn't give her credit for loving you enough, for being strong enough, to be a soldier's wife. I know she picked up on my insecurity

and doubt. I know it fed her own. I'm sorry, Noah.
I just want you to know I'll do anything I can to
further your reconciliation."

"Thank you, Helene. But I think it might be too
late for Megan and me." He went on speaking before
she could protest. He turned slightly so he didn't
have to see the remorse in her eyes. "And at any
rate, our relationship is secondary to Erik's happi-
ness."

"On the contrary," Helene said, "your relationship is of primary importance to Erik. He wants a
family. A real family. The three of you together."

"That's up to Megan," Noah said, unable to filter
the harshness from his words. "It always has been."

"Noah—"

"I think Jamieson will want his coffee by now.
Would you like to meet him?"

She opened her mouth, closed it again and nodded
once, then she turned and preceded him out of the
kitchen.

Jamieson was not alone when they reached the
still-bare deck. Merrick Hardaway was with him.

"Good morning, Commander," Jamieson said,
giving a half salute with two fingers.

"Good morning, Ensign. I hope you slept well."

Jamieson grinned. "Like a baby, sir."

"I see you've met Noah's friend," Helene said to
Merrick as Noah handed the younger man the mug
of hot coffee.

"Yes, my dear. He informs me he's been here
most of the night."

"Kyle Jamieson. My mother-in-law, Helene Hardaway." Noah performed the introductions. "Kyle owns and operates SecurTek Investigations."

"Welcome to Sea Haven," Helene said graciously. "I hope you'll join us for breakfast."

"Thank you, ma'am. I'd be honored."

"Good. That's settled." She eyed his black T-shirt and sweatpants with a critical eye. "Your clothes appear very damp, Mr. Jamieson. Do you have dry clothes somewhere around?"

"Yes, ma'am. In my kit." Jamieson cradled the mug between his big hands.

"Why don't you freshen up in the bathroom at the top of the stairs. Do you need a place to stay?"

"Yes," Merrick seconded. "You're welcome to stay with us for as long as necessary. The nearer you are to our grandson the happier I'll be."

"Thank you, sir. I appreciate that. Now, if you'll excuse me, I'll take you up on that offer of a shower and shave. I'm due at the sheriff's office in thirty minutes. Commander, can you provide me with that sketch of Fielder that your son drew?"

"It's in my study," Merrick answered for Noah. "On the desk. You can't miss it."

"Thank you, sir." He turned back to Noah. "Do you want to be there when I talk to the sheriff?"

"Yes," Noah said. "I'll be waiting in the study. It's the room at the bottom of the stairs."

"I saw Erik's sketch last night," Helene said softly after Jamieson left the deck. "Such an ordinary-looking man." She turned to her husband. Held out her hand. "Wasn't he an ordinary-looking man, Merrick?"

"Ordinary enough, I guess."

"Brown eyes. Brown hair, receding hairline. Middle-aged. A thousand men just like him in every town in the country."

Helene held tightly to Merrick's hand. "I thought. All these years, well, that this Fielder person must be a monster. I kept asking myself over and over, how could I not have seen him? How could I have overlooked someone so evil? I've felt so guilty for so long."

"Did you ever see him, Helene?" Merrick asked, bending his head to her ear.

She shook her head. "No. I never did. And if I had, I wouldn't have given him a second glance. Evil really doesn't show, does it? Now I know there was nothing more I could have done. Nothing Megan could have done."

"No, my love. Nothing at all."

"Now we know who he is. We know what he looks like." Her voice strengthened as she looked up at her husband. "This time we won't let him get anywhere near Erik."

MEGAN AND HELENE were in the kitchen, sitting at the big round table, talking quietly. Talking about him. He didn't have to be listening at the keyhole to figure that out. He was the only thing they talked about, unless Amy was around, and then they talked about the party. Which was back on track, it seemed, since Fred had skipped across Louisiana and trailed off into Oklahoma and Texas, leaving Hurricane Beach pretty much untouched except for some missing shingles and broken windows, and one or two boats washed up on the beach.

Erik didn't think he'd still be here on Saturday. He'd had the creepy feeling he was being watched all day yesterday. And then Noah had told him earlier that morning that Fielder was probably getting close and the FBI had been notified. Now Erik had to leave Hurricane Beach. It was the only way to give his mom and dad a chance to be together and to help keep everybody he loved safe from harm.

"Erik, telephone." His mother was standing in the kitchen doorway holding the portable phone out to him, that worried watchful look in her eyes he'd been seeing since yesterday morning. "It's Kieran. She sounds upset."

He took the phone. "Hi," he said, looking down at his shoes.

"My dad's here," Kieran said abruptly. "He called from the bakery. He's coming to the store. I don't want to see him."

"I—" He stopped abruptly as he looked up and found Megan still watching him.

"Has her father returned?" Megan asked quietly. When he nodded, she continued. "I imagine she's pretty nervous about seeing him."

"Yeah," he said.

She smiled at him. "You can talk her through it," she said, turning around. "Just bring the phone back into the kitchen when you hang up."

"Okay, thanks."

"Erik? Are you still there?"

"Yeah. I'm here."

"I don't want to see him." He could hear tears in Kieran's voice. He didn't know how to deal with her

crying, with any girl crying, but especially Kieran.
But she was his only friend—and she needed him.

"Okay. I'll meet you…at the end of the boardwalk. That's about halfway between Rêve Rags and
Sea Haven."

"Okay. I'll be there in ten minutes. Hurry."

"Okay." He pushed the button to break the connection. Now he was really in a mess. Less than an
hour ago, he'd promised Noah he wouldn't leave the
house while he and Jamieson were at the sheriff's
office. He was breaking his word by leaving, but he
had to be there for Kieran.

He rubbed the bandage over the stitches on his
arm. They itched. He wondered how he'd get them
out after he ran away. God, he hadn't thought of that.
He'd have to take that tiny, sharp pair of scissors
he'd seen in a little zippered manicure case he'd
found in a drawer in his bathroom and take them out
himself. The thought sent a shiver up and down his
back as he walked into the big kitchen, still gloomy
because Merrick hadn't had time to fold back the
storm shutters yet.

"Kieran feeling better?" Megan asked. She was
sitting at the table. Helene was standing at the sink
cutting up a tomato for lunch. Annie wasn't there
today. She had stayed home to supervise the repairs
to a section of her roof where the singles had been
blown off.

"Yeah," he lied. "I think she's okay."

"Poor girl," Helene said. "Just when she and
Amy and Jon were starting to make a family, Nick
Costas has to drop back into their lives and stir ev-
erything up."

"Maybe this time he really does have his life back on track," Megan said as Erik replaced the phone on its stand near the refrigerator.

"We can always hope so," Helene replied, but she didn't sound convinced. "Lunch will be ready in half an hour, Erik," she said, smiling at him.

Half an hour. He could just about make it to the boardwalk, talk to Kieran, and—suddenly the idea hit him—keep on going. He'd *never* have a better chance to get away.

"Okay," he said, avoiding looking directly at either his mother or grandmother. *It was time for him to go.* His hands started shaking. A big knot formed in his stomach and moved up into his throat. He swallowed hard to get it to go back down. "I'll be up in my room. I...there's something I want to work on up there."

"All right." Megan was holding on to her coffee mug with both hands. She looked as if she wanted to say something more, then thought better of it. "We'll see you in half an hour."

"Yeah. Okay. That's good."

It was easier than he thought. He went upstairs two at a time, got his money, the little manicure case, pulled on a pair of jeans and a long-sleeved shirt over his shorts and T-shirt, even though it was still pretty hot out, because he'd need the extra clothes on the road. He walked back down the stairs, quietly. Merrick was dozing in his chair in the study. Megan and Helene were still in the kitchen. Erik opened the sliding glass doors to the deck just enough to slip through, closed them just as carefully and took off down the stairs, never looking back.

"YOU MADE IT." Kieran was huddled in the shelter of the broad, shallow steps leading onto the sand at the end of the boardwalk. Her pretty dark eyes were red and puffy from crying. Her nose looked a little bit like Rudolph's, but he didn't say so.

"I told you I'd be here."

"You think I'm being stupid, don't you?" she said, sitting back down on the damp sand and wrapping her arms around her bare knees. "You think I should see him."

"He's your dad," Erik said, feeling his way. "He's come back to you. He could have stayed away forever, you know."

"I know." She hugged her knees more tightly.

"But that just makes it all the harder if he goes away again."

Erik could understand that. Leaving Sea Haven was the hardest thing he'd ever done. He pulled at a broken stalk of sea grass until it came loose in his hand. He twirled it between his fingers. "I think you should see your dad," he said at last. "You should hear what he has to say."

"I know what he's going to say," Kieran said fiercely. "He's going to say everything's going to be all right. He's going to say he wants to come back to town. Get us a place to live together. He'll go back to work in the bakery so Grandma and Grandpa can retire. And it will be like that for a while. And then he'll start to get lonely and tired, and pretty soon he'll be using again. And he'll go away again—"

"Maybe it will be like that," Erik admitted. "But maybe it won't. You've got to give it a chance." He took a deep breath, concentrated on tying a knot in the grass stalk so that he didn't have to look at her. "Family's the most important thing there is."

"You really mean that, don't you?" She was looking at him but he kept his eyes fixed on the grass blade, watched it blur and waver.

"Yeah. I really mean that." He hadn't left even a note behind, but Kieran would remember what he said and tell the others. "You've got a great family already. There are a lot of you. You don't have to do it alone. They'll all help your dad make it this time, right?"

"I guess so," she said not quite so belligerently. "I still don't know—"

"Give him a chance, Kieran. That's all you have to do."

"I don't have to love him," she said, once more as fierce as some warrior princess from long ago.

"No. Not if you don't want to."

She rose to her knees, turned to face him. Erik dropped the grass stem. He had himself under control. "Okay. I'll do it. Can I call you and tell you how it goes?"

"Sure," he said. Then he remembered he wouldn't be there. "But a little later, okay. I didn't sleep too good last night. I think I'll go home and crash for a while." The lies came easier now. He was getting good at it.

"Yeah. Okay. I'd better let you go right now. It's almost lunchtime, anyway."

"Yeah." She stood up. So did he. Kieran started up the steps to the boardwalk. "I think I'll go back by the road," Erik said. "It was pretty rough going along the beach. The storm really tore it up."

"A ton of really gross stuff will wash up in the next few days." She sounded more like her old self already. "Maybe we can head out tomorrow after school—if your arm feels better—and see what we can find." She swung around to face him. Her eyes were still puffy, her nose still red but she was smiling, and pretty. "Gosh, I can't believe tomorrow is the first day of school. I mean, we should have been in school today except for Fred. That's the kind of hurricane to be in, though. One that blows over a few trees and gets you an extra day of summer vac—"

She'd turned a complete circle while she was talking and was facing away from him again when she stopped dead. Erik looked past her shoulder and saw a man coming toward them. For a scary couple of seconds he thought it might be Fielder, then saw that this man was a lot taller than his nemesis. Tall and thin as a rail, with dark thinning hair and a face that was vaguely familiar. As he came closer, Erik realized the man resembled Amy's husband, Jon. Sort of. Except this guy looked a hundred years older.

"Daddy," Kieran whispered above the wind. She looked back over her shoulder at Erik. "What do I do?"

"Go on," he urged. "Remember. Family. Go to him."

Nick Costas stopped walking. Waited, searching his daughter's face. "Hi, baby," he said, his voice shaky. "I've missed you." Then he spread his hands. And with a strangled little cry Kieran ran toward him and flung herself into his arms.

Erik turned and walked away. Kieran had forgotten he was even there, and that was okay. She'd be fine even if her dad didn't make it. Jon and Amy would be there for her. Family. That made a difference.

He left the boardwalk and trudged across the gravelly sand toward the street. He'd head back down Gulfview for a block or so, and then turn north to avoid the business district. He'd hitch to Pensacola and then catch the bus to—someplace. If he was lucky and got a ride right away, he'd be at the bus station before anyone at Sea Haven even knew he was gone. The thought was like a knife thrust through his heart but he ignored the pain. He was doing the right thing.

He hadn't gone far when a beat-up old pickup was driving slowly toward him. He waited at the side of the road for it to pass. Instead, it slowed down even further, then stopped. Erik wondered if he was going to be lucky enough to get a ride so soon. Then he looked into the open window and saw who was driving the truck, and his heart stood still.

Fielder.

"Get in the truck, boy," he said in the same quiet, even voice he'd always used.

Erik shook his head. All he had to do was yell. Or turn around and run. But he couldn't do anything. His muscles and joints were frozen with fear and loathing. It was as if he was four years old again, and this man had come out of nowhere and swept him up in his arms, squeezing him so tight he couldn't make a sound.

Fielder didn't raise his voice, didn't move a muscle, except for his right hand. He picked up a gun from under a newspaper on the seat and pointed it at Erik's face. "I said, get in the truck, boy. Now."

Erik opened the door and got inside.

CHAPTER FIFTEEN

"MOM, can I speak to Megan, please?"

Amy's voice sounded strained. Helene frowned slightly as she handed the handset to Megan. "Amy wants to talk to you," she said. "Probably some party detail."

Megan tried to ignore the tiny dart of unease that pierced her heart. Every time the phone rang did not mean there was bad news. Helene was probably right. More than likely it was another last-minute party crisis that Amy wanted her help with. "Hi, Amy," she said. "What's up?"

"Is Erik with you?" Amy asked without preamble.

"He's in his room," Megan told her.

Amy didn't reply immediately. "Are you sure?" she said at last.

"Why are you asking that?" Megan realized she hadn't been able to keep the rising panic out of her voice when she saw Helene stiffen.

"What's wrong?" her mother whispered, sitting down in the chair next to Megan's.

Megan held up her hand. Amy was talking so fast her words tumbled over themselves. "And then Maida saw the boy. She was positive it was Erik— she saw the bandage on his arm, even though he was wearing a long-sleeved shirt—get in the truck with the man and head out of town toward Sea Haven.'' She paused, then, ''Are you certain he's in his room, Megan? He didn't leave Sea Haven to meet Kieran, did he? She's been so upset about Nick coming back. She was here at the store a while ago. But now she's gone. I'm not sure where. Could they be together?''

''I—I don't know. Erik promised not to leave the house alone...'' Megan let her eyes meet Helene's for just a moment, and saw her own fear mirrored in their sea-blue depths. ''Mom, could you go call Erik and ask him to come downstairs.'' Helene stood up and hurried out of the room.

''Can Mom hear me?'' Amy inquired, lowering her voice to a whisper.

''No,'' Megan replied. ''She's gone to call Erik down to the kitchen.''

''Maida swears—'' Her sister broke off. Her breathing was harsh, heavy. Fear raced along Megan's nerve endings, invaded her bloodstream and her brain and her heart.

''Amy, what are you trying to say?''

''Oh, Megan. Maida can be so scatterbrained sometimes, but I've never known her to lie. And she has the eyesight of a hawk. She says—'' Amy took a deep breath ''—she *swears*, even though she only saw this whole incident through her rearview mirror as she drove past them—''

''Amy!''

''She swears the man had a gun pointed at Erik.''

''Oh, God.'' She was through the swinging doors before the plea was past her lips. ''Mom!''

Helene was standing halfway up the stairs, staring up—at nothing. No one. "He's not answering."

Megan rushed past her, taking the stairs two at a time, the handset still pressed against her ear. She pushed open Erik's bedroom door without knocking. The room was neat and clean. And empty. Nothing was out of place. Nothing was missing—except her son. "Oh, Amy. He's gone."

"Where is he?"

Megan whirled at the sound of Helene's startled question. She hadn't even realized her mother had followed her into Erik's room. "I don't know, Mom."

Amy was still talking, but Megan's heart was pounding so hard the beats echoed in her ears and she couldn't understand her sister's words. "You said Maida saw the truck head out this way," she interrupted without ceremony. "Toward Sea Haven? That makes no sense. It's a dead-end road. It leads nowhere but the beach property."

"Oh, God, it's that man...Fielder, isn't it? He's got Erik." Helene was unable to remain silent.

Megan held her free hand to her other ear. She couldn't keep track of both their words at the same time. "Amy, Noah is at the sheriff's office. Please call there and tell him what's happened."

"What are you going to do?" The question came from her mother and her sister simultaneously.

"I'm going to get my son," she replied, looking at Helene as she spoke to Amy. "There's *no* way I'm going to lose him again."

HIS ARM HURT like hell. Blood had already soaked through the bandage and was dripping off his fingers into the swampy ground where he was hiding in the tall grass. He'd landed on it, hard, in the sharp stones and gravel at the side of the road when he'd thrown himself out of Fielder's truck. He'd felt the stitches tear out of the flesh, and the blood start to run warm and stinging down his arm. For a moment, thinking about it, Erik got sick to his stomach all over again.

But it had been worth it, a small price to pay for getting away. And it hadn't slowed him down. Much. Yet. He'd made it almost to the dunes that rose up behind the beach, but he was breathing hard, and if he lifted his head, anything he looked at tended to swirl in slow dizzying circles.

He'd never thought he could do it. He'd never thought he could get away from his tormentor. Never thought he'd be able to make his voice work again, let alone get Fielder to believe that the road they were on wasn't a dead end but a shortcut to the highway. But he had. He'd looked the asshole right in the eye and lied his head off. And Fielder had believed him.

At least for a while. Long enough for Erik to make a plan. Then when it became obvious the road went nowhere and Fielder got real quiet and real mad, started driving too fast and got to fishtailing around, that's when Erik had bailed.

He closed his eyes and rested his forehead on the spongy ground. *If only he could have gotten the gun away from Fielder first.* He could have flung the pistol into the swamp and just kept on running until he was safe inside the walls of Sea Haven. But even though he'd had it in his hand, he hadn't been able to hang on to it when he threw himself out the passenger door. Fielder had snatched it back just before he lost control of the truck and ended up with the two driver's-side wheels hubcap deep in the sand.

He lifted his head slowly, blinked hard to clear his vision and looked around, wincing at the pain that shot up his arm. He refused to let himself imagine that there might be snakes this close to the ocean, or that an alligator somewhere nearby had smelled blood and was heading his way.

Fielder was off in the distance, working his way toward the scrub oak and palmettos that edged the pine woods nearer the highway. Erik was going to have to make a run for the beach. It was a straight shot back to Sea Haven. Almost two miles. A long run on a good day. And this definitely wasn't a good day. But he could make it. He had to. All he needed was a couple of minutes' head start and he'd be out of range of Fielder's gun. Only a couple of minutes. Erik took one more look at the man who had terrorized him for so long, saw that Fielder was still moving away from him, obviously convinced that Erik had made for the woods. Erik pulled himself up with a grunt.

He spun around and started running. Even though the dunes were low, he was winded by the time he got to the broad crest. Erik took one quick look over his shoulder, saw Fielder start to turn toward him and threw himself over the top. He rolled halfway down the other side, sand in his mouth, the sound of the angry, storm-tossed gulf loud in his ears.

He picked himself up and looked around, dizzy and nauseated. His arm felt as if it was on fire. He shoved his hand into the pocket of his jeans and looked around, hoping against hope that maybe someone was out walking the shoreline, looking for shells, or storm salvage, or just checking out the damage to the beach. Not a soul in sight. Haze and mist rolled over the sand, obscuring his view of Hurricane Beach in the distance. It seemed very far away, out of reach.

Erik looked the other direction. The same. Nothing man-made anywhere in sight, except the old pier. He stumbled toward it. He had no choice. He wasn't going to make it all the way back to Sea Haven. He needed a place to hide out and get his arm to stop bleeding, rest a little, wait until dark and then try to make it back home.

It might work. Fielder hated water. He couldn't swim. He wouldn't try to wade the ten yards through high surf to get out to the pier. Erik started running again. He sprinted across the wet sand, stumbling through holes eroded by the storm, dodging debris and uprooted clumps of sea oats whose long tangled roots threatened to reach out and wrap around his ankles, bringing him down.

The fence his grandfather had erected along the water's edge was gone, knocked over by the force of the storm waves. Erik stumbled out into the surf, buffered here by the wooden pilings but still strong and treacherous, and fought his way through the thigh-high water to the ladder. He grabbed hold and hoisted himself up one rung, then two. Now he was in water only to his knees. Six more rungs and he had it made. It was going to take some doing to pull himself up with only one good hand, but he'd make it. He had to. He was close. So close.

He turned his head, took one last look over his shoulder. And saw Fielder watching him from the top of the dune. The man had spotted him after all. And he'd run faster than Erik ever thought he could. Or perhaps, his eyes had been playing tricks on him, and Fielder had been much closer to Erik's hiding place than he had appeared. It didn't matter now. His nemesis was almost to the water's edge.

So much for his theory that his kidnapper's fear of water would keep Erik safe on the pier. The man never broke stride, just kept coming. Already knee-deep in the surf, Fielder motioned at him with his gun. "Keep climbing," he ordered never raising his voice, just like always. He reached out to grab hold of the rusty iron ladder. "You didn't really think you'd get away from me that easy, did you?"

NOAH WALKED down the steps of the Hurricane Beach sheriff's office and patted down his shirt pocket looking for his sunglasses. It had stopped raining earlier that morning and the clouds had a watery, luminous sheen to them that bounced off the pale brick and glass of the town hall. If he remembered anything about this climate at all it meant the sun was trying its damnedest to break through.

Obviously the natives felt the same way. Everywhere along Gulfview there was bustle and activity. Fred was gone. A near miss. The town's luck had held. The legend was intact. Storm shutters and taped X's were coming off windows. Planters of flowers and umbrella tables, and their matching chairs were appearing on patios and porches. Stores were open and it was business as usual in Hurricane Beach.

It was time he got back to Sea Haven to help Merrick open the heavy wooden storm shutters. Erik could help. It would give him something to take his mind off Fielder.

His meeting with the sheriff had gone as well as could be expected. The FBI agent from the New Orleans field office would arrive late that evening, or first thing Wednesday morning. The sheriff had informed him that Fielder's Jeep with a blown engine, but no sign of the man himself, had been found in the parking lot of a honky-tonk bar outside of Tallahassee. A '79 Chevy pickup had been reported stolen from the same parking lot sometime over the weekend—the owner had been on a holiday bender and couldn't remember where he'd left it until he sobered up Monday night—and all area law enforcement agencies had been alerted to be on the lookout for both man and truck.

Noah had sent Jamieson off to check out the lead, anyway. He'd left Hurricane Beach about fifteen minutes ago. Noah hefted the cellular-phone case that Jamieson had given him onto the front seat of his car and started to swing into the seat when he heard his name.

"Noah! Noah!" Amy rushed toward him holding her side, as though she'd been running. He slammed the car door, walked round the vehicle and met her at the curb.

"Amy, what's wrong? What are you doing here?"

"Looking for you," she said, panting, leaning one hand on the hood of his car.

"What's happened?" The slight uneasiness that he'd experienced all through the meeting with the sheriff coalesced into ice-cold dread.

"It's Erik. He's gone. Maida saw him get in a truck with a man that could be Fielder. He had a gun. Megan went after him."

God, Megan and Erik both at a madman's mercy. "How long ago, Amy?" he said, willing his voice even, neutral, so that he didn't scare her even more than she already was.

"Just a couple of minutes. Five at the most. I called the sheriff's office, but the dispatcher thought you'd already left. By the time she put me through, you really had, I guess I came running down here, hoping to catch you, somehow." She tried to smile, but only managed a twist of her lips. She was still panting with exertion. "If not, I was going to go inside screaming for help at the top of my lungs." She would have too, he had no doubt. "Hurry, Noah. Let's go tell the sheriff."

"Amy, listen to me. You go inside. Tell the dispatcher and the sheriff exactly what you told me. There's no time to waste. I'm going after both of them."

MEGAN SAW the truck ahead of her, half on, half off the narrow track, its wheels stuck in the mud at the side of the road. She made herself walk up to the open passenger-side window, look inside. There was no sign of the driver. No sign of her son. But there were dark stains on the grass and gravel at the side of the road. She bent down, touched her fingers to the darkness. They came away covered with blood.

Fresh bloodstains. She swallowed hard against a wave of fear and nausea.

Megan rubbed her hand down her shorts, trying to scrub away the blood and control the fear. A movement in the distance caught her eye. A man, not a boy, crossing the dunes. She ran after him. She crested the dune just in time to see two figures climb onto the pier and disappear into the old shack. The second figure was Erik wearing the blue chambray shirt and jeans they'd bought the week before.

Megan dropped to the sand, keeping out of sight, catching her breath. She didn't know what to do, stay where she was and wait for help, or climb onto the pier herself? She closed her eyes, remembered the blood beside the pickup, and made up her mind. She started running again toward the pier, stumbling over the edge of the half-buried chain-link fence, falling to her knees in the heavy surf. She made a grab for the iron ladder as another powerful surge of seawater almost washed her feet out from under her and began to climb.

And then, there was Byron Fielder. He'd waited until she'd pulled herself up onto the splintered wooden planking to step out of the sagging doorway of the shack. He motioned toward her with the muzzle of the pistol he held in his hand. "Who the hell are you?"

"I'm Erik's mother," she said, ignoring the gun, keeping her eyes locked to his. Brown eyes, filled with hostility. Medium height, medium build. Receding hairline, a slight paunch around the middle. He was wearing a plain brown T-shirt and faded jeans and a John Deere ball cap. A very ordinary-looking middle-aged man.

Except for the fact that he was a kidnapper, a child stealer.

Except for the fact that he looked as if he wouldn't hesitate for a moment to blow her to kingdom come.

CHAPTER SIXTEEN

"OH BABY," Megan whispered, kneeling beside Erik after Fielder had pushed her into the shack. Her son was sitting with his back against the wall, his legs stretched out in front of him. His clothes were dark—obviously wet through. "Let me see your arm. I thought you promised me to take better care of yourself," she scolded, trying for a light note, but not quite succeeding.

"Sorry, Mom. I guess I forgot." Erik tried to smile, but all he managed was a grimace that twisted up one corner of his mouth. His eyes were dark holes in his pale face. "I felt the stitches tear out when I jumped out of the truck."

"It's okay," Megan said, smoothing the hair back from his forehead. His skin was cool beneath her fingers, yet clammy to the touch. He was shivering and Megan was sure he was going into shock. "Let me see."

He turned his head to look at his arm. "It hurts."

"I know," she said, laying it back across his lap. He was bleeding badly, but she did her best to keep her fear out of her voice. She looked over her shoulder at Byron Fielder who was standing behind her and a little to the right, blocking the doorway and most of the light. "I need something to bandage his arm. He's losing a lot of blood."

"I ain't got nothing but what I'm standing up in," Fielder said. "Don't look like you've got much to spare, either." His eyes traveled up and down her shorts and sleeveless blouse with casual insolence. "Use the sleeve of his shirt."

Megan reached up and tried to tear the shoulder seam of Erik's shirt, but the fabric was new and strong and refused to yield. Fielder bent down and pulled a wicked-looking hunting knife from a carrier strapped to his boot.

"Get out of my way." She scooted over as he dropped to his knee and cut the sleeve free. "Hurry up. I don't want him passing out on me. He's too big to carry anymore."

He's too big to carry anymore. How many times through the empty years had she and Noah ached to carry their son in their arms. She hated this man with all her heart and soul. Her hands balled into fists, her nails bit into her palms. "Give me that." She jerked the shirtsleeve out of his hand.

Moving far more quickly than Megan thought possible, Fielder reached out and grabbed a handful of her hair. "Don't get mouthy," he said in a voice of quiet menace. "I don't like sassy women."

Megan bit back a sharp reply. She couldn't afford to challenge this man until she had figured a way to get herself and Erik off the pier. "Okay," she said meekly, her eyes downcast. Fielder let go of her hair and it tumbled free of the soft knot on the top of her head. She brushed it back behind her ears with hands that trembled despite her best efforts to keep them steady. "I'm sorry. Just let me bandage his arm."

Fielder watched her through narrowed eyes. "Go ahead. Like I said, he's too big to carry." He turned away to look out the door of the windowless shack.

"Don't get him started," Erik, whispered as she wound the torn sleeve around his arm as tightly as possible. "He wouldn't think twice about hitting a woman. He's done it often enough."

"Just hang on," Megan whispered back, ripping a strip off the frayed edge of the fabric to tie the bandage in place. "Help will be here soon. Your father will come looking for us."

"How did you know I was here?" Erik asked, grimacing with pain as she tightened the knot.

"Maida passed Fielder's truck when he picked you up. She was pretty sure it was you. And she was convinced she saw a gun. She watched him drive off in the direction of Sea Haven and she told Amy." The steady drip of blood down the back of his hand slowed as the makeshift pressure bandage did its work. Megan breathed a sigh of relief. "Then Amy called me."

"Maida's the fat lady from the gallery? With the little dog?" Erik rolled his head from side to side. "I don't remember seeing her."

"I imagine you had other things on your mind. Anyway, what matters is that she saw you." Megan sat back on her heels. The sounds of wind and waves were muted inside the small shack, but she could feel the pounding of the storm surf against the pilings. The whole structure shuddered and swayed when a particularly strong wave roared onto shore. The pier was a death trap.

"I tricked him into coming this way," Erik said as Megan strove to ignore the disconcerting and disorienting movement beneath her. "We drove right by Sea Haven but no one was outside."

"We thought you were safe in your room."

"I thought I could outrun him if I got out of the truck. I would have made it, too, if I hadn't fallen on my arm."

She patted his hand. "We'll get out of this, okay. I promise."

He looked past her to the man in the doorway. "Yeah. Sure." He dropped his voice a little lower. "Mom?"

"Yes?"

"There's something I want to tell you. It's about some money." She hated the way his eyes kept flickering past her to Fielder. "I...I took it from Granddad's safe. In case...in case I needed to get away. I was going to pay it back. Honest."

"It doesn't matter." She wrapped her arms around her knees, made herself stay still and calm.

"Yes, it does. I only took it because I was scared." Once more his dark gaze met hers. "I was going to send it back as soon as I got a job somewhere. I swear it."

"I wish you had come to me or your father. Told us how frightened you were."

He leaned his head against the wall, closed his eyes in exhaustion and defeat. "I wish I had, too. But I didn't want to talk about it. To talk about him. And I didn't want to cause any more trouble between you and Dad. I know...I know you don't want to stay together but you were going to because of me.''

"That's not true, Erik. Your father and I haven't settled anything between us, but we both love you. We love you more than anything else on earth. You believe that, don't you?''

He smiled again, Noah's smile and her heart almost burst with love. "I know that now. I'm sorry. But it doesn't change anything. I knew Fielder'd come for me. I've known it all along. And this time I'll never get away from him. I...I tried before—''

"I know, Erik.'' She brushed her hand over his hair again, let her fingers linger on his cheek for a few precious seconds. "I overheard you telling your father about the gun.'' Had it only been two days ago they had been eating quiche and having a family picture taken? "I wish you would have told me then, too.''

"I didn't want you to think I was a freak. A weirdo, like he is. I couldn't do it. I couldn't kill a man just like that.''

"I know.'' She took his uninjured hand between both her own, squeezed it tight. "You're going to be a fine, strong man, just like your father.''

He nodded wearily. "Tell Dad I—''

"Put a lid on it over there,'' Fielder said, barely raising his voice as he stared out the open doorway. "I'm trying to figure out what to do.''

"I'll tell you what to do,'' Megan said, getting to her knees. Her voice sounded thin and reedy. She took a deep breath to steady it and almost gagged. The heat and humidity in the small, windowless shack was oppressive. The smell of mold and decay was overpowering and beneath it all was the coppery scent of new blood. "You can help me get my son onto dry land, and then you can take my car and go wherever the hell you want to go. I won't try to stop you. I won't send anyone after you. Just go away and leave us alone. Do you hear me? That's what you can do."

Fielder didn't move from the doorway, he simply pointed the barrel of the pistol directly in her face and said, "Shut up. You don't talk unless I tell you to."

Megan ignored the gun. "Look, if you leave now you can get away before anyone spots you. I'm driving a rental. There are dozens of them in town. I don't know the license number or even the make and model. By the time the police get the information from the rental agency you'll be hundreds of miles away."

"I said shut up. I need time to think. And I don't need any half-assed plan from the likes of you."

"Mom." Erik reached out and tugged on the hem of her shorts. "I said don't get him mad."

"Be quiet, boy. I'll deal with you later." Fielder's tone was menacing.

"I'm offering you the only chance you have to get away," Megan went on. "My husband knows where I've gone. Sooner or later he'll find us."

"Husband? You aren't wearing a wedding ring."

"Erik's father will come for us," she said, lifting her eyes from the barrel of the gun to focus on his ordinary—terrifying—face.

His eyes darted to Erik's huddled figure for a moment. "So you found yourself a new old man, too, huh, kid?"

"You're not my old man. You'd better listen to what she's saying," Erik said, meeting Fielder's flat brown gaze. "My dad will come after us. He's a SEAL."

"Hell. A navy SEAL? Well, I'll be damned. Ain't that just my luck."

"We're running out of time. I'll do anything you want. I'll go with you now," Erik said, resignation in his voice. "I'll stay with you forever. Just let my mom go, okay?"

"I can't let her go," Fielder stated. "But you and me are going to leave, all right. Kidnapping's a federal offense. A frying offense, and last time I checked they've got the death penalty in this state. You're the only one who can testify against me. I can't wait around for no hick-town sheriff to catch up with us. Especially if he's getting his orders from a SEAL."

Megan fought down a wave of panic. Had Erik's revelation of Noah's identity pushed Fielder over the edge? She had to do something. She couldn't just sit here and let her son be taken from her again. She searched the calm, almost expressionless face above her. Yes, she thought, horrified, this man would kill without compunction.

"Come on, son. We've wasted too much time here already." Fielder reached out and grabbed Erik by his injured arm, hauling him upright. The boy bit off a cry of pain, stood swaying groggily, then sagged against the wall.

Megan surged to her feet. "Don't call him that, you bastard," she said, feeling heat and anger race through her veins, dilute the paralyzing fear that had kept her on her knees. "He's my son. Not yours. Do you hear me? My son."

Fielder dropped Erik's arm and in the same motion slapped Megan across the mouth. The blow snapped her head back. Spots danced before her eyes, her head spun, she tasted blood from a cut on the inside of her cheek.

"He's my Diana's boy, and don't you go thinking otherwise. He has been since the day I brought him home. I don't want any more lip out of you."

"Mom!" Erik pushed himself away from the wall and his arms came around her. He held her tight, and she felt the frantic beating of his heart against her arm. "Don't you ever touch her again." His voice was steady and hard, a man's voice.

Fielder blinked in surprise at his defiance, but recovered quickly. "Shut up." Fielder unbuckled his belt and pulled the worn leather strap through the belt loops. "Step aside, son. I'll deal with you later."

"No!"

"Erik, do what he says."

"No! I've changed my mind. I'm not going anywhere with him. Never again."

Megan couldn't take her eyes off Fielder's face. His expression was terrifying, and filled with purpose. "Erik. Listen to me. Do what he says."

Fielder was advancing on them, the belt doubled in one hand, the gun, never wavering from her chest, in the other. "I'm just going to tie you up. If your husband's as smart as you think he is, he'll find you soon enough. If he isn't..." He chuckled. "Well, let's just hope you can swim with your hands tied behind your back. Move away, Erik. Now!''

"Go on, Erik." Megan gave him a little push. "I'll be all right."

"That's right, lady. Do what I say and you won't get hurt. Otherwise... I don't much care. Maybe none of us will live through this." His eyes sought Erik's and held his gaze. "His momma. The fine woman who raised him. She'd be right glad to see him in Heaven with her and our little Reggie. I got no qualms about meeting my maker. You might tell them that when they find you. If they find you," he added, smiling at Megan now. "Turn around and cross your hands behind your back."

He stuck the pistol in the waistband of his jeans to deal with her and Megan knew she would never have another chance. She launched herself at him with a strength born of desperation. Caught off guard, Fielder stumbled backward through the doorway onto the rotting planking of the pier, Megan on top of him. She felt the breath go out of him. He lay still for a moment, stunned by the unexpectedness of her attack and the fall.

She twisted her head, saw Erik come stumbling out of the shack, blinking against the strong light, swaying dizzily. "We have to get the gun," she said between clenched teeth.

She made a grab for the grip of the pistol but Fielder was already recovering. His big, hard hand closed over her wrist, grinding bone against bone. She cried out as he rolled over on top of her, trapping her left arm painfully beneath her body as he pinned her with his weight. She tried to scratch his face with her free hand but he pulled the gun out of his waist-band and shoved the barrel against her throat. "You bitch," he snarled, his breath hot and stale in her face. "I ought to kill you for that trick."

"No!" Erik launched himself at Fielder, but he brushed the boy aside like an annoying fly. Erik went down in a heap and didn't get back up.

Megan could see nothing but her assailant's face. She didn't know how badly Erik was hurt. The gun barrel digging into the soft flesh of her throat choked off her breath, the groan and creek of strained timbers and the ceaseless roar of the surf filled her head with the sound and fury. Death stood at her shoulder; she had never been more scared and she had never wanted to live more. She fought to be free of Fielder's weight with all the strength she had left. He grunted in pain as her knee connected with his testicles.

"Bitch," he muttered again. He lifted the pistol above his head. Megan braced herself for the blow of the gun barrel across her cheek. Instead, Fielder's weight was suddenly lifted from her body. A figure, sleek and dark and wet, was silhouetted momentarily against the metallic gray of the sky.

Noah. His name echoed in her head, but she had no breath to speak it aloud.

"Dad!" Erik yelled.

Megan caught a quick glimpse of Noah as she rolled away from the struggling men. He was wearing nothing but a pair of soaking-wet jeans. His face was set in a mask of fierce concentration. Seawater ran in crystal rivulets from his hair and down his arms and the broad expanse of his back as he wrestled Fielder to the decking of the old pier.

Noah's fingers were clamped around Fielder's wrist. He slammed his hand down onto the splintered wood, once. Twice. The third time the gun flew from Fielder's mangled fingers and skidded toward the edge of the pier.

"Get it," Erik said hoarsely in Megan's ear. He was sitting up against the outside of the shack, but his face was as pale as the whitecaps surging past the base of the pier. "Get the gun, Mom!"

Megan scrambled upright as Fielder managed to roll out from under Noah and began scuttling, crab-like, in the same direction. Megan half ran, half crawled, oblivious to the splinters digging into her hands and knees, intent only on reaching the weapon before Fielder did.

She almost made it. She groped for the gun, half blinded by her windblown hair in her eyes. She saw movement at the edge of her vision but couldn't tell what it was. She lurched forward, stretched out her body, her arm. Her fingers had curved around the pistol's grip at the same time as Fielder's foot came down on her wrist. She screamed in pain, pushing at his steel-toed shoe with her free hand. He didn't budge, just reached down to pull the hunting knife from its carrier. Megan ignored the agony of her crushed fingers and grabbed his wrist, frantic to keep him from the weapon.

Then, once more Fielder's weight was lifted from her. She turned her head in time to see Noah, one hand on Fielder's shoulder, one hand hooked in the waistband of his jeans, plant his foot to throw him to the deck. But as he did so the weather-beaten planking gave way. His leg disappeared to the knee. With a grunt he threw himself sideways to keep from dropping through the jagged hole onto the crumbled concrete pilings and angry surf twenty feet below.

Fielder twisted from Noah's grip and landed hard ten feet from Megan. He jumped to his feet, shaking his head groggily. Blood trickled from a cut at the side of his mouth. His face was twisted with fury. His head swung back and forth as his eyes searched for the gun. It was almost under his feet. He took a half step backward, his heel striking the weapon, sending it skittering over the edge into the sea. Fielder swore softly. He groped for the hunting knife at his ankle. He half crouched with it in his hand, waiting to pounce as Noah dragged himself heavily to his feet, his jeans torn, his left foot bloody, his left arm scraped raw from shoulder to elbow.

He was hurt and unarmed, the advantage of his superior height and strength, his familiarity with the martial arts effectively nullified. Fielder, canny and clever, waited patiently for an opening to skirt the gaping hole and move in for the kill.

Megan was between Noah and Fielder. But there was nothing she could do to stop the man. Yet Fielder was vulnerable, too. He was standing only inches from the edge of the pier. If somehow, some way, she could knock him off balance, he might go over the edge. She pulled her knees up against her chest, curling herself into a ball. If she came at him low and hard she just might be able to pull it off. He was so close to the edge. So close.

She braced her hands on the damp, rotting wooden

planks like a runner in the starting blocks as Fielder rose to his full height. She moved her head slightly, felt Noah's dark glittering gaze skim over her for a brief second.

"Megan, No!" he growled, and Fielder's head swung in her direction, assessing the new threat.

It was the opportunity Noah must have been waiting for. He charged Fielder, clearing the jagged edges of the rotten planks, catching Erik's kidnapper low to the ground in a bruising tackle that sent them over the edge.

"Noah!" The scream tore itself from Megan's throat. In less than a second she was at the pier's edge, looking down at a scene that she knew would be engraved on her memory for the rest of her life.

Noah clung to the rusty rungs of the iron ladder, Fielder clamped to his leg, waist-deep in the churning, wave-tossed water. The knife was still clutched in his hand, his face twisted in a grimace of mingled terror and rage. Noah's left arm was useless, his face a mask of stoic calm, intense concentration, almost unrecognizable. Fielder had his legs manacled in a death grip as he attempted to climb past Noah to the relative safety of the pier.

Megan's heart beat wildly against her chest. At the moment Fielder seemed intent only on fighting his way out of the buffeting waves, saving himself from being sucked into the gulf by the treacherous rip currents that swirled around the pier and along the shoreline. But if he regained his purchase on the rickety rust-weakened ladder, he would kill all of them.

"Mom! We've got to do something." Erik was

beside her, stretched out along the pier, a length of broken planking in his hand.

Fielder grabbed Noah's arm, wringing a groan of pain from his lips that tore through Megan like a lance blade. "Noah." Tears streamed down her face, blurring her vision.

Fielder had made it up one more rung. Noah twisted away from him, freeing his leg. With a powerful upward thrust of his knee he caught Fielder full in the rib cage. Fielder's mouth opened in a silent scream. He surged upward, his arm curling around Noah's neck in a choke hold. He lifted his knife hand high overhead, ready to bring it down in a slashing arc that would bury the blade deep in Noah's chest.

For Megan time stood still. Erik's wild cry of fear and denial reverberated endlessly along her frozen nerve ends. For what seemed an eternity, but could have been no more than the merest fraction of a second, her eyes locked with Noah's. His expression had not changed. His message for her was in his eyes, dark, flashing with pain and purpose. And she knew. Knew beyond doubt that he intended to keep his promise to protect their son even if it meant his own death.

Noah twisted in Fielder's grasp, loosening his stranglehold, kicking away from the pier. In that last split second, Fielder knew, too, what Noah intended. The knife tumbled into the sea as Fielder's hand flailed in thin air, striving to find a hold on the ladder. But it was too late, Noah's good hand curved around his shoulder dragging him into the sea, and the angry waves and the currents took them both.

Megan scrambled to her feet, sobbing with terror

and a sense of loss as powerful as what she had felt when Erik disappeared. For a moment, a heartbeat only, she thought she caught a glimpse of a sleek dark head above the wave tops, already a hundred yards or more from where she stood.

"Noah!" She couldn't tell if Fielder was still clinging like a weight around his neck. Noah was a big man and he was hurt. But she was a strong swimmer. She might be able to reach him. She had to try. Megan stood up, keeping her eye on the spot where she thought, hoped, prayed she'd seen Noah surface. She kicked off her shoes, started to run for the far end of the pier. She hadn't taken two steps when a long, bronzed arm circled her waist with a viselike grip and hauled her back against a soaking wet chest and body as hard as reinforced concrete.

"I can't let you do that, Mrs. Carson. The commander would have my hide if I let you dive off this pier into that kind of surf."

Megan twisted her head around to find herself staring up into Kyle Jamieson's blue eyes. His voice was low-pitched, unthreatening, but his expression was the one she'd seen on Noah's face. She didn't even put up a fight.

"He's hurt. He'll never be able to swim against those currents."

"Yes, he will." He gave her a quick grin, a mere curve of his lips. "He'll make it."

She wanted to believe but she could not. "He needs help." She couldn't seem to control the sobs that racked her chest. "Please. Let me go."

"The surf's too heavy now. You'd be committing suicide."

"Then you go. You were a SEAL. You've surely been in seas like this before. Please."

He shook his head. "I can't do that, ma'am. My orders are to stay with you and the boy."

"Oh, God," she whispered, horror and loss rippling through her. "If you had only gotten here a few seconds earlier."

His right hand held a gun she hadn't noticed until then. "I tried," he said quietly. "I couldn't get a clean shot at Fielder from the shore." He dropped his arm, shoving the weapon out of sight at the small of his back. "Commander Carson sent me off to Tallahassee to check out Fielder's Jeep." He wasn't looking at her now, his eyes were searching the angry gulf. "I didn't get more than five miles out of town when he called me on the car phone I gave him and told me to get my sorry ass out here as fast as I could. I think I broke a land-speed record or two on the way. But it just wasn't fast enough."

"You did your best." Her eyes followed his. Nothing. Only a few wind-tossed seabirds skimming low over the roiling waters.

It was too late.

Noah was gone and she had never had the chance to tell him she loved him. For a moment she wanted to die, too. Somehow, what she'd been thinking must have shown on her face.

"Mom!" Erik's voice broke with emotion. He took a shaky step toward her. "Mom, it's okay. Dad'll be okay. But Fielder can't swim. He hates the water. That's why I thought I'd be safe out here. Dad must have figured that out. That's why he did what

he did. To keep Fielder from coming back after us.''
His eyes looked glazed and his knees sagged.

"Erik? Oh God, Erik. Are you all right?"

"He's okay, aren't you, buddy?" Jamieson said,
supporting Erik with an arm around his shoulders.

"Yeah, just a little dizzy."

"We have to get him to the hospital. He's lost a
lot of blood." Megan rubbed her hands across her
cheeks, drying the sting of tears from her face. She
would cry later. When she was alone. She had all the
rest of her life to mourn for Noah. Erik had to come
first.

"The ambulance and the sheriff are already on the
beach. Can you make it under your own steam,
buddy?"

"I'll make it."

"This way, ma'am." Megan followed him in a
daze, climbed down the ladder, let a soaking wet
sheriff's deputy standing in the waist-high surf in full
uniform, help her onto the beach.

She blinked at the number of people at the base
of the pier. For the last hour she'd felt as though she
and Erik and Fielder—and Noah—had been the last
four people on earth. Now she saw her mother and
father coming toward her. The sheriff and at least
three deputies were milling around on the sand. The
emergency medical squad with Hurricane Beach's
beach rescue unit, a dune buggy equipped with a
gurney anchored over the back seat, were advancing
on Kyle and Erik. A Florida State highway patrolman
was talking into a cellular phone, and Amy was
sprinting down the dunes.

Helene hurried toward them, her fine white hair

lifting in the brisk breeze that had begun to blow tattered holes in the cloud cover. "Megan. Child, are you all right? Is Erik okay?" She swept Megan into her arms and held her tight.

Already the paramedics were swarming around Erik. The boy shook his head, staying close to Jamieson who kept an arm around his shoulders. Erik waved off down the beach. "Go find my dad," he told the emergency workers. "He needs help worse than I do."

"We had to come," Helene said. "We couldn't stay at Sea Haven watching first Noah and then the sheriff and the emergency squad and half the town drive by," Helene looked deep into Megan's eyes. "Where is Noah?"

Megan turned her head, her eyes drawn to the endless march of waves along the beach. "He's gone."

"Megan, what happened out there?" Her father had joined them at the water's edge. His voice was a low soothing growl.

"Fielder—"

"Mrs. Carson," a paramedic interrupted before she could answer. "You really should let us treat your son."

Erik had moved a few feet down the beach, still defiantly shaking his head, his eyes searching, searching. Megan held out her arms and he came into her embrace. She kissed his cheek, shut her eyes against the almost overpowering surge of love that washed over her as he rested his forehead against hers.

"Dad's gonna make it. I know he will. I'm going to wait right here for him."

She wrapped her arms tight around him, careful not to jar his injured arm. She smiled for Erik's sake, though her heart was a stone-cold weight in her chest. "We're not going anywhere," she said, shaking her head at the earnest young woman still hovering nearby. "We're not leaving this beach without my husband."

Helene was crying softly as Merrick held her in his arms. The sheriff and his deputies began to shout orders to one another as Jamieson gave them details of what had occurred. Vaguely Megan was aware they were making plans to call in a search plane, contact the Coast Guard. She paid no attention, just kept watching the water, making herself breathe in and out, fighting tears, fighting despair. Waiting with her son for the miracle she didn't believe would come.

And then she felt Erik stiffen, pull away from her. "Mom," he whispered. "Do you see what I see?"

She blinked hard to clear the tears from her eyes. Far down the beach a lone figure emerged from the waves. Erik stumbled away from her. She reached out to pull him back. "Don't go," she warned. "It might be—" Then she fell silent. Her heart was beating hard and fast so high up in her throat her words were stilled.

"That's not Fielder," Erik called back over his shoulder. "It's Dad!"

Noah was walking toward them now, limping slightly, his left arm cradled against his chest. Erik ran full tilt into his outstretched arm. Megan started forward, slowly at first, not daring to hope, not quite daring to believe she'd been granted another miracle.

And then her husband looked at her over their son's head and smiled.

"Noah? Oh, God, Noah." And then she was flying along the beach, rushing to catch up with Erik, rushing to be reunited with her husband and her son.

CHAPTER SEVENTEEN

Saturday evening—The Anniversary Party

THE LOWER LEVEL of the marina's restaurant was filled with friends and neighbors helping to celebrate Merrick and Helene's special day. The room was decorated with gold and white balloons and festive streamers. Fresh flowers floated in crystal globes on the tables, candlelight flickered against the darkened windows.

The party was everything Amy had wanted it to be. Now, seated between her sisters, she surveyed the scene with a satisfied eye, before leaning down to rub her ankle. "Whatever possessed me to wear high heels? I hate high heels. And I've been on my feet for hours."

"You wore them because that drop-dead gorgeous dress would look ridiculous with sneakers." Lisa chuckled, taking a sip of champagne.

Megan smiled at the easy bantering tone of her sisters' exchange. For longer than she cared to remember, a conversation like this would have been impossible between the three of them. But no more. Today they were truly family again. "It *is* a beautiful dress, Amy. And you look lovely in it." The dress was hunter green with touches of beading at the collar and cuffs, both the design and the color accentuating Amy's slender height and the strawberry blond of her hair.

"I'm just jealous," Lisa said. "If I'd known you were going to have such a great dress for the party I would have gone shopping myself." Her tailored gray suit was set off by a persimmon-red silk blouse and chunky gold jewelry. The effect was sleek and sophisticated, a look that suited her well.

"I wouldn't care if you were wearing a feed sack just so long as you're here." Amy continued, reaching past Megan to give Lisa's hand a quick squeeze.

Lisa's smile grew a little brighter, a little softer. "You both knew all along I couldn't stay away, didn't you, big sisters?"

Matt and Lisa had arrived just before lunch and closeted themselves in the study with Helene and Merrick for over an hour. When they emerged, Lisa's eyes were bright with tears, and Helene was openly crying. But there were no more secrets between them, Lisa told Megan later as she perched on the edge of Megan's bed, her fingers tracing the outline of the yellow and blue starburst designs on the coverlet. She and Matt had told Helene and Merrick everything. The past was all out in the open and the healing could begin.

"*Megan* said you'd be here." Amy took a sip of ginger ale from her own champagne flute. "I have to admit I was worried. But Megan said family would always win out in the end. And she was right."

Megan didn't want Amy to start getting sentimental again. Her own emotions were too near the surface these days, she couldn't be certain of her control. "Oh, look," she said. "Mom and Dad are going to dance." The three-man combo in the corner of the room had launched into a Glen Miller medley, and several couples, including Merrick and Helene, were making their way to the dance floor. "Doesn't Mom look beautiful in that dress." Helene's evening suit was a designer original, white with a gauzy overlay heavily encrusted with beading and seed pearls.

"God, I hope I have that good a figure at her age," Amy said wistfully. "And Dad looks like a million bucks in his tux. Where's Ian? He should be getting a picture of this."

"He's photographing the cake," Lisa informed her, rolling her eyes at Megan. "Exactly as you told him to do not two minutes ago, General Costas."

"My mother-in-law would have me tarred and feathered and ridden out of town on a rail if Ian didn't photograph it in all its glory." Amy stood up, craning her neck to spot the diminutive photographer. The cake, five tiers tall and covered with ten pounds of sugar roses and icing latticework, was indeed a sight to behold. Leda and Aurelia Costas had personally overseen its creation from beginning to end, including transportation from the Costas Family Bakery and the final setup on a white linen-covered table that held pride of place in the center of the room.

Before Amy could sit down again, Kieran sailed into view with Erik in tow. "Hey. Look. There's your mom and your aunts all together. Quick, Erik. Take a shot of them."

"Please no," Lisa said, holding up a restraining hand. "I've been seeing spots before my eyes ever since we left the church." Merrick and Helene had renewed their marriage vows in a private candlelight ceremony a few hours before. "No more flashbulbs going off in my face. I'm going on strike. Go bug Jon and Matt."

"They're outside on the deck having a beer."

"Uncle Jon says champagne gives him indigestion. "Pretty please," Kieran wheedled. "Erik needs all the practice he can get."

Erik grinned and held up Helene's camera for their inspection. An inch of gauze bandage stuck out beneath the cuff of his shirt, although he seemed to have no problem using his injured arm. "C'mon, Aunt Lisa. I'm getting pretty good at this despite what Kieran says."

"All right." Lisa gave in with a smile. She smiled much more easily now, it seemed to Megan. She and Matt were planning to marry before Christmas and had already opened their home and their hearts to Julie and her babies, tiny darlings whose pictures Lisa proudly carried in her wallet. God willing, Lisa would someday have babies of her own to cherish, a fulfillment Megan wished for her sister with all her heart.

"Aunt Amy, scoot closer to Aunt Lisa so I can get all of you in the frame," Erik directed.

"Are you suggesting I'm getting fat?"

Erik's face flushed brick red. "No. No way."

"Well, maybe not yet." Amy laughed, touching her still-flat stomach. She moved into the space between Megan's and Lisa's chairs. She leaned over, draping her arms around their shoulders. "Can you get all of us in the shot now?"

"Wow! Great." Erik adjusted the focus.

"The Hardaway girls. Together again," Lisa whispered as she glanced at Megan and Amy from the corner of her eye.

"All for one and one for all! Just like the old days. Now smile and say cheese, everyone," Amy commanded, her eyes shining as brilliantly as her smile.

"Hey," Erik griped from behind the camera. "I'm supposed to say that."

"Just take the picture," Kieran prompted. "We still have to get the cake."

"And we have to cut it," Megan reminded her sisters without moving her lips.

"I'm taking these shoes off first," Amy murmured back.

"Got it!" Erik crowed. "That will be a good one. Come on, Kieran. Let's go."

"Ahhh." Amy kicked her shoes under the table.

"Erik's looking fine," Lisa said, watching the duo as they made their way across the crowded room. "A little pale maybe, but otherwise fine."

"Teenagers bounce back quickly, thank God," Megan said, thinking once again how lucky they'd been.

Less than thirty minutes after Noah had walked out of the sea Tuesday afternoon, Megan had found herself back in Hurricane Beach Hospital's emergency room. Noah had refused treatment for his injured shoulder until Doc Yount had examined Erik, resutured his arm and decided his blood count warranted a transfusion and an overnight stay.

And then in the cool, tile-walled treatment room, Megan discovered, long after she needed any confirmation, that Erik truly was her son. Their blood types

were identical. The transfusion he needed would
come from her. She found herself hustled off to the
hospital lab barefoot, still in her soaking-wet shirt
and shorts. By the time the procedure was completed
and she had showered and changed into dry clothes
Amy had brought from Sea Haven, Doc Yount was
studying X rays of Noah's shoulder, and was saying
that, in his opinion, Byron Fielder could not have
survived the rip currents and storm-tossed waves off
the pier. That no man could, except perhaps a one-
armed United States Navy SEAL.

Noah had also assured her that Fielder was dead.
He had not said how he was certain. She had not
asked him to explain. But until the body was found,
a small terrified corner of her heart could not believe.

So she had not left Erik's side. And Noah hadn't
left hers. Doc Yount had ordered a cot brought into
their son's room and Noah and Megan had spent the
night at the hospital taking turns dozing fitfully on
the hard narrow bed. By morning Erik had developed
a slight fever, and Doc Yount decreed another day
in bed. Megan stayed by him that day as well, watching cartoons on TV, teaching him to play cribbage
and gin rummy. Noah had spent the day with Kyle
Jamieson and Sheriff Ormand, filling out police reports and giving statements.

But Wednesday evening, an hour before Erik was
discharged from the hospital, a Coast Guard search
plane spotted a body floating a couple of miles off-
shore. Just before nightfall the recovery was complete. Megan did not view the body, but she believed
Noah when he told her it was Erik's kidnapper, that
Fielder had died of a broken neck, sustained—in the

coroner's opinion—either as he fell from the pier or as he was dragged down on the rocks by the under-tow. At last Megan could be assured her son was safe.

Through it all there had been no time for her and Noah. No time to talk, to plan. She loved him. Had always loved him, but she still didn't know if there was a future for them together. And then duty called, and Noah left Hurricane Beach to return to Coronado at his commander's orders. She hadn't asked him not to.

Noah always kept his promises. Even at the risk of his life. But she needed more. She wanted all of him, heart and body and soul. And she wasn't certain he would give that much of himself to her. Not after all the years she had held him away, not after all that had gone before.

"Megan?"

Megan turned to Amy. Her sister was frowning at her. "Are you all right? You look as if you're a million miles away."

"What? Sorry." She shook off her memories and her uncertainties. "I'm fine. My thoughts just drifted for a moment."

"He'll be here," Amy said. "He promised."

Megan nodded, not letting herself glance toward the door as she stood up. "Let's go get Mom and Dad and cut the cake. They look as if they would stay out there on the dance floor all night if we let them."

Lisa smiled at their parents, still dancing, still in each other's arms. "Isn't it romantic? They're looking at each other as if there's no one else in the world."

"I'm going to make sure Ian gets a shot of them that way," Amy said.

"Amy!" Lisa and Megan said simultaneously.

"All right. All right. No more pictures."

"What? You aren't going to insist on another big family portrait while we're all here in our best bib and tuckers?" Lisa asked teasingly.

"Well." Amy looked sheepish, then lifted her chin a notch. "It would be nice. It all depends on whether or not Noah gets back in time. But I'm not going to worry about it. If there's one thing I've—" Amy interrupted herself as they bore down on the massive confection in the center of the room. "Oh, good. Ian's getting a shot of Mom and Dad."

"So's Erik," Lisa said, pointing at the two teens also zeroing in on the dancing couple.

"What were you going to say, Amy?" Megan asked as her sister bent beneath the table to pull out a box that contained lace-trimmed organdy aprons. Lisa made a face but tied hers around her waist and picked up the sterling-silver knife lying beside the cake.

"Yes, Amy. Finish your thought."

"I was going to say that I've learned something over this past summer."

"A life lesson?" Lisa murmured, stretching to lift the top layer from the cake to set it aside for Merrick and Helene. "I think I've picked up on one or two of those myself lately."

"What's yours, Amy?" Megan said, shaking out the folds of her frilly apron.

"That family pictures are wonderful things."

Lisa tilted her head. "That's it? That's the Secret of the Universe?"

"No, silly. Family pictures *are* wonderful things." Amy smiled and gestured for Merrick and Helene to join them as the music ended. "I'd like to have a new one every year if I could. They're wonderful because families are wonderful. But I've also learned that this family is always going to be together from now on. Maybe not always in the same picture—not always in the same place." Amy shook her head at her sisters' expressions. "Don't laugh. I know that didn't come out very well. But, what I meant was we used to be apart even when we were together, and now..."

"I'm not laughing." Lisa leaned into Merrick's arm as he came up and gave her a quick hug. "I agree with every word you said. From now on we'll always be together even when wc're apart. Chocolate or coconut, Dad?"

"Chocolate."

"Merrick—"

He smiled wickedly at his bride. "I said chocolate—with no icing."

"What am I going to do with you, Merrick Hardaway?"

"Keep me around for another fifty years, I hope."

Helene reached up on tiptoe and kissed the tip of his nose as he bent toward her. "At least that long, my love."

Megan smiled as she picked up a server, only to have it lifted out of her hands by Amy. A slight prickling at the back of her neck should have told her what she would see when Amy turned her toward the door. "Noah's here. Go," she said softly, untying the apron and pulling it from Megan's waist. "We can manage the cake."

"But the pictures—" She didn't know if she wanted to be alone with Noah, not yet. She wasn't ready.

"Pictures can wait," Amy said, making a shooing motion with her hands. "Didn't you just hear what I said. Go to your husband, Megan."

Megan looked across the room to the tall uniformed figure standing just inside the doorway. She took a step forward, then another, her feet seeming to move without orders from her brain. Noah stood quietly, waiting for her to come to him. He held his hat in his hand. The sling Doc Yount had insisted he wear, barely noticeable against the white of his uniform coat, the burnished gold of his trident-and-eagle emblem gleamed above the row of decorations on his chest.

Other heads were beginning to turn, other women beginning to notice the tall, handsome naval officer. "God, if that isn't a walking recruiting poster," she heard someone say as she passed.

Megan stopped three feet away, just beyond arm's length. "Did you have a good flight?" she asked.

"A little turbulence over Louisiana," he replied, bending slightly forward to hear her above the background noise of the party.

"Was the traffic bad getting out of Pensacola?"

"No."

"Oh." She was running out of small talk.

"Where's Erik?" His dark eyes hadn't left her

face, but she could read nothing in their shuttered depths.

"I…" She spun around, glad for the distraction. "He's there. At the buffet. With Kieran."

"No aftereffects from the transfusion?"

"He's fine. No more fever. No infection. Do you want me to go get him?"

"Later, Megan," he said. "We need to talk first, don't you think?"

"Yes."

He held out his hand. She hesitated for a few long seconds, then let him fold his strong fingers around hers. He opened the door and let her precede him into the warm darkness. When the glass door closed behind them, the soft night sounds of wind and water replaced the music and muted laughter of the party.

They climbed the steps to the boardwalk level in silence. A few other couples were enjoying the cool of the September night. Megan and Noah walked along, still in silence until they were alone. Noah stopped. Megan turned to look out over the gulf, pretending to watch the waves rolling into shore.

"It looked as if the party was a big success."

"Yes," she agreed. "It's all going very well. How…how did it go for you…I mean, the meeting with your commanding officer?"

"What are you asking, Megan?"

No more hesitating. No more beating around the bush, too much depended on her speaking her mind. "I guess I'm wondering what your orders are." Would he be returning to duty right away? Would he expect her and Erik to go with him? Would he even ask them to come with him?

"The Old Man's thinking of retiring," he said. She could feel him looking down at her, but she wouldn't—couldn't—meet his eyes. "They offered me his job. If I agree to sign on for another hitch."

"I see. Congratulations. I'm happy for you." She hated herself for mouthing the polite words. She wasn't happy, she was devastated. Had he decided he could be satisfied with a long distance relationship with his son now that the danger of Byron Fielder was gone forever?

"It's a great opportunity," he said evenly. Megan barely heard him. Why hadn't she told him she loved him that day on the beach? She should have followed her heart, told him then and there that she wanted nothing more than to be his wife again, in thought, and word, and deed.

But there had been Erik's injury. And Noah's. And all those people. The terror they had just experienced, the uncertainty about whether Fielder was really gone. All those things had conspired to keep her silent.

Now it was too late. Noah had chosen the navy. She had lost again.

"I know it's what you wanted."

Noah made an exasperated sound at the back of his throat. He spun her around. "*You're* what I want, Megan. What do I have to say and do to get that through that thick Hardaway skull of yours?"

"It's too late, Noah," she said miserably. "I'm not so ignorant that I don't know you don't just have to extend your hitch to take a position like that. You have to promise them the next ten years of your life."

"And you can't deal with that."

"I'm sorry. I can't. I...I've made plans to stay here in Hurricane Beach." She'd taken a gamble on his coming back to them and she had lost. "I've already faxed my resignation to Graceway. I've enrolled Erik in school. I...I asked Doc Yount to recommend a therapist for him—" Her voice broke slightly and she willed it strong. "For all of us. I hoped—" She couldn't finish.

He lifted her chin with his hand, but she closed her eyes to block out the sight of his face, the mesmerizing darkness of his eyes. "What did you think, Megan Marie?"

She opened her eyes, drawn by the heat of his touch, the sensual lilt in his words.

"I want you," she said, walking out from behind the last of her emotional barricades. "I love you. I've always loved you. I was lying each and every time I said otherwise." Her voice dropped to a whisper. "I want us to be together."

"That's all I've ever wanted, too," Noah said, bending to touch his lips to hers.

"But I can't—"

"I haven't asked anything of you yet, Megan Marie." He pulled her against him with his good arm. The crown of his hat dug into her hipbone. Megan took it from him and wound her arms around his neck, letting the hat dangle from her fingertips behind his back.

"What are you asking, Noah?"

"I'm asking you to marry me again. I'm asking you to start over again as the wife of a retired navy SEAL."

"Retired?" Her pulse rate accelerated a little more. "You mean—"

"I told Harrison Mannley he should postpone retirement. He's only ten years older than I am. He can train someone else to take his place. It won't be me."

"But what will you do? The teams have always been—"

"My life?" he finished for her.

"Yes," she said as his hand moved lower, cupping her bottom, fitting her tightly against him.

"The navy was all I had," he said quietly.

"Oh, Noah. What will you do?"

"A little fishing maybe? A little shrimping. I was planning on my wife supporting me."

His wife. Her. She didn't think she would ever get tired of hearing those words. "What if I'd said I was planning on returning to Nebraska?"

Without hesitation, he replied. "I would have gone there, too."

"Thank you," she said simply. Noah couldn't have proved his love more conclusively. She knew his decision to leave the military had not been reached easily despite his teasing words. She knew, because her own decision to leave Graceway had caused her similar pangs of regret. The regret was quickly overtaken by joy and hope for the future of her small family. "But I'm staying here. In Hurricane Beach. It's going to be pretty slim pickings for us. I'm going to manage Lisa's new group home when it's up and running. I took a huge pay cut—"

"Megan," he said, his smile doing strange and wonderful things to her insides. "I'm kidding about living off your wages. I've got a few prospects. There are people who are willing to pay big bucks for my kind of job experience.''

"Noah! You're not talking about becoming a mercenary, are you?"

He laughed, looking intrigued. "I hadn't considered that possibility."

"Then don't!"

"I was thinking more along the lines of doing some consulting work for the navy and multinational corporations. There are a couple of agencies run by ex-SEALs that deal in that kind of work. It's strictly paper warfare from now on, I promise. I might be traveling some, but it won't be often. And it won't be for long periods of time."

"Then I'll have all my wishes, won't I?" Megan said softly, letting her head fall against his chest, listening to the strong steady beat of his heart, speaking aloud the dreams she'd never before dared to put into words. "A home here in Hurricane Beach. My parents. My sisters. My son."

"Our son," he corrected in a low rasping growl that sent shivers racing up and down her spine. "Our son," he repeated, wonder in his voice and in his eyes. He tipped up her face for his kiss.

"Our son," she whispered. "And the man I love." This time his kiss was neither soft nor gentle.

"Do we have to go back to the party?" Noah asked, sounding slightly breathless as he lifted his mouth from hers.

Megan thought it over, her heart pounding, her body aching for more, much more, than just one kiss. "We probably should."

Noah groaned, bringing his hand up to his injured shoulder.

She reached up, laid her hand on his breast. "Where does it hurt?" she asked.

"Not there." A rumble of laughter escaped him. She had forgotten what a sexy laugh he had, how it made her skin tingle and her thighs ache. There was so much she had to learn about him again, so much they needed to share. "My shoulder's fine, but no one has to know that."

"No," she said, feeling deliciously wicked and happier than she had been for twelve long years. "No one has to know that. And if we don't stay away too long, it will be all right."

"There's a key in my pocket," he said, with a smile that turned her knees weak and interfered with her breathing.

"Which pocket?" she asked, feeling herself blush but meeting his gaze.

"This one." He closed his big hand over hers above the trident emblem on his breast. "I didn't plan far enough ahead." She reached inside his jacket, extracted a key with a Sand Dollar Cabins plastic key ring attached. "I paid the rent until the end of next week."

"That was good planning," she said, letting the key ring dangle from her fingers.

"It was, wasn't it." Noah slipped his arm around her waist, pulling her close, holding her tightly against him as if he would never let her go. "Come with me, Megan Marie. Let's start planning the rest of our life."

"Yes," she said, her heart so filled with love she

could barely speak. She slid her arm around his waist, holding him as tightly as he was holding her. "My thoughts exactly."

"ISN'T THAT your mom and dad making out down there on the boardwalk?" Kieran asked, leaning over the railing of the upper-level deck of the restaurant.

"Where?" Erik felt the back of his neck getting red. It was his mom and dad, all right, and he didn't like the idea of spying on them.

"Whew. It's just like Richard Gere in *An Officer and a Gentleman*. You do know who Richard Gere is, don't you?"

"Yes," he said absently as he watched the scene below.

His dad moved a little bit away from his mom as the kiss ended and the light from a lamppost across the boardwalk fell on her face. She reached up and touched her fingers to his cheek. She was smiling. She looked young and pretty—as if she was in love. His dad put his arm around her waist and they started walking, down toward the shadows at the end of the boardwalk. Erik started smiling, too. Just like his mom. He knew everything was going to be all right. She wouldn't be smiling up into Noah's eyes like that if it wasn't.

"That is absolutely the most romantic thing I've ever seen." Kieran sighed. "Better than *An Officer and a Gentleman*. Better than *Casablanca*." Her voice softened, grew wistful. "You're going to have a real family now, Erik."

"Yeah. I am. I wonder if…"

"What?" She'd turned her head to watch one of

her family's fishing boats rocking gently at its moorings alongside the dock on the other side of Alligator Creek.

"Would everyone think I'm nuts if I told them I...I want my old name back?" He couldn't look her in the eye, so he stared straight down at the dark water swirling around the lower-deck supports.

"You mean you want us to start calling you Derek again? Just when everyone got used to Erik? You've been Erik for a long time. Why change now?"

"Because Fielder made me Erik. He's dead. I don't have to be afraid of him anymore. I don't have to do what he tells me anymore. I'm *not* Erik Fielder."

She nodded. "You're back in Hurricane Beach where you're supposed to be. You're back with your mom and dad. With all your family. You're supposed to be Derek Noah Carson."

"I *am* Derek Noah Carson," he said.

"Then go for it. What else is family for if you can't make them learn a new name for you every month or so."

"Kieran!"

"Just kidding," she said, and gave him a little punch on the shoulder. "Lighten up, Derek."

"Okay, I will," he said, feeling happy because what she said about his family was true. Then he looked at his best friend and asked, "What about your family, Kieran?"

"It went okay with my dad," she said, knowing what he was asking. "He didn't make all kinds of promises I knew he couldn't keep. He says he's got to take it one day at a time. He's not coming back

to Hurricane Beach. At least not right away. I know
that makes Grace sad, but she's handling it okay.
He's not going to run the bakery and that makes
Grandma and Grandpa sad, but they're okay, too.''

"You've got Jon and Amy.''

"Yeah. And what with the new baby and all, it'll
be okay.'' She smiled. "It'll be better than okay. I'll
be set for life. Or at least I'll have a bundle of money
stashed away by the time I'm ready for college.''

"What are you talking about?'' he asked, exasperated by her mercurial changes of subject. Girls.
He didn't think he'd ever understand them.

"Babies.''

"Babies?'' Now he was more confused than ever.
"How do you get from stashing away a bundle of
money for college to babies?''

"You men can be so dense,'' she said. "You get
money from baby-sitting, stupid. I have the feeling
this extended family of ours is going to be hip-deep
in babies by this time next year. Amy's already pregnant. And I overheard Amy and your mom talking
about how Lisa wants a baby really bad, so I bet she
and Matt don't waste any time trying to have one.''
She ticked the points off on her fingers then gave
him a sly little glance from the corner of her eye.
"You better start learning how to change diapers and
burp babies, too, if you know what's good for you.''

"Why?''

"You saw the way Noah and Megan were kissing.
Maybe kissing doesn't make babies, but it's sure a
good start. Think about it.'' Kieran laughed gaily at
his flaming-red cheeks, and turned to go down the

steps and back to the party. "Come on. I want a piece of cake before the chocolate's all gone."

"Okay. Go ahead. I'll be there in a minute," he said, and watched her walk away.

Babies. A baby brother or sister. He had to think about that one for a minute. And the more he thought about it, the better he liked it. A little brother or sister he could help to grow up strong and safe and happy. Derek knew exactly what he'd say the first time he saw it, too. He looked around, checking to see if he was alone so he could try out the words with no one to hear but the night birds and the stars.

"Hi there, little guy," he would say. "I'm your brother, Derek. Welcome to the family."

He changes diapers, mixes formula and
tells wonderful bedtime stories—he's

Mr. Mom

Three totally different stories of sexy, single
heroes each raising another man's child...
from three of your favorite authors:

MEMORIES OF THE PAST
by Carole Mortimer

THE MARRIAGE TICKET
by Sharon Brondos

TELL ME A STORY
by Dallas Schulze

Available this June wherever
Harlequin and Silhouette books are sold.

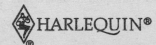 

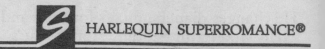

HARLEQUIN SUPERROMANCE®

WOMEN WHO *Dare*

*They take chances, make changes
and follow their hearts!*

WHERE THERE'S SMOKE... (#747)
by Laura Abbot

Jeri Monahan is a volunteer fire fighter in her Ozarks
hometown—and Dan Contini, former navy officer, is the
fire chief.

Jeri's a natural risk taker—and Dan's a protector, a man who
believes women shouldn't be exposed to physical danger.

Jeri's a woman who wants it all, including marriage—
and Dan's a divorced father embittered by his ex-wife's
unfaithfulness.

There are a lot of sparks between Jeri and Dan—and a lot of
problems, too. Can those sparks of attraction be fanned into a
steady fire?

Find out July 1997 wherever Harlequin books are sold.

TAYLOR SMITH

Who would you trust with your life? Think again.

A tranquil New England town is rocked to its core when a young coed is linked to a devastating crime—then goes missing.

One woman, who believes in the girl's innocence, is determined to find her before she's silenced—forever. Her only ally is a man who no longer believes in anyone's innocence. But *is* he an ally?

At a time when all loyalties are suspect, and old friends may be foes, she has to decide—quickly—who can be trusted. The wrong choice could be fatal.

THE BEST OF ENEMIES

Available at your favorite retail outlet in June 1997.

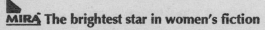

MIRA The brightest star in women's fiction

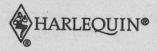

And the Winner Is...
You!

...when you pick up these great titles
from our new promotion at your
favorite retail outlet this June!

Diana Palmer
The Case of the Mesmerizing Boss

Betty Neels
The Convenient Wife

Annette Broadrick
Irresistible

Emma Darcy
A Wedding to Remember

Rachel Lee
Lost Warriors

Marie Ferrarella
Father Goose

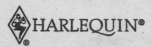 

It's hot...and it's out of control!

BLAZE

Beginning this spring, Temptation turns up the *heat*. Look for these bold, provocative, *ultra*sexy books!

#629 OUTRAGEOUS
by Lori Foster (April 1997)

#639 RESTLESS NIGHTS
by Tiffany White (June 1997)

#649 NIGHT RHYTHMS
by Elda Minger (Sept. 1997)

BLAZE: Red-hot reads—only from

HARLEQUIN®
Temptation.